*The steps of a good man are ordered by the Lord,
and He delights in his way.*

—Psalm 37:23 (NKJV)

Savannah Secrets

Savannah Secrets

Southern
Fried Secrets

NANCY MEHL

Guideposts

Danbury, Connecticut

Prologue

Letter from Ambrose Sedgwick to his wife, Abigail, dated 1773

To my beloved Abigail,

I received your letter, which I prize. I pray daily for the welfare of our family. I know you are caring for Thaddeus and Mercy with loving attention. I cannot tell you when I will be home. I am blessed to work alongside the most splendid British gentleman, James Oglethorpe, a true philanthropist who has founded a new city near the Savannah River, in the province of Georgia. He has been joined by Colonel William Bull of South Carolina. Together, they have designed a truly remarkable town. It is made up of public squares. The design will help the immigrants who will live here to defend themselves against attack since all the houses will face forward and will allow for seeing imminent raids. I also believe it will promote neighborly discourse and connection. It is truly remarkable. I am counting the days until I can return home to you.

Your loving husband,
Ambrose Sedgwick

Chapter One

MEREDITH BELLEFONTAINE FROWNED AS SHE watched her partner in Magnolia Investigations stare at a file on her lap. Julia Foley had been in her office all morning going through their files, trying to whittle down any unnecessary paperwork and put them in order. It was clear her heart wasn't really in it. She sat in one of the two chairs in front of Meredith's desk, using the other chair to stack the files she'd cleaned out.

Outside the rain tapped on the roof and drizzled down the large floor-to-ceiling windows in Meredith's office. Usually she loved rainy days, but for some reason, this dreary Monday morning just added to the feeling of boredom she felt. It wasn't just the weather and the tedium that bothered Meredith. She had to admit to herself that she missed Quin Crowley. He was a friend. Maybe a little more than that, but she wasn't sure. A corporate attorney, he was out of town for a week, working. She tried to push thoughts of him away. It would certainly help if they had a case. Something else to think about.

Meredith liked to keep the temperature in her office a little chilly, but in deference to Julia she'd started a small fire in the fireplace. It crackled and popped, adding to the cozy ambience of the room.

"You know Carmen can take care of that," Meredith said, pointing at the files. "It's actually her job, remember?"

"I realize that, but she's not here, and I need something to do."

Carmen Lopez, their receptionist, had been out for over a week with the flu. Chatty, funny, and extremely competent, she added a sense of fun to every day. She was certainly missed.

"We need a case," Meredith said, stating the obvious.

Julia sighed. "No kidding. I've gone through these files so many times, I think I've memorized them."

Meredith laughed and looked at her watch. "It's almost eleven. Maybe we should take an early lunch and—"

The front door opened, and a few seconds later a tall man stepped into Meredith's office. She was surprised to see he didn't have an umbrella. Water dripped off his longish dark hair and beard. When his eyes met hers, Meredith realized she knew him. "Davis," she said with a smile. "How nice to see you."

"You're Davis Hedgerow," Julia said. "You write that wonderful column in the *Savannah Tribune*, Searching Savannah." She stood up and shook his hand. "I never miss it."

Davis wrote about well-known Savannah attractions as well as places even older residents didn't know about. "I haven't seen you since the funeral," Meredith said.

"I know," Davis said. "Sorry. I've wanted to stop by and check on you. Maybe you could come over one day soon. You know how much Sylvia loves to cook."

He grinned at her, and Meredith giggled. "Davis's wife is very brave in the kitchen," she said to Julia. "Let's just say that some of her more complicated recipes aren't always successful."

"In other words, they're awful," Davis said. "Like the vegetarian gumbo with tofu. She proved that gumbo with tofu isn't gumbo at all. I still can't believe you and Ron ate an entire bowl. I wasn't brave enough to make it across the finish line."

Davis and Julia laughed, but then Meredith watched as his expression changed. "Have a seat," she said, gesturing to one of the chairs in front of her desk. Julia picked up the files she'd put on the seat and carefully placed them on the floor next to her.

"I'm here," he said as he sat down, "because I…might need some help."

"Might?" Meredith asked.

Davis reached into the pocket of his lightweight overcoat and pulled out an envelope. "This was given to the receptionist at the paper last week. And before you ask, no, she doesn't remember anything about the person who gave it to her. All kinds of packages and mail are delivered to her throughout the day, and she also answers tons of phone calls. Eventually the letter was sent upstairs to me." He handed the envelope to Meredith, who opened it slowly.

"So this went through quite a few people before you got it?" Meredith asked.

"I suppose. The receptionist. The mail room where the mail is sorted. The guy who delivers the mail… I would say it traveled quite a bit before I got it." He frowned at her. "Why?"

"Fingerprints," Julia said. "Now add Meredith and you to the list." She shrugged. "Too many people have touched it. I doubt seriously we can get anything from it."

"I don't think you'll find any fingerprints from the person who delivered the letter. The video showed he wore gloves."

"If he was trying to keep his fingerprints off the envelope I'm pretty sure he didn't leave any on the letter either." Meredith carefully removed the folded piece of paper, using a tissue to hold it. She opened it and began to read. PUBLISH YOUR NEW BOOK AT YOUR OWN PERIL. IF YOU DON'T STOP ITS PUBLICATION YOU'LL BE SORRY. VERY SORRY. Block letters. Plain white paper. Nothing distinctive about it. She handed it to Julia, along with the tissue. "No signature of course."

"Do you have any idea who wrote this?" Julia asked after reading it. She gave it back to Meredith.

Davis shook his head. "Not a clue. I mean, my upcoming book is mostly a compilation of my past articles about Savannah attractions. Not some kind of exposé that would compromise anyone."

"Maybe he has a similar book coming out?" Julia suggested. "Could this person be afraid your book will steal sales from him?"

"The same thought occurred to me, so I did a little poking around. Couldn't find anything like that. Besides, I think most people in Savannah look to me for this kind of information. I really can't see a legitimate publisher signing someone to compete with me. I don't mean that to sound egotistical. I'm just stating facts."

"I understand," Meredith said. "This could be a prank, you know. It may mean nothing."

"I realize that, but even before the letter arrived I had a weird feeling. Like I was being watched."

"Watched?" Julia echoed. "What do you mean? You think this person followed you to the newspaper?"

"No, not necessarily." Davis rubbed the back of his neck with his fingers. He was clearly under stress. "The other night when I got home, I was convinced someone was hiding in the bushes that run along my property line. I went outside to check it out, but no one was there. I talked myself into believing it was the neighbor's cat. But then it happened again the very next night." His eyes sought Meredith's. "Sylvia is alone a lot because of my work. She gets out some, but all in all, she's a real homebody. I'm...I'm not sure she's safe."

Meredith put the letter back in the envelope and handed it to Davis. "You need the police, Davis. Not us. We're investigators, not bodyguards."

"I realize that. But what if this really is some kind of a prank and word gets out? I'm in the public eye. And besides... Well, I'm afraid my publisher might get cold feet if I come off like some kind of nut afraid of his own shadow. Or even that I'm lying in an attempt to draw attention to my book."

"But wouldn't attention to your book be a good thing?" Julia asked.

"Not if the publisher thinks I made it up. Makes me look unprofessional." He sighed deeply. "I know I sound paranoid, but this same publisher recently had an author who faked cancer because she thought more people would purchase her book. When the truth came out, they took a big hit. I don't want this to remind them of that fiasco."

Davis slumped down in the chair. "This book is really important to me. And not just because of the money I hope it'll make. I've given my publisher a proposal for a line of books, each one highlighting attractions in other cities. Sylvia and I would get to travel together on their dime. She's had a tough time lately. Her mother passed away suddenly. They were very close. I think getting away from Savannah and visiting other places would really help her. I just can't allow anything to ruin this deal." He put the envelope on Meredith's desk. "I'm convinced that this effort to stop publication is connected to one of the five new businesses mentioned in the book."

Meredith wasn't convinced Davis was on the right path. "Davis, I'm just not sure about this. Did you write something negative about any of these new places?"

"No. I only highlight attractions I believe people will enjoy. If I investigate it and feel it's not exceptional, I don't write about it."

"I'm confused," Julia said. "How would anyone know what's in a book that isn't available yet?"

"The publisher has sent out quite a few ARCs—advanced reader copies. They go to TV stations, other publishers, and, of course, to anyone associated with the sites in the book. A few copies were mailed to the Chamber of Commerce so they could mention the book and the new attractions on Savannah's official website."

"Could this be someone you decided not to include in the book?" Meredith asked, trying to come up with any reasonable possibilities.

"I thought about that, but there isn't anyone. Every one of the new sites was recommended by a friend or reader who had either visited the place or who had heard about it from someone else. No one was rejected."

"What about a past business that didn't like what you wrote?" Meredith asked.

"No. There's no one like that. For the other locations I just gave my editor the original article I wrote on each one, and she included them without any changes. If any people at those sites are upset about what I wrote, they would have said something long ago, when their article first came out. All of them were thrilled for a mention." He clasped his hands together. "I know in my gut someone connected with one of these five new places is behind this letter."

Although he didn't appear angry, Davis was firm. Meredith could see he wasn't going to budge. She wanted to help her old friend, but was this a case they should take? Were the parameters Davis had given them too narrow? Would it end up being a wild-goose chase, or were his instincts right? Meredith looked at Julia. Her expression echoed Meredith's hesitation. What were they getting into?

Chapter Two

"Look," Davis said, softening his tone. "I've researched every other possibility. I'm not trying to be unreasonable."

"Okay," Meredith said slowly. "So no complaints from these new places? Nothing that made you suspicious?"

"No." He paused a moment. "Well, one person asked that we retake a picture because he didn't like the way the first one came out, but that was it. Nothing serious enough to threaten me." He sighed deeply. "Meredith, you know I was an investigative reporter for many years before I took over this column. I did my research here, trust me. But if anything else pops up, something that doesn't have to do with these five spots, I'll call you immediately and let you know." He leaned forward in his chair. "I'd look into this myself, but I can't spend any more time on it. Sylvia needs me right now. I try to go home immediately after work because I know she's grieving alone. Besides, I think having fresh eyes take a look may be exactly what's needed."

"Can you tell us about the new sites mentioned in the book?" Meredith asked.

"Sure. There are two B and Bs, each claiming they're the most haunted place in Savannah. I doubt Moon River Brewing Company has anything to worry about, but I still found them interesting."

Davis's mention of the Moon River Brewing Company made Meredith smile. Known as one of the most haunted spots in the world, it was part of Savannah's Haunted Pub Crawl and Ghost Tour. Ron and Beau, Julia's husband, used to make fun of tourists who hoped they might stumble upon some old Southern specter. Ron would have loved this case. It would have been great fodder for his jokes.

"Then there's the Book Worm," Davis continued. "I've never showcased it before, but I've wanted to. They're adding a coffee bar and pastries. There's some opposition to it, I guess, but nothing serious. People who don't want to see it change. It's been an institution in Savannah for seventy years."

Meredith knew the bookstore. The mention of it brought a wave of wonderful memories along with a quick stab of pain.

He paused for a moment. "Oh, then there's a story about a statue being dedicated to Ambrose Sedgwick," he said. "A man who served with General James Oglethorpe."

Julia nodded. "The man who founded Savannah."

"Right. Through old letters and diaries recently discovered, Sedgwick's story was uncovered. According to new information, Sedgwick was the one who suggested Savannah be laid out in grids. Some historians are upset that someone else is being credited with this architectural element. They claim Oglethorpe is the only one who should be recognized as the creator of one of Savannah's most interesting features."

"Interesting. That's four. So there's one more."

Davis's forehead wrinkled as he thought. Finally, he smiled. "Oh yeah. Might be my favorite. Peachie's Diner just reopened."

Meredith's eyebrows arched. "Really? I used to love that place." She smiled at Julia. "Both of us did."

"Peachie's granddaughter decided to bring it back. She's using all of her grandfather's old recipes. Trying to keep it authentic."

Meredith grinned. "I hope so. It was the only place in Savannah that made a great lemon milkshake. My favorite. I'd love to have another one."

"Leopold's has lemon custard ice cream," Davis said. "They'll make a milkshake with any of their flavors."

Meredith nodded. "I've had it. It's very good and their ice cream is yummy, but there was something about Peachie's lemon shake. I don't know. It was just perfect."

Julia frowned. "Who would be upset about Peachie's coming back? It was a small place, not much competition for Leopold's."

Meredith nodded. "Besides, the people who own Leopold's are really nice. I can't see them being upset about a small place like Peachie's reopening. They make hamburgers, sandwiches, and other food. Ice cream was just part of their menu, not something they specialized in."

"Yeah, you're right. That doesn't seem likely," Julia agreed.

Davis reached inside his jacket and pulled out a book, which he put on Meredith's desk. "Here's an ARC of the book." He took a pen from the desk and opened the book to the index. "I'm putting a star next to the new places I mentioned." When he finished, he put the pen down and held out the letter Meredith had given back to him.

Meredith took it from him. "I still think you're narrowing it down too much, but if that's what you want, we'll do what we can."

He shrugged. "I guess if you can't find anything and another possibility presents itself, okay. Look into it. But let me know first before you follow it. And if you don't uncover something credible in connection to these five locations, and I don't hear anything from this person again, I'll throw the letter in the trash and assume this was some kind of hoax."

"We'll have to look not only at the owners of these businesses," Julia said, looking at Meredith, "but employees and other people who have a connection to them."

Meredith nodded. She hoped that list wouldn't be too long.

"I'm concerned about your wife," Julia said to Davis. "Just in case the threat is real..."

"I'm trying to get her to visit her sister for a while. She's wanted some time with her ever since the funeral. I think they will be able to comfort each other. So far she's resisted. She says she needs time at home with me. I don't intend to tell her about the letter. If I do, she definitely won't leave town."

"At least call the police and tell them you think someone has been in your yard," Julia said. "They can send patrol cars past your house so you'll feel safer."

"Okay, I'll do that. So you'll help me?"

"We'll do our best," Meredith said.

He got up from the chair. "Great. You know, Ron was an incredible investigator. If you have picked up even half of his skills, I know I'm in the right hands. Of course I realize this might be a wild-goose chase, but I'd feel better knowing it was checked out. Just in case."

"We understand."

Davis said goodbye and left. They no sooner heard the front door click shut when Meredith said, "I really want to help him, Julia. Davis and Ron were good friends." She took a steadying breath. Davis's comment about Ron had shaken her. Was she as good an investigator as he had been? She wondered frequently if he would be proud of her. She hoped so with all her heart.

"He's not asking us just to find out who sent the letter. He wants us to look over five possibilities and nothing else. I don't know, Meredith. We need to be certain we can actually help."

"He's really concerned. If nothing else maybe we can put his mind at ease." Meredith paused a moment. "He was a great reporter in his day. Maybe we need to trust his instincts. I've had to do that many times, and it's never led me astray."

"I understand, but putting such restrictions on where we can look? I'm not comfortable with that."

"I'm not either, but what he says makes sense. We probably would have arrived at the same conclusion...if he'd allowed us to." She shrugged. "At least we know where to look. Maybe it will make things easier."

"Why do I feel like saying something about famous last words right now?"

Meredith laughed. She had the same concerns Julia did. However, she wasn't certain she was being completely honest about her intentions. Right now all she could think about was a lemon milkshake.

Chapter Three

ABOUT THIRTY MINUTES LATER MEREDITH and Julia were seated at the Sentient Bean Coffee Shop, a small café not far from the office. A vegetarian restaurant, it was a favorite among Savannah residents. Meredith ordered the Greek tacos and a cappuccino. The tacos were scrumptious, stuffed with hummus, feta, spinach, tomato, kalamata olives, and tzatziki sauce. Julia asked for a cheddar potato with sour cream. Since the restaurant didn't serve Diet Dr Pepper, Julia's favorite drink, she asked for chai tea. Meredith sipped her coffee and flipped through Davis's book while they waited for their food.

The book was beautifully put together. The pictures sparked Meredith's pride in her city. The historic district, Forsyth Park, the Cathedral of St. John the Baptist, all of the incredible homes in the city. She turned the page and found the first B and B that Davis had mentioned.

"Okay, here's one of the new places," she said to Julia. "'The Magnolia Blossom Inn,'" she read. "'Located in Savannah, a ten-minute walk from Madison Square, the Magnolia Blossom offers four-star accommodations with a hot tub, free WiFi, and a garden. Rooms feature a flat-screen TV and a private bathroom with shower and a hair dryer. Some rooms include a seating area and/or a balcony.'"

"Is there a warning about not using the hair dryer in the shower?" Julia asked dryly. "Maybe that's how they got their ghosts."

Meredith rolled her eyes and continued reading. "'Breakfast consists of Southern favorites, including grits, corn bread, scrapple, and Southern spoon bread. Our homemade sausage is incredible, and you'll love our fried apples!

"'Popular points of interest near the accommodation include Oglethorpe Square, Colonial Park Cemetery, and the Owens-Thomas Museum.

"'Located in a renovated Italianate-style home built in the 1800s, the Magnolia offers the best of Italian architecture, including modest country features and lavish ornamentation.

"'There are daily ghost tours throughout the public rooms, where you might catch a glimpse of Colonel Lincoln Morgan and his wife, Clementine, the first owners of this magnificent structure. Our tour guide will share the story of their tragic love story. If you listen carefully as you're snuggled into your large four-poster bed at night, you may hear them walking down the hallways, calling each other's names.'"

Meredith looked up from the book and grinned at Julia. "Wonder why they have to call each other's names if they wander the same halls. You think they'd have found each other after all these years. They must be really stupid ghosts."

Julia laughed. "I think I know where this is. There are several Italianate-style houses in Savannah, including yours, but there's one that was being renovated last year. I'll bet it's the same one." She took a sip of her tea. "You remember. The big orange house I pointed out when we visited the cemetery?"

"Oh yeah. I do remember that. Boy, renovating that place would take a lot of money."

Julia nodded. "My guess is that whoever bought it might be pretty frantic to recover their investment." She arched one finely shaped eyebrow. "So why would they want Davis to pull his book off the market? Wouldn't they want the exposure?"

Meredith considered Julia's point and had to agree. She stared down at the picture in the book before scooting it toward Julia. "Nothing in that picture that should concern anyone, is there?"

"No. I don't think so. It's just a house. Beautifully refurbished." She chuckled. "Maybe old Lincoln and Clementine don't like their home invaded by strangers."

Meredith shook her head. "Let's put that possibility on the back burner, okay?"

Their waitress stepped up to their table with two plates in her hands. She gave the Greek tacos to Meredith and cheddar baked potato to Julia. When she walked away, Meredith went back to the book.

"Okay, let's keep going." She flipped through several pages. "Hey, here's the article about Peachie's." She smiled. "I think we need to investigate. How about we go there for supper tonight?"

Julia shook her head. "Sorry, not tonight. We're having dinner with one of Beau's doctor buddies. I'm not looking forward to it, but there wasn't any way to get out of it. Beau likes the guy, although his wife leaves a lot to be desired."

Meredith frowned. "What do you mean?"

Julia looked around as if she suspected someone was listening. "She's a real Southern belle. Rich, spoiled, and overly impressed with her heritage. You know the type." She sighed. "If I have to hear one more time about how her ancestors helped Oglethorpe found Savannah, I may just throw up all over my nice lace tablecloth."

Meredith burst out laughing. "Oh, Julia. Really."

"I'm not trying to be rude, but that woman would test the patience of a saint."

"Hey, maybe you could ask her about..." She flipped through the pages of Davis's book. "What was his name? Oh yeah. Colonel Ambrose Sedgwick. You know, the guy who's getting the statue dedicated to him?"

Julia's eyes widened. "Why don't you come? That way you could bring the subject up. If she gets upset we can blame it on you."

"Gee, thanks. Not sure I like that idea."

"I just meant... You know, since her husband is a friend of Beau's..."

"You just meant that you'd rather have me take the heat. Then if it goes sideways, Beau can't get upset with you. But what about me?"

"Oh, Meredith. He loves you to pieces. Don't worry about that. Besides, he knows how nosy you are."

"Nosy?"

"I don't mean it that way," Julia said. "I meant...inquisitive. Of course, you have to be in our line of work."

"You've done your fair share of investigating too, my friend."

Julia grinned. "Okay, we're both *inquisitive.* Now, are you coming?"

"You already know I will. I'd love to dig up some information about this Ambrose Sedgwick."

"Hopefully, you can get a word in edgewise."

"What's her name?" Meredith asked.

"Dixie."

"No," Meredith said, drawing it out. "You've got to be kidding."

"I wish I was. Dr. Franklin and Dixie Vanderkellen."

"Oh my."

Julia nodded. "Oh my, indeed."

"You're cooking?

"No. Having it catered by Justine's, that new French place on Oglethorpe Avenue?"

"Yeah, I've seen it. Is it supposed to be good?"

Julia shrugged. "Hey, it's French, Dixie's favorite, and I don't have to cook. Win-win. Besides, it doesn't matter what I serve, she'll criticize it."

"I don't remember you mentioning these people before. Why not?"

Julia sighed. "The last time we had dinner with them was five years ago."

Meredith burst out laughing. "Five years? You talk about her like you saw her last week."

Julia scrunched up her face. "Just wait. An evening with Dixie isn't easily forgotten."

"Hmm. Maybe I won't come after all."

Julia pointed at her. "You might be able to get me through tonight in one piece. You *have* to be there."

"Okay, but what about Peachie's?"

"We'll go for lunch tomorrow."

"Okay." Meredith sighed. "I still remember when Ron and I went there on a date before we were married. We shared a lemon shake. And afterward..." She smiled.

"And afterward he told you he loved you for the first time," Julia finished for her.

Meredith nodded. "I sure miss that man."

Julia reached across the table and covered Meredith's hand with her own. "I know you do. He'd be proud of you, you know."

"Thanks, Jules. Sometimes I just don't know what I'd do without you."

"Oh, phooey. You'd be fine. But let's not find out, okay?"

Meredith smiled. "Okay. This would be easier if we could find fingerprints."

"I agree. But you know the police won't help us unless we have some real evidence that proves a crime has been committed."

"It doesn't matter," Meredith said. "I'd bet a lemon shake he wore gloves when he wrote it, and you know how much I value those. Let's nose around a bit before we bring the police in. We need to check out each of these five possibilities. Take pictures, talk to people. See if something pops up. Something suspicious."

"Please tell me we don't have to stay at the B and Bs."

Meredith wrinkled her nose at Julia. "Why not? Just tell Beau we're on a case."

"Most cases don't last overnight."

Meredith laughed. "Then invite him along."

"Maybe…," Julia said slowly. "He might be willing to go. He's been restless lately. Ever since he arranged my surprise birthday party at the Mansion."

"Did you ever tell him you figured it out *before* the surprise?"

"He was so pleased with himself. I would never let him know. It was such a lovely evening. He really threw himself into arranging everything."

"And it was wonderful. Too bad he sprained his ankle when he decided he wanted to dance in the dining room. I meant to ask, what did the doctor say at the last visit?"

"No golfing or fishing until it's healed. He can still walk, but the doctor told him to stay off it as much as possible. He's so bored." Julia paused for a moment. "You know, visiting these B and Bs might be just the thing to get him going. A ghost hunt!"

Meredith gestured at Julia with her fork. "Like us, he's not a believer in ghosts. Are you sure he'll go with us?"

Julia laughed. "He loves making fun of people who do. I think he'll want to be involved. I'll ask him."

"Good. I'll call them and make reservations. But tonight… Colonel Ambrose Sedgwick. Who is he really, and is anyone upset enough about this statue to threaten Davis?"

Julia went back to her potato while Meredith ran the names of the five new Savannah attractions through her head. Who could get upset about Davis's book? Although she and Julia saw this case as something fun and interesting, could Davis be in real danger?

Chapter Four

Meredith arrived at Julia's early. Even though Julia wasn't cooking, she would still be setting the table and putting the food onto platters and plates. She drove into the driveway and pulled up close to the garage, leaving enough room for the Vanderkellens to park.

As she got out of the car, she smoothed the light blue silk blouse she wore under her black jacket. She loved the blouse and felt it looked good with her blond hair and blue eyes, but it was easily wrinkled. Maybe she should have picked something else, but it was too late to do anything about it now.

She grabbed her purse and walked up to the large front porch that graced Julia's lovely Southern-styled home. She rang the doorbell and within seconds was greeted by Julia's husband, Beau. Although he was in his late sixties, Beau had the vitality of someone much younger following his recovery from triple bypass surgery.

Beau grinned widely at her. "So glad you could come, Meredith. Julia's in the kitchen. You'd think she's cooking all the food herself the way she's carrying on."

Meredith laughed. "I came early so I could help her."

"I tried, but she kicked me out. I think you're just the person to settle her down." As Meredith stepped inside, Beau closed the door.

"Can I take your jacket?" he asked.

"Thanks, but I'll keep it on."

Beau smiled and waved toward the kitchen. Meredith noticed that he had a slight limp as he favored his left leg. Meredith passed through Julia's beautiful dining room with its high ceilings and cream-colored satin wallpaper with small blue flowers and off-white wainscoting. The chandelier shimmered as the setting sun shone through the windows, making the raindrop crystals sparkle like diamonds. She called out Julia's name before stepping into her huge kitchen with its gorgeous dark wood cabinets and large island in the middle. The white and gray granite countertop was filled with plastic containers and assorted plates and utensils.

"Everything okay?" Meredith asked as she walked up to the island.

Julia threw her hands up in the air. "How do I keep everything warm? If I put it on plates now, it will be cold by the time they get here."

"I'll help. We'll figure it out."

Julia paused and shook her head. "Please don't mention the word *microwave*. I just can't do that to these wonderful dishes. Sometimes the results just don't taste right."

Meredith pulled out a drawer in the island and took out an apron. "You set the table. I'll take care of the food. And by the way, you look incredible."

Julia wore a soft dark blue blouse with flowing sleeves and gray slacks that matched her perfectly styled silver hair. She always looked so elegant that many times Meredith felt sloppy next to her.

Julia smiled. "You look lovely too. And thanks. I'm so glad you're here. See how much I need you?"

"Don't be silly. You don't need me at all. You just need to take a breath and calm down."

"You're right. But you make it possible. Thanks."

Meredith winked at her. "Anytime."

After turning on the oven to 200 degrees, Meredith quickly poured some crushed ice into several of Julia's crystal wine glasses. Then she hooked several large shrimp on the rims of the glasses, along with a lemon slice on each one. She put the cocktail sauce in small glass sauce containers. All of this went into the refrigerator. The wedge salads were transferred to the salad plates Julia had set out. Her beautiful Marchesa Gilded Pearl china made everything look so stylish. The salads went into the fridge as well. She placed the coq au vin, lardons, pearl onions, mushrooms, asparagus, and potato purée onto the large dinner plates and then put them in the oven to keep warm. The French cheesecake was already in the refrigerator.

Meredith stepped into the dining room. "Once we've started dinner I'll pop in here and take the cheesecake out of the refrigerator," she told Julia. "You want it to be cool but not cold when you serve it." She looked at the beautiful table Julia had set in the dining room. The white lace tablecloth was perfect on the antique mahogany table. Julia's wonderful silverware matched the crystal glasses with their silver rims. Julia had folded the cloth napkins and secured them with silver napkin rings. Crystal goblets were filled with ice water and a pitcher of tea sat on the table. "It's perfect," Meredith told her. "And the food is ready. When they get here we'll take the plates out of the oven. The food will be just right."

"That's wonderful," Julia said. "I'm okay now. Don't know why I get into such a dither sometimes. It's not like I've never had a dinner party before."

"I think this Dixie person really gets to you for some reason."

"You're right. I don't know why. It's ridiculous."

Meredith was glad to see Julia had relaxed some. She could get upset, but it never lasted long.

In her mind Meredith double-checked everything. They hadn't made coffee, but Julia had the kind of machine that brewed single cups so everyone could choose what they wanted.

At that moment, the front doorbell rang. "I'll get it," Beau called out.

Julia grabbed Meredith's arm. "Here we go. Stay close. If I start to say something snarky, pinch me."

"You? Snarky? Never," Meredith said with a grin.

"Hush up."

Meredith heard the front door close. A large man with white hair and a beard stepped into the dining room. He reminded Meredith of a carefully groomed Santa Claus. The woman with him was dressed to the nines. She wore a black dress with a diamond choker and dangly diamond earrings. Her hair was blond with silver streaks, and her silver nails were obviously done professionally. She smiled widely when she saw Julia.

"Why, Julia, honey," she said with a thick Southern drawl. "I am *so* glad to see you. It's been way too long."

"I'm happy to see you too, Dixie. This is my friend and partner, Meredith Bellefontaine."

"Nice to meet you, Dixie," Meredith said.

"And you as well, sugar." Dixie looked at Julia and Meredith with a slight frown. "I apologize. I thought we were to dress for dinner." Except she said "dinnah" and her disapproval was obvious.

"Well, Dixie honey, I can't imagine where you got that idea," Julia said with a slight accent. "I… Ow!"

Meredith's pinch on her arm stopped Julia before she could say anything else.

"Sorry. I think something bit me," Julia said, her face red. "I just want everyone to be comfortable. And you look gorgeous, Dixie."

"Bless your heart, honey," she said. Then her forehead furrowed. "Are there bugs in the house, Julia? If we need to come back another time…"

This time, Julia pulled her arm away before Meredith could pinch her again. "No, no bugs in the house. Sometimes I accidentally carry an ant inside when I add mulch to my garden." She swung her gaze toward Beau. "Beau, why don't you get the drinks? We're almost ready to eat."

"So soon?" Dixie asked, a look of amazement on her face. "Surely we'll have a little time to relax before dinner?"

"Dixie," her husband said in a low voice. "Be still."

Dixie's lips thinned, and her jaw tightened. Obviously, she didn't like to be corrected. "Why, I'm so sorry, Julia. Whatever you want. Can we at least take our coats off?"

Meredith was doing all she could not to laugh. She knew Julia didn't think it was funny, but Meredith thought Dixie was hysterical.

"I'll tell you what you can do," she muttered under her breath before she turned on her heels and went into the kitchen. Meredith followed her. Since the kitchen was open to the dining room, she had to be careful. She covered her mouth with her hand while she laughed lightly.

Julia glared at her. "I don't see what's so funny."

"Sorry. I think she's hysterical."

Julia finally grinned. "You're right. So what do we do? Serve drinks? Ask the servants to serve *dinnuh*?"

The way she said it started Meredith laughing again, but when Julia turned around, Meredith watched as her expression changed. She looked into the living room and realized that Beau and the Vanderkellens had overheard them. Beau was staring down at the table, but Franklin was frowning at them. And Dixie—well, if looks could kill…

Not knowing what else to do, Meredith started removing the salads from the refrigerator and carrying them into the dining room. As she put them around the table she didn't dare look at Dixie. "Would you like to eat your salads before or during dinner?" she asked, trying to sound as innocent as possible.

"Before please," Beau said somberly.

"Okay." She smiled, wondering if she should say something or if it was wisdom to keep quiet, pretend nothing unusual had happened. She turned around and almost ran into Julia, who had the other three salads. She put them on the table, then sat down.

Meredith started to sit down too when she noticed Dixie staring at her with a disapproving look. She followed her gaze and realized she was still wearing Julia's apron.

"Oh, excuse me," she said. "I didn't realize." She jumped up and hurried into the kitchen, putting the apron down on the counter. As she walked back toward the table she said a silent prayer that God would somehow bless this evening. She and Julia really wanted to find out more about James Oglethorpe and Ambrose Sedgwick.

So far, things didn't look promising.

Chapter Five

THANKFULLY, AFTER A FEW BITES of salad, conversation began. Beau and Franklin were commiserating on the way young doctors today handled patients.

"Get 'em in, move 'em out," Franklin was saying. "Not much personal attention anymore. Not like we provided."

Beau nodded. "I always tried to meet patients before surgery. Answer any questions they might have. Most people never see their anesthesiologist until they get to the operating room. That's if they get a glimpse of them at all."

"Yeah," Franklin agreed. "Of course, you were the best anesthesiologist I ever worked with."

"I'm sorry, Franklin," Julia said. "I don't remember Beau mentioning your specialty."

"I was a proctologist," he said. He laughed at her expression. "It's okay. I'm used to strange looks. It's an important profession. I'm not embarrassed by it."

"I'm sure it is," Meredith said. "Are you retired like Beau?"

He nodded. "Yes, I had to retire. I was always a little behind on my work."

There was a long silence before Dixie said, "Franklin Reginald Vanderkellen, stop telling that awful joke. No one wants to hear it."

Meredith bit her lip, trying her hardest not to laugh, but she finally lost the war. She was relieved when everyone else laughed too, including Dixie.

"You can't go into proctology unless you have a sense of humor," Franklin said.

"What made you choose it?" Meredith asked.

"My father followed the same path," he said. "I really respected him. He was a wonderful doctor. I wanted to be like him."

"That's impressive," Julia said. "Good for you."

It seemed all the salad plates were about empty. "Are we ready for our main course?" Meredith asked.

When everyone indicated they were, she and Julia got up and went into the kitchen. Meredith got pot holders and began to remove the warm plates from the oven. Julia picked them up and began transferring them to the dining room.

Meredith got the shrimp cocktail out of the fridge and carried those in. She also took the cheesecake out so it could warm up a bit.

When she and Julia were finished, they joined the others at the table.

"Oh, coq au vin," Dixie said breathlessly. "One of my favorite dishes." She frowned at her plate. "My goodness. This looks just like the coq au vin at Justine's."

Julia just smiled at her. "Well, let's hope it's as good."

Meredith waited a while, letting the conversation flow, hoping any earlier tension had resolved itself. Dixie kept looking at Julia, giving her what Meredith's parents had called "the stink eye" until they were halfway through the dinner.

Regardless of where the meal had originated, everything was delicious. According to Julia, Dixie loved to talk about her ancestor James Oglethorpe, but so far, not a peep about him. Meredith was hoping to bring up Ambrose Sedgwick once an opportunity presented itself. She glanced over at Julia, who gave her a small shrug.

When there was a lull in the conversation, Meredith decided to take the bull by the horns. "Julia tells me you're related to James Oglethorpe, Dixie. How wonderful."

Dixie put her fork down and smiled. "Yes ma'am. I'm very proud of my roots. Oglethorpes have been important citizens in Savannah from its foundation."

"I don't suppose you've heard of a man named Ambrose Sedgwick," Julia said. "I heard the strangest thing the other day."

Dixie's smile disappeared as quickly as her fake Southern accent. "What did you hear?" she demanded.

Julia faltered a little, so Meredith picked up the thread. "We heard that he is being honored with a statue. That he is the person who really laid out Savannah's grid design. Of course, that takes nothing from your ancestor. I mean, goodness gracious. Oglethorpe founded the entire city. Much more important than anything this Sedgwick person may have done."

Dixie's cheeks had turned red, and her eyes were wide. "Where did you hear about this?"

Julia stared at her. Finally, she said, "Someone mentioned that a statue was being dedicated to him. I found it odd that I'd never heard of him before."

Dixie reached for her iced tea glass and downed half the contents. When she put the glass down, she seemed better composed.

"This turn of events has upset my Dixie very much," Franklin said. "Supposedly, some distant relative of this Ambrose Sedgwick found a diary and some other papers that made her believe this man actually suggested the layout of Savannah. Of course, everyone who knows anything about James Oglethorpe is aware that he alone was primarily responsible for designing Savannah."

"But most historical references to Oglethorpe don't even mention Ambrose Sedgwick," Meredith said. "Is it really that important?"

"It's important because it isn't true!" Dixie exclaimed. "The SOS is fighting the placement of this statue in Savannah."

"The SOS?" Meredith asked.

It was only then that she noticed Julia trying to get her attention. Although Meredith tried to read Julia's lips, she couldn't make out what she was saying.

"Yes, the SOS. The Sisters of the South. We are united in our goal to preserve our history. These people who claim this Sedgwick person had *anything* to do with establishing Savannah are trying to change truth into fairy tales. We will not allow it."

Her last sentence was said with emphasis. Meredith didn't want to stir her up any more than she already was, but she wondered how far Dixie was ready to go to achieve her goal. Before she could find a way to ask the question diplomatically, Julia said, "How can you stop it, Dixie? The statue is already up in Forsyth Park. My understanding is that it will be dedicated this weekend."

"You know, maybe we should change the subject," Beau said. "Seems this topic is a little too volatile for dinner conversation."

Meredith could tell Julia was ready to press the question, but she wanted to quietly investigate this SOS group and was afraid to push

Dixie too far. She didn't want her to be suspicious. She slipped her shoe off and stretched her foot under the table, finally nudging Julia until she finally took another bite of her coq au vin. Meredith could tell Julia was irritated, but she kept it together. Better to keep things sociable in case they needed to talk to Dixie again.

Beau deftly redirected the conversation to something more palatable. Recent restaurant openings in Savannah's Historic District had not only ignited interest from Savannah foodies, but also consternation from those who weren't sure if they would fit the flavor of the area. Dixie and Franklin had very strong opinions about what kind of food was truly Southern and what was gauche. Although Meredith had her own views on the subject, she was happy to allow everyone else to talk while she turned over the idea of Dixie writing that letter to Davis. Although it was a possibility, she wondered if perhaps it might be someone else in the SOS.

"I have cheesecake for dessert," Julia said when there was a lull in the conversation. "And several kinds of coffee. What do you like?" Beau picked his favorite dark roast blend while Franklin asked for a light breakfast blend. "Not a problem," Julia said. Now all eyes were on Dixie, who hemmed and hawed a while before saying, "I don't suppose you have Speculoos, hon? It's an espresso with spice and brown sugar cookie flavor."

Julia's triumphant smile tickled Meredith. "Why, certainly I have that," she said with a smile. "I'll be back in a bit with your coffees."

Meredith had a suspicion Dixie tried to pick something she thought Julia wouldn't be able to provide. Dixie looked disappointed.

"Can I help?" Beau asked.

"Thanks," Julia said, "but Meredith and I can take care of it. You go on and visit."

Meredith got up and helped Julia carry the dishes into the kitchen. "Dixie was pretty sure I didn't have Speculoos coffee," Julia whispered as they put the dirty dishes on the counter. "I'll bet she was going to try to make me seem like some kind of…" She suddenly stopped and stared at Meredith with her mouth open. "Oh, Mere. I sound awful. What's the matter with me?"

Meredith patted her shoulder. "You're not awful. She just brings it out of you." She sighed. "Do you think she wrote that letter, Julia?"

"I think we have to keep her as a suspect. I wish I could get into one of those meetings."

"I doubt she'd let either one of us within ten feet of her little club."

Meredith began to cut the cheesecake and put the slices on dessert plates while Julia brewed the coffee. As much as she wanted to believe Dixie wrote the letter Davis received, she had no proof. There was certainly some animosity about the Sedgwick statue, but would Dixie and her group feel so strongly about Davis's book that they would actually threaten him?

She picked up two of the plates and carried them into the dining room. She'd just entered when she heard Dixie say, "Did you hear that Davis Hedgerow, you know the man who writes that dreadful column in the newspaper…what's it called?"

"Searching Savannah," Franklin said with a frown.

"Yes, that's it. Did you know that he has a book coming out that includes that horrible statue of Ambrose Sedgwick?"

Meredith almost dropped one of the dessert plates. She set it gently in front of Dixie, who picked up her fork and jabbed it in the air. "SOS will be speaking with his publisher this week. We intend to tell them that they'd better stop that book's publication or at least remove the story about Ambrose Sedgwick. If they don't they'll be sorry. Very sorry."

Meredith looked at Julia, who was carrying two more dessert plates. Her eyes were wide with surprise. Dixie Vanderkellen had just echoed the exact words used in the letter.

Chapter Six

AFTER DIXIE AND FRANKLIN LEFT, Meredith and Julia huddled together in the kitchen.

"Did you hear what she said?" Julia asked as soon as Beau closed the door behind their guests. "She's got to be the letter writer."

"Not necessarily," Meredith said. "She may have inadvertently echoed the letter writer, but that doesn't mean she's the one we're looking for."

"Well, I think she should be at the top of our list."

Meredith laughed. "Our list? We've only looked at one person. Not a very long list."

Julia smiled. "Okay. Good point."

Meredith stood up from one of the chairs that sat next to the island. "Let's get these dishes in the dishwasher. I'm beat."

"You didn't have to help," Julia said. "I didn't ask you over so you could work. But I have to say, you saved the day."

"It was nothing, really. Everything was wonderful. Absolutely delicious."

"I shouldn't have let Dixie intimidate me," Julia said. "Next time I'll cook. Maybe I can use some of the recipes from Grandma Gertrude's cookbook. They might not be fancy, but they're good Southern food. If Dixie doesn't like it, tough."

"I'd be glad to help you," Meredith said. "I could bring some side dishes and bake a cake. Maybe my Lemon Charlotte cake?"

Julia raised her eyebrows. "Not sure Dixie deserves that cake, although you can make it for me anytime." She sighed as she scraped food off the dirty dishes. "So, what now?"

"We go to Peachie's tomorrow." Meredith patted her stomach. "I'll have to skip breakfast so I'll be hungry. If I remember, they used to make pretty good cheeseburgers. I'll splurge and eat really healthy the rest of the day."

Julia scraped another dish, sending the food into her garbage disposal. "I can't imagine anyone at Peachie's wanting to stop the publication of Davis's book. It's free publicity."

"I agree," Meredith said, "but we still need to check it out."

"You just want a lemon shake," Julia said with a grin.

Meredith laughed as she placed the scraped dishes in the dishwasher. "I can't argue that point, but I do believe we need to investigate every new attraction in case we can locate our letter writer."

Julia stopped what she was doing. "I'm still not sure Davis is on the right track. What if the person who wrote that letter wasn't someone connected to one of these new places?"

Meredith sighed. "Let's hope we're looking in the right place. Frankly, Leopold's isn't threatened by Peachie's. And Moon River Brewing Company isn't worried about two small bed-and-breakfasts. I can't figure out why anyone would be afraid of a mention in Davis's book."

"Speaking of bed-and-breakfasts…"

"I made reservations for the three of us this Friday." Meredith smiled. "I assume Beau is coming with us."

"Oh, Meredith, I haven't asked him yet."

"Haven't asked who what?"

Beau's voice from behind them made Meredith jump. She turned to see him carrying a stack of dishes in from the dining room.

"Thank you, dear," Julia said, "but you need to get off your foot for a while."

"I will. No worries. It was a wonderful dinner." Beau put the dishes down and kissed Julia's neck. Meredith smiled at them. She loved seeing them together even if it did make her ache for Ron.

"Now, what didn't you ask who? Why do I feel I'm the *who* in that question?" He leaned against the counter with his arms crossed, his face creased into a frown. "What are you getting me involved in?"

Julia quickly shared their visit from Davis Hedgerow and the letter he received. "We're checking into the five new attractions being included in the book. For now, that's the scope of the investigation, but that may have to change." She cleared her throat. "Friday night Meredith made reservations at the Magnolia Blossom Inn. It's supposedly haunted."

Beau's eyebrows arched. "Now you're talking. That sounds like fun." He sighed. "Frankly, until the doctor releases me for more active pursuits, I'm up for anything."

At that moment their cat came into the room. She immediately went to Beau and began rubbing up against his leg. He reached down and picked her up.

"Hey there, Jack," he said.

Although their rescue cat was named Bunny, Beau called her Jack, short for Jackrabbit, because of her long legs.

"Where has she been?" Meredith asked, walking up to Bunny. As she stroked the beautiful cat under her chin, she purred loudly.

"Dixie doesn't like cats," Julia said. "We put her in the bedroom. I just let her out." She put a plate in the dishwasher. "A few times I thought about letting her out on purpose."

"Oh, Julia," Beau said. "I know Dixie can be irritating, but she's had a tough time. Breast cancer seven years ago. She almost didn't make it."

"I'm sorry about that, truly," Julia said. "But everyone struggles sometime in their life, Beau, yet they don't act the way Dixie does."

Beau shrugged. "You're right. Just give her a little slack."

"I hope I don't have to *give her slack*," Julia said, a hint of frustration in her tone. "You haven't seen Franklin in years. Let's just keep it like that, okay?"

Beau didn't say anything, but he looked uncomfortable and wouldn't meet Julia's gaze.

"Beauregard Eugene Foley," she said slowly. "What have you done?"

Meredith reached over and took the plate Julia held in her hand. No sense taking a chance it might get broken.

"Now Julie-bean. I had no choice. I had to…"

"They invited us to their house," she said flatly. "Didn't they?"

"Dinner. A week from Saturday." His glance slid over to Meredith. "You're invited too."

"Julia, if we haven't uncovered anything about her by then, it might be helpful. I hate to wait so long, but in the meantime, we'll be looking at some of these other places." She shrugged. "Hey, maybe we'll have this solved by then and you can make up a reason to cancel."

"Are you thinking Franklin and Dixie had something to do with the letter to David Hedgerow? I've known Franklin a long time. He'd never be involved in anything like this."

"We're not saying he is," Julia said, "but we're interested in SOS and their attitude toward the Ambrose Sedgwick statue."

"Okay, I get that," he said, "but I don't want to cancel dinner at their house, Julia. Franklin is a friend of mine."

At this point Meredith decided silence was her best defense. This was between Julia and Beau. She began rinsing dishes and putting them where Julia could reach them.

Julia didn't say anything for a couple of minutes, just kept loading the dishwasher. Finally, she said, "Have you heard about this group? SOS? Do you know anything about them?"

"Sisters of the South?" He shrugged. "I'm certainly not an expert, but I haven't heard anything negative about them. I think they do a lot of charity work." He snapped his fingers. "Remember that children's home that was broken into last Christmas?"

Julia nodded. "Someone got in and took electronic equipment, cash in the office, and even loaded up the gifts under the tree that were meant for the kids."

"I remember that," Meredith said. "It made me so angry."

"A lot of people wanted to help," Beau said, "but before anyone could coordinate something, a group stepped in and replaced everything that was lost. Not only that, they upgraded the computers and the gifts."

"SOS?" Julia asked.

Beau nodded. "SOS."

Julia put the last plate in the dishwasher and leaned against the lower cabinets. "I'm impressed."

"I think there's a lot more to Dixie than you realize. I've never met anyone who was all bad. We're all a work in progress. I think Dixie acts the way she does because she's afraid."

"Afraid of what?" Meredith asked.

Beau sighed. "Afraid no one likes her. It's easier to push people away and blame others for their negative reactions than to take responsibility for your own actions."

Julia was quiet. Then she walked over and wrapped her arms around Beau. "You're pretty smart, you know that?" she said. She kissed him on the cheek then smiled at Meredith. "Let's have dinner with Dixie next Saturday." She wriggled out of Beau's embrace, laughing. "I forgot to tell you earlier," she told Meredith. "I was too busy being upset with Dixie, I guess. I invited Maggie Lu to have lunch with us tomorrow."

Meredith smiled. "Oh good. I haven't seen her for a while."

"I haven't either," Julia said. "Maggie Lu is a wealth of information. We can ask her about Ambrose Sedgwick and SOS." She sighed. "Of course, we need some solid evidence before we deliver our suspect to Davis. It needs to be reliable enough so that the police can get involved, or Davis can confront the letter writer himself."

"Can't you get any information from the letter?" Beau asked. "Can you match the handwriting...or look for DNA on the envelope?"

Meredith smiled as Julia chuckled. "Not so fast, Columbo," Julia said. "First of all, we need some real proof that a crime has been committed—or that there is a credible threat. The police won't run the letter for DNA or fingerprints unless we do. And even if they find fingerprints, which I doubt, the letter writer has to be in the system. In my opinion, someone who used a letter to threaten another person probably won't be in the police database. If he were violent, he would have approached Davis in person."

"But surely intimidation like this isn't legal," Beau said.

"No, it's not, but all we have is a letter. We have to find the letter writer and prove he wrote it before he can be prosecuted."

"The letter writer used capitalized block letters," Julia added. "Really hard to match that to anyone."

"Can I see it?" Beau asked.

"It's in my briefcase," Meredith said. She went into the living room and retrieved the case she'd brought with her. She'd planned to go over the evidence tonight after leaving Julia's. She took out the letter, which she'd put into a large baggie to protect it, and carried it back into the kitchen. She handed it to Beau. He read it, then carried it over to a small built-in desk in the kitchen where Julia kept recipes and made her store lists. He turned on the desk lamp and turned to look at them. "Can I take this out of the bag?"

"Yes," Julia said. "Just be careful."

He nodded at her and opened the bag. He gingerly removed the letter and then held it close to the lamp.

"See this?" he said, gesturing at the paper. "It looks like an imprint."

Julia and Meredith came over and stood next to Beau. Meredith peered at the paper, trying to see what Beau referred to.

"This paper came from a pad of paper and part of what was written on top of this sheet shows up," he said. He looked up at Meredith.

"Just what is it you think you see?" Julia asked.

"In the upper part of the paper, before the words, it looks like someone wrote, BID in capital letters."

"BID means twice a day," Julia said to Meredith. "It's a doctor's notation when writing a prescription."

"Yes, or maybe someone's just using the word *bid*," Beau said. He shrugged. "I can't be sure, but it's possible your letter writer is a doctor. Or works with one."

Meredith caught Julia's eye. "Dixie is looking guiltier and guiltier."

Julia nodded. "You're right. Could we have found our main suspect on our first try?"

Meredith didn't say anything, just smiled at her partner. Had they been handed what they needed to crack the case? If so, why did she feel it was far from being solved?

Chapter Seven

MEREDITH WAS HAPPY TO FIND Carmen in the office Tuesday morning when she arrived. "Glad you're on the mend."

"*Buenos días*," Carmen said. "Boy, I felt like something that needed to be thrown out. It was awful." She smiled, her brown eyes sparkling. "*Gracias* for the chicken soup. I guess that old chestnut has truth to it. The first sip made me decide life might be worth living after all."

Meredith laughed. "I can't take too much credit for it. That's one of Grandma Gertrude's recipes." Julia's grandmother Gertrude had left behind a collection of her wonderful recipes with personal comments written in the margins. Julia treasured it and had shared several of the recipes with Meredith.

"Well, Grandma Gertrude was a whiz," Carmen said. "The soup was *muy bien*. I had no idea her recipes had healing powers."

"Who has healing powers?" Julia asked as she joined Meredith.

"Seems Grandma Gertrude should have been licensed as a medical professional," Meredith said.

"Oh really. Let me guess. Grandma Gertrude's chicken soup?"

Carmen pointed at her. "*Sí.* It's so good I almost want to get sick again just so I can have some more."

Julia laughed. "I don't think that will be necessary. I'll write down the recipe for you. You can make it yourself."

"Not sure it will be as good as Meredith's, but I'm willing to try. *Muchas gracias*, boss."

"You're welcome."

"Now I have a question," Carmen said, frowning. "Who messed with my files while I was gone?"

Julia's eyes widened. "I...I was just cleaning them out. I wanted to make sure they were all up-to-date."

Carmen folded her arms across her chest. "And were they?"

"Pretty much. I removed a few things," Julia said softly. "I put everything I took out in a separate folder."

Meredith had to look away to keep from laughing. Julia's guilty expression was comical.

"Some of those papers you removed were possible future contacts," Carmen scolded. "We may not use them, but what if we need them later? And I had everything in a specific order. "First contact report. Personal report. Case notes. You put the case notes first."

"I'm sorry, truly," Julia said. "I was so bored..."

Carmen groaned. "*Aye-yi-yi!* Next time, get a hobby." She pointed at a stack of files on her desk. "It will take me all morning to fix this."

Meredith and Julia were used to Carmen's frank way of communicating. Although it sounded like she was being disrespectful, they knew her well enough to realize she didn't mean to be.

"Okay. Point taken," Julia said. "And you quit getting sick. See what happens when you're not here?"

Carmen's slightly sour expression vanished. "I'll do my best." She grabbed some of the files she'd been working on and began putting them back in the filing cabinets. "You ladies really do need me."

"Yes, we do," Meredith said. "We were lost without you."

When Carmen turned around, Meredith was happy to see her smile.

Julia followed Meredith into her office and closed the door behind her. "So Dixie Vanderkellen and her SOS group are at the top of our list?"

"A very short list so far." Meredith opened her briefcase and took out the letter sent to Davis. "I'm still going to protect this just in case we're able to check it for fingerprints or DNA. Like I said last night though, I doubt seriously that will work. Add the fact that our guy wore gloves when he dropped off the letter to the newspaper. My guess is he's been very careful with this."

She put it on the top of her desk and moved her desk lamp over it. She opened another drawer and found her magnifying glass. Using it always made her think of Sherlock Holmes. The image made her giggle.

"Sherlock?" Julia asked with a grin.

Meredith nodded. "Sherlock." She held the glass up to the paper. Now that Beau had pointed out the imprint, Meredith could easily see it. "I'm so glad Beau noticed this. Why didn't we see it earlier?"

Julia leaned over the desk and stared at the letter. "Because we were so focused on what the letter said."

"I think there are other images on the paper, but the writing blocks them." She squinted, trying to make out something else on the page. "Why wouldn't a doctor use a prescription pad if we were ordering medicine? Why use a regular pad of paper?"

"That's a good point," Julia said. "Maybe someone was just talking about a bid for something, or maybe the letters stand for something. You know, like SOS means Sisters of the South."

"An acronym? Yeah, could be." Meredith shook her head. "Let's keep this in mind as we check out these places. But we can't use it as an important clue because it may mean nothing. We have no idea where this pad of paper was and who had access to it."

"Okay," Julia said. "I get it, but I still think it points toward Dixie."

"Maybe. Maybe not."

"So where do we start?" Julia asked. "What about Peachie's?"

Meredith sighed. "I still can't come up with a reason they wouldn't want to be included in the book. I'll bet it sells like hotcakes. People love to visit Savannah, and a book that points out some of our best features?" She reached over and picked up the ARC lying on her desk. "Look at this. Forsyth Square, Bonadventure Cemetery, Cathedral of St. John the Baptist, there are beautiful pictures from the Historic District...." She closed the book and looked at Julia. "Local citizens will buy this book and so will people who are planning a visit. Again, why would any of these people not want this book to see the light of day? It just doesn't make sense. Every single new attraction should want visitors."

"Even the statue of Ambrose Sedgwick?" Julia asked. "You know who we need to talk to?"

"The people behind the statue."

"Yes."

"Can you get on the phone and find out who they are?" Meredith asked. "Call the mayor's office. They would have had to approve it."

"I'm on it." She walked toward the Meredith's office door.

"What time are we supposed to meet Maggie Lu at Peachie's?" Meredith asked.

"I asked her to meet us there at twelve thirty."

Julia nodded. "Good. I'll get back to you and let you know what I found out."

"Thanks."

After Julia left, Meredith made a call to Davis to get permission to discuss the letter with Maggie Lu. She was extremely knowledgeable when it came to goings on in Savannah—past and present. She wasn't a legal professional, but she certainly qualified as a real historian. Davis welcomed any help they could get and gave the okay.

After she hung up the phone, Meredith picked the book up again and slowly thumbed through it as if the answer to this mystery was printed on its pages. At this point she definitely suspected Dixie, but was sending a threatening letter her style? For some reason Meredith couldn't see it happening. Dixie would approach city officials and try to stop the dedication of the statue that way. Something occurred to her so she got up and walked down the hall to Julia's office. Julia had just picked up her phone when Meredith walked in.

"While you're at it," she said, "ask the mayor's office if they've heard from SOS. Have they tried to stop the statue and the dedication? I'd also like to know anyone else who's voiced a complaint."

"Good thinking. I'll let you know."

Meredith nodded and headed back to her own office, stopping first at the coffee bar situated between their offices. She got a cup of coffee and carried it back to her desk. Then she began looking through the ARC again, this time making notes about anything that might give someone a reason to want Davis to back off. Although it seemed as if she hadn't been at it that long, she was surprised when Julia opened her door. She had her coat on.

"Ready?" she asked.

Meredith looked at the clock on her wall. Twelve fifteen. Where had the time gone? "Sure. Let me get my coat and my purse."

On the way to Peachie's Julia filled her in on what she'd discovered from talking to people at the mayor's office.

"I spoke to the mayor's publicity guy," Julia said. "That was a waste of time, but when I asked the mayor's administrative assistant, I got an earful." She smiled. "Sheila and I went to school together."

"What did she tell you?"

"The family of Ambrose Sedgwick advocated for the statue. They even hired the artist who created it. The Sedgwick family was a major contributor to the mayor's reelection campaign." Julia shrugged. "Sheila wouldn't say that the mayor approved the statue because of that, but she didn't deny it either."

"Did you find out how we can contact the family?"

"I did," Julia said, "but I'm not sure they will talk to us. Sheila says they're pretty private. However, I was able to find out that Ambrose's great-great-great… Well, it goes on and on. Anyway, it's a lot of greats, granddaughter, Elise Sedgwick, owns…" She tossed Meredith a grin. "Wait for it…"

"Oh, for crying out loud, Jules, just tell me."

"Okay," Julia said. "She owns the Magnolia Blossom Inn."

"The same B and B we're going to Friday night?"

Julia nodded.

"What a coincidence." Meredith wasn't sure that made Elise Sedgwick a suspect, but it was certainly an interesting turn of events.

"And yes, the mayor has heard from SOS on many occasions. According to Sheila, the mayor just ignores them. Sheila hasn't heard of any other group protesting the statue."

"Okay, thanks, Julia."

Meredith was silent as she pulled into Peachie's parking lot. She was happy to see the building had been carefully restored. All the fluorescent lighting was working again. The name, PEACHIE'S, was displayed on a large, colorful sign over the front entrance. Although Meredith wanted to bask in the joy of seeing one of her favorite places in Savannah brought back to life, she was stuck on the information Julia had given her.

"So the family behind the Ambrose Sedgwick statue also owns the Magnolia Blossom Inn." She turned and frowned at Julia. "That's a really big coincidence."

"There's more," Julia said. "Eloise is on the outs with her family. She owns the B and B, but her family has nothing to do with it."

"So maybe she has a grudge against them?"

"Maybe," Julia said, "but now we have two reasons to visit the inn Friday night."

"I guess we do." Meredith looked at Julia and smiled. "This case just got really interesting."

Chapter Eight

WHEN THEY ENTERED PEACHIE'S, JULIA grabbed Meredith's arm. "Oh, Mere. Look at this place. It looks just like it used to." Julia's voice cracked a bit. "Sorry. I guess I didn't realize how much Peachie's meant to me. Remember how many times we sat in here, talking about...well, all kinds of things. Mr. Walsh never complained about how long we sat in a booth, even when we didn't order food."

Meredith laughed. "I think we made up for it with all the milkshakes we bought."

"You could be right."

A girl walked up to them, dressed in a '50s themed outfit, peach-colored with frilly black lace around the hem and outlining the white apron. She wore short sleeves trimmed in the same black lace and a jaunty hat that sat on top of her brown hair, which was pulled back in a ponytail.

"Just two of you?" she asked.

"We'll be joined by someone else," Meredith started to say when she heard someone call her name. She looked toward the back of the dining room and saw Maggie Lu sitting in a booth.

"I take it you're with Maggie Lu?" the waitress asked.

"You know her?" Julia asked.

The waitress smiled. "She was my teacher at Spencer Elementary. She was the best teacher I ever had."

Meredith wasn't surprised by the waitress's praise. Maggie Lu was loved by almost every child she'd ever taught. In 1998 she'd received a Teacher of the Year award.

"You go on over," the waitress, whose name tag read MOLLY, said. "I'll bring you menus."

"Thank you," Meredith said.

As she and Julia went over to join Maggie Lu, Meredith looked around the restored restaurant. Everything was the same as she remembered. The huge counter up front with red plastic-covered stools in front, the big fluorescent clock on the wall that touted a popular soft drink, waitresses in '50s costumes, the Formica tables with shiny silver legs and chairs with white and peach-colored striped vinyl. The wood booths against the walls looked completely restored, with laminate tabletops, paper placemats, and tabletop jukeboxes on each table.

"It's exactly the same," Meredith said softly, more to herself than anyone else.

When they reached the booth, both women hugged Maggie Lu before sitting down. "We could have picked you up," Meredith said.

Maggie Lu, who didn't drive, just smiled. "Now why would I let you do that when the bus is so convenient? Besides, I just love talking to everyone. The driver on my route was one of my students, you know. His mama's been so very ill. I like getting updates. Helps me to know how to pray."

"I hope she's improving," Julia said.

Maggie Lu nodded. "Much better, thank the good Lord. Kenny thinks she'll be released from the hospital any day now."

"That's good news."

Molly came up to the table and handed Meredith and Julia menus. Meredith noticed a butterfly tattoo on her arm. "That's lovely," Meredith said.

"Thanks," the girl said. "I tried to cover it up when I came to apply for a job, but my boss saw it. I was afraid I wouldn't be hired, but she doesn't have a problem with tattoos. Some people do, you know."

"Well, I think it's beautiful too, child," Maggie Lu said. "Just like you."

Molly smiled at her. "Do you know what you want to drink, ladies?" she asked.

"I've been waiting years to say this," Meredith said. "May I have a lemon shake, please?"

Molly grinned. "You bet. And for you?" she asked Julia.

"I'll have a Double-Dutch Chocolate Shake," she said. It had been one of Peachie's most popular shakes.

"Will that be it for you ladies?" Molly asked. "Or do you also want to order food?"

"I'm sure we will," Julia said.

"What about water?" she asked Julia and Meredith.

"Yes, please," Meredith said.

"Okay. I'll get your shakes now, and Morris will get your lunch order. I'll bring those waters too." She smiled at Maggie Lu. "You'll order lunch with them?"

Maggie Lu nodded. "I will, thank you, honey. It's been such a blessing to see you again."

"You too, Mrs. King. Hope you come back a lot."

"I will. Maybe we can have lunch together one day when you're off?"

Molly's smile widened. "I would love that, thanks."

As she walked away, Julia remarked, "Your students really love you, don't they?"

"Most of them do," Maggie Lu said. "Of course, not everyone appreciates being challenged. At first, Molly was one of them, but a little attention and some encouragement changed that child. She's only working here part-time, you know. That girl's got gumption. Molly's in college now, studying to be a teacher."

"That's wonderful," Meredith said. "She's following in your footsteps."

Maggie Lu shook her head. "No, she needs to walk her own path. Become whoever God created her to be. My granny used to tell me, 'Maggie Lu, everyone is special. They just need to discover the gifts God put inside them.'"

Meredith smiled at her. "I love spending time with you. I always leave feeling better."

Maggie Lu took a sip of her iced tea, then focused her brown eyes on Meredith. "Is there some reason you're not feeling up to par?"

Meredith sighed. "No, I'm fine. We're working a case."

"You want to tell me about it?"

"Yes, we're looking into some new Savannah businesses that may not want publicity for some reason."

Maggie Lu's eyebrows shot up. "Now why in heaven's name wouldn't any business not want publicity? They must be hiding something."

"But what?" Julia asked. "That's the question we need to answer."

Maggie Lu smiled. "I have a profound faith in you two ladies. You'll figure it out."

Molly showed up with their milkshakes. When she placed the shake in front of Meredith she felt herself getting a little emotional. It wasn't about the milkshake. It was from the memories of sharing one with Ron.

Molly gave Julia her shake and walked away.

"Are you all right?" Julia asked Meredith.

"Fine. Sorry. It's silly."

Maggie Lu reached across the table and took Meredith's hand. "Bless your heart. My sweet Darwin used to buy me Mary Jane candies because he knew I liked them. Hardly ever see them now, but a few stores carry them. Whenever I run across them I think of him. It will always be that way. We just have to look upon those memories with joy. That's what they'd want us to do, isn't that right, Meredith?"

Meredith smiled at her and squeezed her hand. "You're right. Thank you."

Maggie Lu let go of Meredith's hand just as a tall young man stepped up to the table. He was good-looking, with long black hair pulled back in a ponytail. His name tag read MORRIS. He smiled at them.

"Do you ladies know what you want to eat?" he asked.

Maggie Lu ordered a bacon, lettuce, and tomato sandwich while Julia and Meredith asked for cheeseburgers.

"Our cheeseburgers are great," Morris said. "You'll enjoy them."

"Do they come with grilled onions like they used to?" Julia asked.

"Absolutely." He grinned. "Kathy is pretty strict about making everything just like her grandfather did."

He held out his hand and took their menus. "I'll bring your food as soon as it's ready."

"Thank you," Julia said.

He'd just walked away when a woman walked up to their table. She was short, a little chunky with curly blond hair and bright blue eyes. "Everything to your liking, ladies?" she asked.

It didn't take much of a leap for Meredith to guess that this was the owner, Kathy Walsh. "I take it you're Mr. Walsh's granddaughter," she said.

Kathy smiled. "Yes. Did you know him?"

"Yes," Meredith said. "My friend and I used to come here all the time when we were younger. We were just talking about how your grandfather used to let us stay for hours. Never kicked us out."

Kathy's mouth dropped open. "You're the lemon shake girls."

"What?"

"Yeah, Granddad used to talk about two girls who came into the diner and would order lemon shakes. He didn't originally make lemon shakes, you know. He came up with that just for you two. Turned out other people like it too. That's why we still offer it."

"I never knew that. What a sweet man. My husband and I came here when we were dating. This place means a lot to me. I was so sorry when your grandfather died." She smiled up at Kathy. "We attended the funeral."

"A lot of people did," Kathy said. "I was pretty little, but I still remember all the people who showed up."

"Kathy, one thing I've always wondered," Julia said, "where did the name Peachie's come from? Your grandfather's first name was Eddie, wasn't it? And your grandmother was Kathleen?"

"Yes." She grinned. "Peachie was the name of Granddad's cocker spaniel."

"You're kidding," Meredith said, laughing.

Kathy shook her head. "Nope. Granddad loved that dog."

Maggie Lu smiled at Kathy. "Your grandfather was very special to me as well. He always welcomed me and my family when we came in."

"Granddad welcomed everyone," she said. "He loved people. He was the best."

"So how long have you been open now?" Meredith asked.

"Three weeks," Kathy said. "We're still trying to find our footing. Granddad was a whiz at running this place. It's taking five of us just to do what he did by himself."

Meredith looked around the restaurant. Although there were several customers, it certainly wasn't full. "Have you done any advertising?" she asked.

"A little. To be honest, it's taken almost every penny we have trying to get up and running. But Davis Hedgerow, you know the newspaper columnist? He's writing a book about some of Savannah's best attractions. He's including us. And he also promised a follow-up interview in the paper." She clasped her hands together. "The best publicity we could get. I'm thrilled. I know we have a lot of empty tables now, but after that book comes out, things will change, I'm sure of it." She chuckled. "He showed up with a photographer for the book without warning us. I'm not so sure how we'll look. A couple of my staff begged me to ask him to come back and redo the photos when we were a little better prepared."

"And did you?" Meredith asked.

Kathy shook her head. "I tried, but he insisted the pictures were great and that we'd love them. I hope he's right."

Meredith was jolted by the sound of glass breaking. Molly stood behind Kathy, holding one glass of water, but the other had hit the floor and shattered.

The color had drained from her face. She looked frightened.

Chapter Nine

WITHOUT SAYING A WORD, MAGGIE Lu slid out of the booth, took Molly's arm, and made her sit down. "Get this child a glass of orange juice, please," she said to Kathy.

Kathy nodded and hurried toward the kitchen. "Put your head down, honey," Maggie Lu told Molly. She looked over at Meredith and Julia. "Diabetes. Her blood sugar is too low."

A few seconds later Kathy came jogging up to their booth, a large glass of orange juice in her hand. "Here," she said holding it out to Molly.

Molly raised her head and took the glass. Her pale complexion and the sweat that had broken out on her forehead alarmed Meredith. "Will she be okay?" she asked Maggie Lu.

"Yes, she sometimes had bad reactions when she was in my classroom. Back then, I kept oranges and candy bars in my desk in case she needed help. Of course, if this had gone the other way, we would have had to give her a shot to stabilize her."

When Molly finished drinking, she said in a shaky voice, "I'm sorry about the glass. I'll clean it up."

"Don't be silly." Kathy waved Morris over.

"Is everything all right?" he asked, staring at Molly. He looked concerned.

"Yes, it's fine. Would you ask Jeffrey to clean this up?"

"Of course." After casting one more worried glance at Molly, he went into the kitchen.

"I'm usually very careful," Molly said. "This has never happened before. I hope it won't affect my job."

"Oh, Molly," Kathy said. "What do you take me for? Of course it won't. But I do want you to tell me the next time you're not feeling well. Just stop what you're doing and take care of yourself. And maybe…put down whatever you're holding?" She chuckled when she finished speaking, and Molly sighed with relief.

"Thank you. I'll do that."

"Let's go in the back. I have a cot in my office," Kathy said. "You need to lie down for a while."

"But Morris and I are the only ones working," Molly said.

"I can cover for you," she said. "We'll be fine."

Kathy waited for Molly to stand up and then took her arm and guided her toward a door not far from the counter. She took keys out of her pocket and unlocked it, then she and Molly went inside.

"I'm sure Molly was having a reaction," Meredith said under her breath, "but did you see her expression? Was it all physical or was it a reaction to what we said?"

"I don't know," Julia said slowly.

"What are you two talking about?" Maggie Lu said. "I told you Molly has diabetes."

"Well," Meredith said, "someone in the city is trying to stop the publication of a book that showcases important sites in Savannah. Peachie's is one of those sites. Molly looked shocked when she over-heard us talking about that very thing."

Maggie Lu sighed dramatically. "You two are wonderful investigators, you really are, but you also have pretty big imaginations. That girl looked shocked because when someone's sugar is low, they can pass out. She was just afraid of fainting with her hands full."

A young man with Down syndrome came over and began cleaning up the water and shattered glass next to their booth. Meredith smiled at him.

"Are you Jeffrey?" Maggie Lu asked.

"Yes, Jeffrey," he said with a smile.

"Thank you for helping us," she said. "We certainly appreciate it."

A smile spread across Jeffrey's face. "You're welcome. I like my job."

"Do you like everyone you work with?" Meredith asked. It wasn't as if Jeffrey was going to point them to someone who might be the letter writer, but what did it hurt to ask?

"Yes," he said. "Except for Carl the cook. Sometimes Carl is mean."

"I'm sorry to hear that. Jeffrey. Do you know Carl's last name?"

He nodded slowly then looked around him. He must not have seen any of his coworkers because he said, "Finney. Carl Finney. But he doesn't want anyone to know his last name. It makes him mad if you say it."

"Then we won't say it," Maggie Lu said, looking at Meredith through narrowed eyes.

Jeffrey dumped all the glass he'd swept up into a cart. Then he took some paper towels and mopped up the water. "There you go," he said with a satisfied smile. "If I can do anything more to help, let me know. Just ask for Jeffrey."

"We will, thank you," Julia said.

As the young man walked away, Maggie Lu said, "I'm gratified to see Peachie's is willing to hire people with disabilities." She arched an eyebrow at Meredith. "You won't involve Jeffrey in your case, will you?"

"Of course not," Meredith reassured her.

Maggie Lu sighed. "Good. I get a little sensitive about young people like Jeffrey. They have enough challenges to deal with every day."

"We feel the same way you do," Julia said. "But I think we need to check up on Mr. Finney. I don't like hearing that he's mean to Jeffrey."

"I agree," Meredith said.

Just then Morris walked up to their booth with a large tray, which he set down on a foldout table he carried under his arm. Meredith marveled at his dexterity. He began passing out the women's orders. Maggie Lu's BLT looked wonderful. But the cheeseburgers were incredible. Big and dripping with melted cheese. The smell of grilled onions actually made Meredith's stomach growl. She didn't eat like this very often because of her heart attack scare over a year ago, but occasionally she still let herself indulge.

Morris placed Maggie Lu's plate on the table and then leaned across Meredith to put Julia's plate in front of her. He was so close to Meredith that she could smell his aftershave. He really was nice looking even though she thought he needed a haircut. She noticed a small earring in his ear that looked like a diamond but probably wasn't.

After setting her plate down Morris said, "Do you ladies need anything else?"

"Maybe a couple of glasses of water," Julia said with a smile.

Morris grinned. "I guess the last ones didn't make it all the way to the table, did they? I'll get them right away."

As he walked away, Julia said, "Nice young man."

"Yes, he is." Meredith pulled the bun back on her cheeseburger and asked Julia for the mustard. She squirted some on her patty, added the pickles that were on the side of her plate, then closed it up. Julia picked up a packet of mayonnaise. Meredith sighed.

"You don't have to make that noise." Julia rolled her eyes and smiled at Maggie Lu. "Meredith doesn't approve of mayo on hamburgers."

Maggie Lu laughed. "As my granny used to say, 'whatever it takes to get it down, do it.' Of course, she was talking about medicine. That woman loved castor oil. Believed it cured everything." She shuddered visibly. "I hate to even think of that vile stuff."

"Not sure we should be talking about castor oil while we're eating," Meredith said. "It's not very appetizing."

"I agree," Maggie Lu said. "Let's think about delicious things… like this good food the Lord has provided."

"Maggie Lu, how much do you know about James Oglethorpe?" Meredith asked before popping a fry in her mouth. "I mean, the kind of man he was."

Maggie Lu shook her head. "I taught my students that he was a good man who felt that too many people were being tossed into prisons in Britain, many of them because they were poor and desperate. He brought them to the United States, along with refugees from other countries, and arranged for them to have their own land. To provide for themselves and their families. He developed a close friendship with Chief Tomochichi, chief of the Creek Indian village of Yamacraw. He also outlawed the use of enslaved people in the settled areas. He believed slavery to be inhumane. Unfortunately, when he left the antislavery edict was rescinded." She took a sip of her tea. "That dear man was ahead of his time."

"Have you heard of a man named Ambrose Sedgwick?" Julia asked.

"Yes, I have. He was a colonel who served with Oglethorpe. Someone who was instrumental in helping Oglethorpe found Savannah. But I never heard a word about him having direct involvement with the way the city's laid out. It's always been believed that Oglethorpe came up with the idea of creating a city designed on grids. Not long ago, Sedgwick's family claimed to discover some journals and papers that seem to point to Sedgwick as the man who had more to do with Savannah's planning than Oglethorpe himself." Maggie Lu took a bite of her sandwich and chewed slowly, her eyes narrowed.

"You don't look convinced," Meredith said.

After she swallowed, Maggie Lu put her sandwich down.

"The original story is that Oglethorpe and Colonel William Bull designed the new city, Bull being the main architect. But now, because of this new discovery, it seems Sedgwick may have been the man who originally came up with the grid design with Bull taking credit for it."

"What do you think?" Meredith asked.

Maggie Lu shrugged. "Pretty hard to know the truth. I haven't seen the papers or the diary. It sure surprises me though."

"It would be tough to get our hands on these papers," Julia said. "I'd love to see them."

Maggie Lu sighed. "I doubt you will get your hands on them, but you can see them. They're going to be on display at the Georgia Historical Society beginning this weekend. The Savannah Historical Society is sponsoring it. Goes along with the dedication of the statue this Saturday."

"I find it hard to believe the city approved the placement of this statue," Meredith said. She didn't mention the rumor that the family had donated to the mayor's reelection campaign. At this point it was just gossip.

Maggie Lu shrugged again. "Seems the Sedgwicks have offered to donate a million dollars toward restoring the Georgia Historical Society's building. That much money buys a lot of favor, you know."

Meredith gasped. "That seems like a conflict of interest. Are you sure about this?"

Maggie Lu nodded. "As sure as I can be."

Meredith thought for a moment. "How do we know these letters and this diary are real?"

"Well, we don't," Maggie Lu said, "and that's the problem. Trust me, not everyone is happy about this, you know. Even your replacement is perturbed by this turn of events."

"So the Queen Bee has a problem with Ambrose Sedgwick?"

Beatrice Enterline had taken over Meredith's position as the president of the Savannah Historical Society. She could put Dixie to shame as a genuine Southern belle. Meredith smiled at the idea of the two of them together. That would be something but definitely too much *sugah* for her.

"Something amusing about this?" Julia asked her.

"No, just a random thought." She took a bite of her cheeseburger and sighed with pleasure. "Oh, Julia. It tastes just like it used to. I've really missed this place."

Julia grinned and nodded at her. Julia was the classiest woman Meredith knew. So to see mayonnaise dripping down her chin made Meredith laugh. She picked up a napkin and handed it to her.

Julia put her burger down and took the napkin. "There is simply no way to eat this burger with an ounce of elegance," she said, laughing. "And I don't care."

Meredith agreed. "I almost feel like we're back in college, don't you?"

Julia snorted. "Not really, although I understand why you'd say that."

Maggie Lu shook her head. "You two can be really entertaining, but I need to get back to the library." She pointed her finger at them. "I hope your enjoyment of this place won't keep you away from the diner." Maggie Lu's daughter, Charlene, owned the Downhome Diner, one of their favorite restaurants.

"Well, I don't see shrimp and grits on Peachie's menu," Meredith said, "so I think Peachie's will be an addition to our eating pleasure, not a replacement."

Maggie Lu smiled. "Good. Charlene loves seeing your smiling faces in the diner. She thinks the world of you."

"Maggie Lu," Julia asked, "how's Jake doing?"

She smiled. "He's doing just fine. Full of spit and vinegar. I feel very blessed," she said. "And I love babysitting when Charlene and Clarissa are busy."

Meredith reached down to pick up the bag she'd carried in with them. "We both got something for Jake. I put both gifts in one bag to make it easier for you to carry."

"Bless your hearts," Maggie Lu said. "Thank you both. I'll take them to Clarissa."

"Before you go," Meredith said, handing her the bag, "I have a question. Have you ever heard of an organization referred to as SOS? I think it means…"

"Sisters of the South," Maggie Lu said. "Yes, I know about them. Why?"

"They're vehemently opposed to the narrative about Ambrose Sedgwick. They don't believe it's true."

"Vehemently opposed?" Maggie Lu echoed. "Do you know why?"

"I'm not sure," Meredith said. "I'm wondering just how far they might go to stop someone claiming Oglethorpe and Bull weren't responsible for Savannah's unique layout."

Maggie Lu picked up her purse and scooted to the end of the booth. As she stood to her feet, she said, "I'm not sure what they're capable of, but when they asked me to join I turned them down."

"Why?" Meredith asked.

Maggie Lu sighed loudly. "I don't know. Seems like there's some odd things going on in that group. I mean, they do a lot of good, but…well. A friend of mine is a member. Seems the Sedgwicks also gave SOS a nice donation, probably trying to win their approval.

It didn't work, but they took the money anyway. Now it's possible the books aren't adding up."

"You mean money's missing?" Meredith asked.

"Could be." Maggie Lu shrugged. "Of course, this is second-hand information. Might not add up to a hill of beans. I wouldn't mention it to anyone except you."

"Who handles the money? Julia asked.

"Their treasurer is Dixie Vanderkellen. You wanted to know someone who might do something to keep any attention coming toward Ambrose Sedgwick? You might want to look closely at Dixie."

With that, Maggie Lu walked away.

Chapter Ten

"WHAT DOES THAT MEAN?" JULIA asked as she and Meredith watched Maggie Lu leave the restaurant.

"I'm not sure, but we need to find out." Meredith shook her head.

"Oh, Meredith," Julia said, "could the letter writer actually be Dixie?"

Meredith pushed her food to the other side of the table where Maggie Lu had been. It felt silly for her and Julia to sit together on one side of the booth. She got out and slid across the seat until she faced Julia.

"I'm not sure," she said, "but it's possible. But if Dixie is stealing money, that's something the group needs to address, not us."

"True, but could she be trying to stop the publication of the book so no one will look too closely at her group?"

Meredith considered her question. "I thought so, but the more I think about it, I'm not so sure. Won't the dedication of the statue and the display of Sedgwick's papers and diary at the historical society bring loads of attention? Probably more than the book will. So why target the book?"

Julia was silent for a moment, obviously turning Meredith's words over in her mind. Finally, she said, "I see your point. On the other hand, I take Maggie Lu's opinions seriously."

"Yeah, me too." Meredith decided to concentrate on her cheeseburger and lemon shake. By the time she finished, she was so full she was uncomfortable. She noticed that Julia also looked a little distressed.

"I shouldn't have finished that cheeseburger," Julia said.

"But you did," Meredith said with a grin. "So let's walk it off."

"I'd rather lie down and take a long nap."

"Me too. But instead why don't we check out the Book Worm? It's not far from here."

Julia sighed deeply. "Okay, but if I suddenly lie down on the sidewalk and start snoring, please just push me out of the way."

Meredith laughed. "I promise."

After leaving a nice tip on the table, they paid for their meals and left. The Book Worm was only two blocks away. Thankfully, it wasn't raining, but it looked as if it could start again at any minute. As they walked, Meredith marveled once again at how beautiful Savannah was. Especially the historic district. Januaries were chilly, usually not getting any higher than sixty or lower than forty. Today it seemed as if they were getting close to that lower temperature. The icy rain hadn't helped. Meredith buttoned her coat against the wind that made it even colder.

"So where are we so far?" Julia asked. "Peachie's has no reason to worry about Davis's book. I guess Dixie might have a reason, and her husband is a doctor."

"*Was* a doctor," Meredith reminded her. "Why would a retired proctologist be writing prescriptions?"

Julia was quiet for a moment. "Maybe the pad was old?"

"I don't know," Meredith said. "I suppose it's a possibility."

"Let's move on from Dixie for now," Julia said. "We'll keep her on our suspect list, but I'd like to check out other possibilities. Maybe someone will jump out at us."

"I hope you're speaking figuratively," Meredith said with a smile.

Julia laughed. "Yes, I was."

"So we have two B and Bs and the bookstore left," Meredith said. "We're visiting one of the B and Bs Friday night. I wonder what Beau would say if we booked the other one for Saturday."

Julia grinned. "I don't think you want to know. Let me check with him to see if he's made plans for us." She stopped as they reached the crosswalk. As soon as the light changed, they hurried across the street to the next block. The Book Worm was only half a block away.

"Why don't you let me go alone to the John Farmer House?" Meredith said. "I'll keep in touch with you."

Julia hesitated a moment before saying, "It might be best. Beau's overdoing it on that ankle. The doctor told him to elevate it and ice it, but he rarely does that." She frowned at Meredith. "Are you sure about going alone?"

Meredith smiled at her, hoping to relieve her concerns. "I'm positive. Like I said, I can call you or text you while I'm there." She slipped her arm through Julia's. "I'll be fine. It's an adventure. I'm looking forward to it."

Meredith steeled herself to enter the Book Worm again. She and Ron used to love strolling through the rows of new and used books.

But since his death she hadn't been back. Time to bite the bullet and go inside. When they reached the bookstore, Meredith took a deep breath and walked toward the entrance. The automatic door swished open, and they stepped into a large room with rows and rows of books on dark oak shelves that began at the first floor and reached up to the second. Two spiral staircases led to the upstairs. Overstuffed chairs and small tables dotted the bottom floor. One area had a large plush couch with several comfy chairs that circled it, creating a conversation area. Meredith had seen book clubs gather there to discuss their latest discovery. Her eyes drifted to a grouping of two chairs and a small table near a fireplace. She and Ron had sat there more than once. She remembered one rainy day when they spent the entire afternoon just talking. No one ever asked them to leave. Of course, they left with books. They both loved mysteries. Ron had picked out two books that still sat on a shelf in their bedroom, unread. He died before he could get to them.

Julia reached over and put her arm around Meredith. "You haven't been here since..."

"Since Ron died," she said softly. She hugged Julia. "I'm okay. Let's do what we came here to do."

"Okay." Julia gestured toward a spot in the back corner of the shop. "Look. That must be the new coffee bar."

They walked toward an area that was obviously under construction. The counter was in, and a glass case in front of it ran all the way across. Behind the counter, large coffeemakers waited to be used. The display was actually charming. As they looked it over, a girl walked up to them. She was young, had blond-streaked hair, and wore jeans with a long pink sweater and matching heels. Meredith didn't remember seeing her before.

"We plan to have this open by the end of the month," she said. "It should increase our traffic."

"I've heard some people don't like the idea of changing the store," Julia said.

The girl wrinkled her nose as if she were smelling something unpleasant. "We all need to be more progressive," she said. "Keeping things the same just because you don't like change? Well, it doesn't make much sense, does it?"

"Sometimes people don't want change because they fear things they value will be lost," Meredith said. "It's not because they're actually afraid of something new."

The girl, whose name tag read TRACY, shrugged. "I don't think offering coffee and snacks will change the Book Worm. Like I said, this new addition will bring in more customers. People who work in the area can eat their lunch and buy books at the same time." She took a step back and studied Meredith and Julia with a critical look. "You're not part of that group, are you?"

"What group?" Meredith asked.

Tracy rolled her eyes. "The Book Worm Warriors. Some days they walk back and forth in front of the store, carrying signs, protesting the coffee and snack bar. It's not like we're burning books or anything."

"Is there a problem here?"

Meredith turned to find a tall man with black glasses and dark hair frowning at them. She recognized him from her previous visits with Ron.

"Not a problem," Meredith said. "We were just asking about the changes being made in the store. It seems some people are opposed to them."

"I remember you," the man said. "You used to come in here with a man. You sat over there."

"You have a good memory," Meredith said. "That was my husband. He passed away a couple of years ago."

"I'm so sorry," the man said graciously.

"Thank you. I recall you too. You were very nice to us. We stayed here for hours. You could have insisted we leave."

"Why?" he asked. "You were comfortable and enjoying a rainy day in my bookstore. That's why I put the chairs in."

"It will always be a good memory. Thank you."

He turned to Tracy. "I'll take care of these customers," he told her. "Why don't you get back to inventory?"

"Okay." She smiled at them. "Nice to meet you," she said before taking off.

"You too," Julia called after her.

"I'm Alex Hemmings," he said holding his hand out.

"Meredith Bellefontaine." She shook his hand.

"I'm Julia Foley," Julia said, also shaking his hand.

"Can I ask why you're interested in the Book Worm Warriors?" Alex asked. He sighed loudly. "I detest that title. As if we're in a war. We're not. I mean, how can coffee and a scone destroy our store's ambiance? We're not changing anything else." He shook his head. "Sorry, I digress."

"You asked why we're interested in...that group," Meredith said with a smile.

"Yes." Alex pointed toward the area with the couch and chairs. "Would you like to sit down?"

After walking to the store from Peachie's, Meredith's feet were a little sore. She didn't realize she'd be hiking and had worn heels. "That would be lovely," she said.

She and Julia followed Alex and were soon seated on the comfortable furniture. "It's not like we didn't already make drinks available," he said, pointing to a nearby vending machine that offered soft drinks and water. "And we also have a pot of coffee with creamers and sugar. We didn't serve food, but sometimes my wife, Robin, made cookies, and I'd bring them down here. They were very popular."

Meredith and Ron had taken advantage of the coffee and soft drinks. "I remember eating cookies when we were here. Snickerdoodles, weren't they? Delicious."

Alex nodded. "It's been a while since she's felt good enough to bake. She's going through chemo treatments. They leave her weak and tired."

"I'm so sorry," Julia said. "We'll pray for her."

"Thank you," Alex said. "I appreciate that."

Meredith, who felt comfortable with Alex, decided to be straight with him. "Alex, we run Magnolia Investigations. We have a client who has written a book highlighting some of Savannah's popular spots. You're included in the book."

Alex smiled. "Yes, we got an advanced copy. It's a wonderful opportunity. You know, running a small local bookstore when there are big chain stores that sell books so cheaply can be difficult. We're doing okay, but I think this mention in Mr. Hedgerow's book will be very helpful."

"I hope you're right," Meredith said. "Do you know anyone who might try to stop publication of that book? How far would these Book Worm Warriors go to stop the modifications?"

The surprised look on Alex's face seemed genuine. "I'm not sure what you mean. Are they dangerous?" He paused for a moment. "No, I don't think so. I mean, they love the store, but they've never done anything that made me or my employees feel unsafe. They're passionate about their love of the store, but not the kind of people I would fear in any way."

"So you don't believe there is anyone in the group that would go to extremes?" Julia asked.

"No, I…" Alex paused for a moment.

"Did you think of someone that concerns you?" Meredith asked.

Alex breathed in deeply and let it out slowly. "There is one woman. Her name is Patricia Ivers. She used to work here. She was my assistant manager. I hesitate to even mention her, but eight months ago I had to let her go. It was a very difficult time. She was very unhappy with me."

"Can I ask why you fired her?" Meredith asked.

"I don't feel comfortable discussing the reasons, but let's just say I lost confidence in her…honesty."

"Alex, is she still angry?" Julia asked. "I mean, to the point where she might push the limits because of her resentment toward you?"

He shrugged. "I would hate to think that, but the truth is…I'm not sure what she's capable of. It's possible her anger has grown over the last several months. She's tried more than once to talk to me. To get her job back, but I refused to give in." He took a deep breath. "If you think about it, organizing that group and walking up and down in front of the bookstore is... Well, it's a little nuts, isn't it?"

Meredith glanced over at Julia, whose expression mirrored her thinking.

Had they just found another suspect?

Chapter Eleven

WHEN THEY GOT BACK TO the office, Meredith began a background check on Patricia Ivers. Julia waited with Meredith in her office while she worked.

"So we're thinking that this Patricia Ivers might be our letter writer?" Julia asked. "But her beef is with Alex, not Davis."

"But keeping Davis's book from being published might be a way to strike back at him. I'm sure his book will have excellent sales in the city. Especially at the Book Worm. It could bring in a lot of new business to the store. It's also a great way for the shop to introduce their new food and beverage additions." She shrugged. "I know it sounds petty, but maybe it's the only thing she could think of."

Julia paused as if considering Meredith's conjecture. "Okay, you've got a point. And the protests are designed to hurt the store. Maybe Davis is just collateral damage. The real target is Alex."

"But how far would she push it?" Meredith asked. "I'm not sure she would really do anything to hurt Davis. So far, we haven't found anyone whose beef is directly with Davis."

"Well, Davis asked us to look into this. Even if we end up telling him we believe the letter writer isn't a threat to him personally, at least we've given him some peace of mind."

Meredith watched as information came up on her computer screen. "Hmm. Patricia Ivers's employment seems to have stopped after leaving the Book Worm. A couple of her neighbors have filed complaints to the city about her property. Grass not cut, trash in the yard, and a dog that runs loose." She looked over at Julia. "That's it. Nothing criminal."

"When did this begin?" Julia asked. "Before or after she lost her job?"

Meredith swung her gaze back to her screen. "After."

"Sounds like someone who may be depressed." Julia sighed. "I wish we knew why Alex fired her."

"I do too, but we can't invade her privacy." Meredith gestured toward the computer screen. "No criminal charges here. If she'd stolen something I'd think Alex would have contacted the police."

"What was it he said?" Julia asked. "Wasn't it something about losing confidence in her honesty?"

"Yes," Meredith said. "I guess that could mean almost anything." Meredith shrugged. "Guessing about it won't help us."

Julia chuckled.

"Something funny?"

"I had a thought, but it's probably ridiculous."

Meredith's interest was piqued. Usually, Julia's ideas were quite helpful. "Tell me."

"Okay, we need to know more about Patricia Ivers and Dixie Vanderkellen, right?"

"It would be helpful."

Julia grinned. "I'll see if I can join the Sisters of the South and you can get involved with the Book Worm Warriors."

Meredith's mouth dropped open. Maybe she was being too gracious about Julia's ideas. "Are you crazy?" she asked.

Julia's smile slipped a little. "I don't think so. I thought it might help us get some information that could help us."

Meredith turned Julia's idea over in her head. Actually, it wasn't that crazy. "But I'd have to walk around outside the bookstore with a sign. What if someone I know sees me? Or even worse, what if the media shows up?"

Julia eyebrows shot up. "Didn't you tell me once that we should be willing to do anything for our clients?"

"Can I take that back now?"

Julia burst out laughing. "No, you can't. Besides, your part's the easiest. I'd have to spend time with Dixie. Now *that's* a real sacrifice for our client."

Meredith snorted. "Okay, I think you win." She leaned back in her chair and crossed her arms. "I feel like we're missing something. I mean, does the SOS hate the discovery about Ambrose Sedgwick's part in the designing of Savannah so much they'd try to stop the publication of the book? To be honest, I guess it would give the idea credence, wouldn't it? You know how people are. If it's in a book, it must be true." She paused for a moment. "Or does Patricia Ivers want to hurt Alex so much that she would write that letter?" She frowned at Julia. "We need to find out just how angry they are. And if they're capable of writing an anonymous letter like the one Davis received."

"I agree," Julia said, "but what if it's someone else in the group? Not Dixie or not Patricia? Maybe someone who has taken things to another level? Frankly, I would hate to miss checking everyone out and see Davis or his family hurt."

Meredith sighed. "Okay, okay. I see your point. I guess I better get out my good walking shoes if I'm going to be marching back and forth in front of the Book Worm."

"If it helps, the weather forecast predicts rain through Friday. And you can't march on Saturday because you have plans."

"Actually, that does help," Meredith said, giggling. "Well, at least I'm not bored anymore."

"Me either. So how do we get involved in…"

Julia stopped when she heard the front door open. Carmen walked down the hall to Meredith's office. "Davis Hedgerow is here. Wants to know if you have time to talk to him."

"Of course," Meredith said. "Send him in. Thanks, Carmen."

She grinned. "He's cute."

"He's married," Julia said.

Carmen winked and left. A minute later Davis came into the office.

"Hi, Davis," Meredith said. "Have a seat." She could see by his expression that he was upset.

"Is something wrong?" Julia asked.

Davis took off his coat and put it on the back of the chair before sitting down. "Yes. You know, after I talked to you yesterday, I began to wonder if I was making something out of nothing. But it wasn't just the letter. I really felt as if someone was hanging around outside my house. I did contact the police about that as you suggested. That's helped some."

"Did your wife leave town to see her sister?" Julia asked.

"Not yet, but she plans to go this weekend."

"We don't have much to tell you yet," Meredith said. "We're following several leads...."

Davis waved his arm, as if trying to sweep Meredith's comment away. "I'm not here to check up on you. It's only been a day. Something else has happened." He slumped down into the chair.

"Tell us," Meredith said.

"Someone called my publisher. Insinuated that there were some...uncomfortable facts in my past that would ruin sales if this book was released."

"Did they mention what these *facts* were?" Julia asked.

Davis shook his head.

Meredith leaned forward in her chair and fastened her gaze of Davis. "And is there anything in your past that could cause problems?"

"I...I don't know. I mean, all of us have things we'd rather keep to ourselves. We all make mistakes. But something that would embarrass my publisher? I really don't think so."

Meredith watched Davis swallow hard. He also looked away, avoiding her eyes. "You're hiding something, Davis. If you want us to help you, you must be honest."

He took a deep breath. "When I was eighteen, I was involved in a traffic accident. A young woman pulled out in front of my car. I had three friends in the car. We were going to a party. At first, the police thought I was drunk and wanted to charge me with vehicular homicide." Davis blinked away tears. "But after they investigated, they found that I had no alcohol in my body and she was over the limit. She really did pull out in front of us. I tried to stop as soon as

I saw her, but I hit her anyway. In the end the police determined that she was at fault, and that there was nothing I could have done."

"But if you got off…," Meredith said.

"There were a couple of people in the media that tried to keep the story going. Claimed the police covered up for me because my father wrote for the paper. He had quite a following and was very pro-police."

"So no charges were ever filed?" Julia asked. "How could anyone use this against you?"

"Again, my publisher doesn't want negative press about a writer. True or not."

"So how did your publisher react?" Meredith asked.

"He hasn't heard about it yet. His administrative assistant is a friend of mine. She didn't pass the message along."

"If he finds out…"

Davis ran his hand through his hair. "I told her I didn't want her to put her job in jeopardy, but she insists that part of her job is to keep phone calls or mail from 'nuts' from her boss. He has asked her to do that. She filed the phone call under the 'nuts' category."

"Couldn't your publisher find out about it if he does an internet search?" Julia asked.

"I don't think so. I wanted to go to college and was afraid my brief notoriety might follow me. I changed my name from Ronald Davis to Davis Hedgerow. I had an ancestor named Hedgerow. He assisted in the Underground Railroad. He had three daughters. No one to carry on his family name. That's why I picked the name. My parents approved. My family and a few close friends are the only people who know. I trust you won't tell anyone."

"Of course not," Meredith said.

"So how could the person who phoned your publisher know about this? I mean, if only a few people are aware of the accident and your name change…"

Davis shook his head. "I suspect they don't. My gut tells me this was a shot in the dark. I mean, most of us have something in our past we'd rather keep secret."

"So at least for now, it's not a problem," Meredith said.

"Yes, but at some point I'm going to tell my publisher about the accident. Better they hear it from me rather than through someone who has it out for me."

"What about that woman's family?" Julia asked. "How did they react to you being exonerated?"

"Believe it or not, her parents were very supportive. Seems their daughter had a severe drinking problem. They never blamed me. They moved away many years ago."

"Okay," Meredith said. "So no threats against you personally because of the wreck?"

Davis thought for a moment. "There was a brother who blamed me. Said some nasty things. But eventually, he stopped. I haven't heard from him in many years."

"Do you remember his name?" Meredith asked.

Davis shook his head. "Like I said, he disappeared years ago. I doubt he'd suddenly show up now. Besides, I truly believe he was the kind who would have settled problems with his fists. Not by writing letters. I'm not sure he even knew how to write." He looked at Meredith. "Sorry. I'm being unkind. It was an awful time. One I'd like to forget. I don't think we need to worry about him. He drank too. He's probably dead by now."

"Okay," Julia said slowly. "Someone hanging around your house, and now a call to your publisher. At least we know this person is serious. It's not a prank."

"Did your friend at the paper get the number of the person who called?" Meredith asked.

"No. It said *unknown*."

"How many people know about this?" Julia asked.

Davis shrugged. "It was all over the news. Anyone could have looked up the story."

Meredith exchanged a quick look with Julia. They hadn't thought to run a background check on Davis. It seemed that was a mistake.

"Davis, do you know anything about a group called Sisters of the South?" Meredith asked.

He nodded. "They're the people who oppose the statue of Ambrose Sedgwick being erected. They're pretty passionate about their claims of fraud."

"So you talked to them?" Meredith asked.

"Yeah. To a...Dixie...something. Can't remember right now. I need my notes."

Meredith and Julia exchanged glances.

"If you're thinking these ladies are involved, I'd have to disagree," Davis said. "I mean, they didn't blame me for what was happening. They were angry at the family who discovered their long-lost relative's diaries and notes. I might be wrong, but they seemed too..."

"Cultured? Refined?" Meredith suggested.

"Wow. When you say it that way, it makes me sound like a snob. But yes, I guess that's what I meant."

"But what she had to say didn't make you change your mind about including the statue in your book?" Julia asked.

"No. She couldn't offer any proof of her claims. I checked it out myself, but I couldn't find a legitimate reason to remove the article from the book. I can't go by the word of one person, no matter how sincere they seem to be."

Meredith kept her thoughts to herself, but in her experience, people like Dixie, who believed she was a step above everyone else, were capable of pretty inappropriate behavior, no matter how sophisticated they appeared to be. "And what about a group called the Book Worm Warriors?" she asked.

"The people who oppose the Book Worm from adding a coffee and snack bar?" Davis laughed. "Have you met them?"

"No, not yet."

He got to his feet and took his coat off the back of the chair. "When you do, I doubt you'll consider them suspects." He shrugged. "But who knows? I don't seem to be able to figure out who's doing this. Maybe the answer will surprise me." He put on his coat. "Thanks, ladies," he said before walking out. "I'll be in touch."

Meredith trained her eyes on her partner. Julia sighed deeply.

"Yeah, yeah," she said. "I'll call Dixie. Should I ask Carmen to make you a sign?"

Meredith shook her head. "Let's hope the rain keeps me from that humiliation."

"Well, let's get busy," Julia said as she stood to her feet.

As Julia walked out and headed toward her own office, Meredith thought she heard her mumble something like "God give me patience," but she wasn't certain.

Chapter Twelve

MEREDITH GRABBED THE ARC DAVIS had given them. Maybe if she kept going through it she'd find a clue as to who might be intimidating Davis. She'd written notes on the pages of new attractions. She still hadn't contacted the other B and B. "The John Douglas Farmer House," she read. "It is a restored 1834 federal-style townhouse with ten guest rooms and suites. The inn is furnished with museum-quality antiques displayed in splendid parlors and dining rooms, which guests are encouraged to enjoy. The rooms have custom mattresses, lush fabrics, and modern baths. Breakfast is served in a carefully constructed room that echoes the style of the early 1800s. The walled garden is a respite with trickling water and ancient plantings. It provides a relaxing atmosphere for visitors to enjoy after a day of touring Savannah's treasures. The John Douglas Farmer House provides an elegant Savannah experience with grace and charm appropriate to the period. Every afternoon, a selection of vintage wines is available in our garden, along with an assortment of delicious appetizers.

"The John Douglas Farmer House boasts of another spirit, but this one walks the halls. The ghost of John Douglas Farmer, a famed attorney who disappeared in 1825, still resides in what was once his home. His body was never found, and it's said he is still searching for it. If he knocks on your door at night, just yell, 'I don't know where your body is, John Farmer!'"

Below that was the address and booking phone number for the inn. Despite finding the information about the ghost a little silly, Meredith also found it highly amusing. She could just see herself calling out, "I don't know where your body is, John Farmer!" She laughed out loud and then picked up the phone. She would rather have company Saturday night, but she couldn't ask Julia and Beau to give up two nights of their lives for this investigation, especially with Beau's bum ankle. Besides, she wasn't going home to anyone except her cat, GK. She figured he'd forgive her absence for a couple of nights.

She called the number listed and got the reservation. January wasn't a big tourist time of the year. If it had been spring, she would have been put on a waiting list. Meredith reserved a suite for Saturday night.

When she hung up, she looked up John Douglas Farmer. As the book stated, he was an attorney in the early 1800s who disappeared. He was thought to have been murdered by an unhappy client. She didn't find much more about him except a drawing of a handsome man with a handlebar mustache who looked well-to-do.

"Well, the deed is done," Julia said as she walked into the office.

"What does that mean?"

Julia sighed. "Unfortunately, the Sisters of the South meet on Thursday evenings. This week they'll be at Dixie's house." She scowled at Meredith. "I have a feeling I'm going to wish I'd never volunteered for this."

Meredith laughed. "I have complete confidence that you'll persevere. And maybe we'll find out something useful."

"I hope so. If I thought I had to spend a couple of hours with Dixie for no reason…" She sat down on the edge of Meredith's desk. "So how are you coming along with your delightful group?"

"Haven't called them yet."

"Excuse me?"

"Don't get yourself in a state," Meredith said good-naturedly. "I booked a night at the John Douglas Farmer Inn." She opened the book again and read the description. Although she didn't want to laugh, she couldn't help it when she saw Julia's face. "Julia Foley. I know you don't believe in ghosts."

"Maybe not, but don't you find that a little bit…creepy?"

"No, I find it a lot creepy. But funny."

"And if someone knocks on your door?"

Meredith grinned. "I'll call out, 'I don't know where your body is, John Farmer!'"

"Seriously?"

"Of course," Meredith said. "Why not?"

"And if they ask why you're staying with them?"

"I've been thinking about that. I'll just tell them that I've been working so hard lately I needed a night off. A night to relax. It's the truth, actually."

Julia looked a little doubtful. "I guess, but you might try to come up with something a little better than that. Did you give them your real name?"

"Yes. I realize they might look me up, but if they do, so what? There's nothing written that says a woman who runs an investigation agency might not need a rest."

"Hey, it's up to you," Julia said. "Just be careful or one of these days visitors might have to say, 'I don't know where your body is, Meredith Bellefontaine!'"

Meredith laughed. "Will never happen. I have you as a partner. You'd find me."

"Oh, Mere. Stop. Maybe I should come with you."

"Don't be silly. You and Beau will be with me Friday night, and you're working Thursday night. I won't ask more of you than that. Besides, I don't want to make Beau cross with me."

"Don't be silly. Beau loves you."

"I'm sure there are times he doesn't."

Julia crossed her arms over her chest. "Let's not worry about Beau right now. If you're going alone Saturday night, I want you to stay in touch with me, okay?"

"I already told you I would. I hope you're not worried about the ghost of John Douglas Farmer."

Julia sighed. "Don't be ridiculous. No, I'm worried about *you*. Remember, we don't know who has been trying to stop Davis from publishing his book, and we really don't know how far they'll go to stop him." She sighed. "I almost wish they'd do something more threatening so we could bring the police into this."

"I know, but we're not there yet."

Meredith looked up Book Worm Warriors on a search engine. She didn't expect to find anything and had assumed she'd have to call Alex for contact information, but she found a short story that had been on a local newscast. Meredith clicked on it and saw the brief report about customers protesting changes at the Book Worm. A woman with frizzy blond hair who was standing outside with a sign that read PROTECT THE BOOK WORM! had a microphone stuck in her face. "The Book Worm is a Savannah institution," she said in a rather high-pitched voice. "We don't need a new millennial coffee bar. We want things to stay the way they are."

Then the report switched to an interview with Alex, who tried to assure everyone that the Book Worm wouldn't change much at all. He made the point that adding coffee and a few snacks didn't constitute a complete renovation of the store. He appeared clear-eyed and rational while the woman, who turned out to be Patricia Ivers, seemed a little crazed and out of touch with reality. At the end of the story the TV station ran the name of the group protesting, along with a phone number. Meredith paused the screen and wrote down the number. Then she looked at Julia and took a deep breath. "Maybe you should pray," she said.

"You're on your own. I'm going to be stuck with Dixie and her merry band of Sisters. I have no compassion for you."

Meredith stuck her tongue out at her partner and then entered the number. The phone rang a few times, and a woman answered. "Yes, my name is Meredith Bellefontaine. I saw the report on channel seven from the other night and would like to get involved. My husband and I used to love going to the Book Worm. I'd like to find out more about your group."

"We've had several people call who saw the story," the woman said with a note of triumph in her voice. "Of course you can attend a meeting. We're getting together Thursday night. Would you like to come?"

"Yes, I would," Meredith said. "Where will you be?" She wrote down the address and the time of the meeting. "And can I bring anything?"

"Everyone usually brings some kind of dessert, but since it's your first time, don't worry about it. Just come as our guest."

"Thank you so much. I'll see you Thursday at seven."

After she disconnected the phone, she frowned at Julia. "Does every group in town meet on Thursdays? What's the deal?"

Julia shrugged. "Maybe having people in your house on Thursday means you have four days to clean. And it doesn't mess up Friday and Saturday so you can still plan things for the weekend."

"It disturbs me that you've figured this out."

"Very funny," Julia said. "Oh, and it doesn't interfere with Wednesday night church meetings. There may be a method to what seems like madness."

Meredith leaned back in her chair. "I hope that by Friday, we have more of an idea who is trying to intimidate Davis Hedgerow."

"Hopefully, we'll have enough evidence to involve the police," Julia said. "In Georgia, actionable threats have to make the victim feel as if he is in imminent danger and our guy hasn't actually threatened Davis with bodily harm of any kind." She shrugged. "At this point, the worst he can get is a fine, probation, and community service. In the end, it will be up to Davis to contact the police."

"I hate waiting to see how far the person behind this intends to push it," Meredith said. "That's why we have to keep going, Jules. If something happened to Davis..."

"I know." Julia smiled at her. "We'll find the truth, Meredith," she said. "Don't worry."

Meredith returned the smile but wasn't as sure as Julia that they were going to find their quarry soon. Were these threats innocuous? Or was Davis in real danger? She wasn't certain, but one thing she did know. They needed to find this person fast.

Chapter Thirteen

MEREDITH KNOCKED ON THE DOOR of a house in one of Savannah's new construction areas. The neighborhood was beautiful but wasn't Meredith's taste. She loved the old, historic homes. Of course, it was difficult to buy one now. There were a lot of new developments like this one. She was a little surprised to find that Patricia Ivers lived here. The house was very nice. Meredith had expected Patricia's tastes to be more toward the historic areas in Savannah. It seemed her passion for the history behind the Book Worm didn't extend to her personal life.

She knocked again, and the door was opened by the woman Meredith had seen in the video. The woman smiled at her. "Meredith?"

"Yes. And you're Patricia?"

The woman nodded. "Please, call me Pat." Her blond hair was cut short and styled attractively. It must have been humid the day the news channel interviewed her. She was younger than Meredith expected.

She stepped aside. "Please come in."

"Thank you."

Meredith walked up the stairs of the bi-level home. She could hear children playing downstairs. At the top of the stairs she stepped into a lovely living room with overstuffed chairs and a dark gray sectional couch. Whoever decorated this room had done a great job. Comfortable but attractive.

There were four women sitting on the couch. Pat gestured toward one of chairs that complemented the couch. "Please have a seat. Can I get you something to drink? We have tea and coffee."

"Try the tea," one of the women said with a smile. "Pat brews it herself. It's delicious."

Meredith smiled at her. "Thank you. I'd love to try the tea."

"Anything in it?" Pat asked.

Meredith shook her head and sat down. There was a man sitting in a chair that matched hers on the other side of the couch. He watched her through narrowed eyes. His expression was far from friendly. She tried smiling at him, but he didn't respond. Who was he? She turned toward the women, who were talking excitedly about their next protest. One of them, an older woman with tightly curled hair, looked over at her.

"Why are you interested in joining us?" she asked.

Her question wasn't confrontational. She obviously wanted Meredith to let them know what the Book Worm meant to her and why she didn't want it to change. Trying to be as truthful as she could, Meredith told her about Ron and the time they'd spent together in the bookstore. As she talked, Pat came back with a large glass of iced tea.

She set it down on a side table next to the chair. Then she sat down on the couch and listened to Meredith talk.

"I know that may not sound like a good reason to not want the shop to change," Meredith said after sharing her experience with

Ron. "But I guess I want the Book Worm to stay as it is because it makes me feel that…" She was surprised to feel a tear run down her cheek. She hadn't realized how emotional this might be for her. It wasn't the store she missed. It was Ron. She took a deep breath and finished her response. "It makes me feel that part of my husband is in there. I don't want to lose that if I can help it."

"We understand, Meredith," Pat said. "We all have memories of events inside that building. It's special to us. We don't want it to end up a meeting place for people who have no respect for its history or its tradition."

The women on the couch voiced their agreement, but the man in the chair across from her continued to stare at Meredith. What was it with him?

"Let's introduce ourselves," Pat said to the group. "Tell Meredith what the Book Worm means to you. Then Meredith can tell us more about who she is. I'll start." Pat smiled at Meredith. "I'm Patricia Ivers. I'm married with three children—a teenager and eight-year-old twins. I love to embroider and read, especially cozy mysteries. I used to work at the Book Worm. I was the assistant manager. Alex Hemmings, the owner of the store, fired me because I opposed the changes to the Book Worm. It was horribly unfair." Her eyes caught Meredith's. "I'm not doing this to get back at him, believe me. I only want to protect the shop."

Then Pat nodded toward the woman next to her, who introduced herself as Astrid. Meredith tried to listen as the other women introduced themselves, but she was distracted by the man in the chair. When it got to him, he cleared his throat.

"I'm Scott Dallas," he said. "An attorney hired by Mrs. Ivers. We plan to file a lawsuit against Hemmings for wrongful termination."

"Do you mind if I ask what the grounds are for your lawsuit?"

"Why, Mrs. Bellefontaine? Is Mrs. Ivers under investigation? You do own Magnolia Investigations, don't you?"

So that was it. Meredith frowned at him. "Yes, I do. Does that mean I can't care about a bookstore that is beloved by many people in Savannah?"

"No," he said. "But it certainly makes me suspicious."

Meredith stared at him for a moment, trying to figure out what to do. Then she had an idea. She picked up her purse and rose to her feet. "I wasn't sure about joining this group in the first place. But when I saw Pat on the news... Well, I think we have a lot in common. However, maybe it's best that I leave." She looked at Pat. "I'm sorry. I hope you're successful in this endeavor. I wish I could have been part of it."

Meredith turned to leave when Pat said, "Meredith, wait. I'm sorry. Scott is suspicious of everyone. Please sit down. I want you in the group."

Meredith stood for a moment as if she wasn't sure what to do. Then finally, she walked back to the chair and retook her seat. "I'll stay for now, but if anyone here wants me to go, just say something. I didn't come here for some kind of confrontation."

Scott started to say something, but Pat hushed him. Then she said, "Scott, why don't you go on home? I'll talk to you tomorrow. It's late. I'm sure Betty and the kids would like to see you."

Meredith saw something flash across Scott's face, but he didn't argue. Just got up, put on his coat, grabbed his briefcase, and walked out of the house.

"Again, I apologize for Scott," Pat said. "He really is the most suspicious person I've ever known" She sighed. "He believes I can get a pretty big payout from Alex, but… Well, what if it costs him so much the store ends up closing? I don't want that." Her eyes grew shiny. "The truth is, I just want my job back."

"Tell her why you were fired, Pat," Astrid said.

Pat didn't respond right away, which seemed to encourage Astrid to continue. "She saw her boss's wife out with another man," she huffed. "When he found out she hadn't told him, he got rid of her."

Pat took a deep breath. "I just couldn't. Soon after that she was diagnosed with cancer. How could I say something? I knew how much it would hurt him, and with everything else…" She sighed. "I decided to leave it between Alex and Robin. But then she confessed to the affair. I'm not sure it was because of her illness or because she was afraid I'd spill the beans before she did, but she told him I knew about it. He was so, so angry and in so much pain." She blinked quickly. "Not just with his wife. With me. He said I should have come to him. That he thought we were friends." She paused for a moment. "I tried to explain to him why I'd kept quiet. I mean, I wasn't completely sure of what I'd seen. I had no proof they were having an affair. And with Robin so sick… He wouldn't accept my explanation." She picked up a napkin on the table and wiped her eyes. "He said he would never trust me again and that meant he couldn't work with me. He made me get my things and leave right then and there. In front of everyone. It was humiliating."

"Oh, Pat," Meredith said. "I'm so sorry." She was pretty sure Alex was taking out his hurt and anger on Pat instead of dealing with it directly. And Pat was fighting to keep the store from changing because she wanted things to be the way they used to be, when she worked there. The situation was sad, but Meredith couldn't see anyone here upset about the book.

"Thank you. I think it's your turn to introduce yourself, Meredith," Pat said.

"Of course. I'm Meredith Bellefontaine. As I said, I'm a widow. My husband ran Magnolia Investigations. After he died, I took it over. I run it with my best friend. It keeps me busy. I love what I do, but I miss Ron every day."

"I'm sorry for your loss," Pat said. "Thank you for sharing."

"So what's our next move?" Astrid asked.

Pat picked up a file that was on the table. "I want to protest in front of the store again," she said. "But the weather forecast calls for rain the next few days. I think we need to write letters for now."

"To who?" an attractive redhead asked. What was her name? Meredith searched her memory. She finally pulled up the name Jerri.

"The local paper, TV stations, radio stations. Any media outlets you can think of. The report on channel seven helped us more than you know."

"I really don't think the owner will back down on the coffee, snack area," Meredith said. "I went by the store to check it out. It's already built. They're putting the last touches on it." She looked at the six sets of eyes staring back at her. At least five of them seemed interested in what she was saying. She decided to push ahead. "I think you're fighting a losing battle here. Instead of being completely against the changes, why not ask for specific things? Like what they serve. What hours it's open, you know, things like that. Maybe the owner will capitulate to your suggestions. Could you all live with that?"

"We've talked about it," Pat said. "But at the time the changes hadn't been made yet." She sighed. "I don't know, maybe you're right. I hate to give up, but at this point…"

"By the way," Meredith added, deciding to go all the way, "have any of you heard about a book coming out that features the Book Worm? I believe it's by that guy who writes a column for the paper, Davis Hedgerow?"

Pat's expression tightened as her gaze swung to the other women. "No," she said sharply. "We don't know anything about it."

Although most of them didn't react, Astrid did. Her eyes widened, and her mouth became a thin line.

Pat suddenly stood. "I think that's enough for now, everyone. Let's think about these suggestions and talk about them at our next meeting."

Surprised, Meredith picked up her purse and got up from her chair. After saying goodbye to the group and thanking Pat for the invitation, she walked down the stairs that led to the front door and let herself out. When she reached her car she got in and looked back at the house.

Pat was obviously lying. She knew about the book. Why hadn't she admitted it?

Chapter Fourteen

MEREDITH ARRIVED AT THE OFFICE early. She needed to share last night's meeting with Julia. She'd wanted to call her last night, but she was afraid of phoning while Julia was still meeting with the SOS.

She'd been working at her computer for a while, looking up any information she could about Patricia and her friends. What she uncovered was more than interesting. It seemed that Scott Dallas had recently moved to Savannah from Atlanta. His father, the owner of the firm where he'd worked, had recently passed away. His mother was still living, as was one brother. He had a sister who had passed away over thirty years ago.

Not long after his father's death, he'd moved back to Savannah where he was born and raised and opened his own legal firm. One of his biggest clients was the Savannah Chamber of Commerce. Meredith knew they had received ARCs of Davis's book. She turned this information over in her mind. But why wouldn't he want the book to come out? Meredith couldn't think of a reason that made sense. Maybe he didn't care anything about it, but Pat seemed to. Was she a suspect? To Meredith, Pat seemed to be someone who wanted to hurt the Book Worm out of revenge, yet she didn't seem dangerous. Not someone who would want to physically hurt Davis or his family. Besides, her beef was with Alex, not Davis.

Meredith sighed. The only person at the meeting who'd really made her feel uncomfortable was Scott Dallas. He seemed…too intense. Too angry.

She looked up the other members. The ones whose names she remembered, but she couldn't find anything concerning.

When Carmen arrived and passed Meredith's office door, she didn't look surprised to see Meredith already working. "How about a fresh cup of coffee?" she asked.

"You're an angel," Meredith answered with a wink.

"I know it. Forgot to bring my halo today though."

Meredith laughed. "That's okay. We'll just pretend you're wearing it."

"Thanks."

Carmen came over and picked up Meredith's coffee cup. Julia walked into Meredith's office carrying a box. "Beignets, cream puffs, and éclairs. Conference room. Now."

"Etienne's?"

"Etienne's."

Etienne's Bakery was a small shop just down the street from the office. Their pastries were incredible. Meredith was a decent baker, but Etienne's was a step above her skills. Meredith left her desk and headed toward their conference room. Once Ron's office, it had been converted, but Ron's touches were still there.

The wallpaper was a pale yellow silk, and in the center of the room was a gorgeous rosewood table. Meredith had been told it once graced the dining room in the governor's mansion. She wasn't certain the story was true, but it didn't matter. It was lovely. Four matching chairs sat around the table. The two armchairs that were part of the set had been placed on either side of the fireplace.

Meredith loved this room. The memories of Ron were strong here. She'd tried to keep things that had belonged to him. Ron's plat map of historical Savannah hung over the fireplace. She smiled as she remembered when he bought it from the Georgia Historical Society. He'd been so excited. Meredith couldn't part with it. It reminded her of him.

Julia put the box of pastries on the long antique table in the middle of the room. Carmen came in with some paper plates, napkins, and forks from the coffee bar area. She left and then returned with coffee for Julia and Meredith.

"Thank you," Julia said with a smile. "Help yourself."

"I planned to." She reached in and took a beignet and a cream puff. "Way to start off a Friday," she said. "Thanks."

"Yeah, way to start off a Friday," Meredith said, laughing. "I'm tired this morning. A sugar rush is just what I need."

Meredith took a bite of a beignet covered with powdered sugar. Awesome. She put the pastry down and took a sip of coffee.

"So who goes first?" Meredith asked.

"You go," Julia said. "I stopped for pastries. I deserve a chance to eat some."

"Can't argue with that," Meredith said with a grin.

She opened her notebook and took Julia over the meeting she'd had with the Book Worm Warriors the night before. "Everything seemed to be on the up-and-up at first. I even felt sorry for Pat. But this Scott Dallas guy bothered me. I looked him up. One of his clients is the Chamber of Commerce. Specifically, the Office of Special Events, Film & Tourism."

"So they would have an ARC of Davis's book?"

Meredith nodded. "I called Davis last night, and he confirmed it. I decided to ask the Book Worm Warriors about the book. Boy, if people could turn into statues, it would have happened right then and there. They knew about the book, and they weren't happy I brought it up. I was summarily dismissed from the group."

"That *is* interesting," Julia said, wiping some cream from her chocolate-covered cream puff. She washed it down with coffee and opened her own notebook. "May I just say that you owe me forever and ever?" She sighed dramatically. "If we could have just added Beatrice to the mix, my misery would have been complete."

Meredith laughed. "I'm so sorry. I hope you did better than I did."

"I guess it depends on how you judge the meaning of 'better.' If wanting to run from the room screaming counts, then yes, it was better."

"Okay, you were miserable," Meredith conceded with a grin. "What did you find out?"

"Let me start with the good news. Most of their time is spent doing charitable events."

Meredith's mouth dropped open. "Okay, I am truly surprised. Dixie doesn't seem like the charitable type."

"Oh, she was insufferable. That's the awful part of the evening. She was constantly bragging about her house, all her antiques, and her lengthy Southern roots." Julia put her hand to her mouth and giggled. "By the way, I did a little research on our Southern belle.

Her great-grandfather was a porter on the railroad, her grandfather was a barber, and her father owns several hair salons. I couldn't find any familial ties to James Oglethorpe. Oh, and the real money comes from her husband."

"Julia," Meredith scolded. "That's not part of our investigation. Shame on you."

"I know, I know. She just pushed me past my limits, Meredith."

"Well, let's disregard that information and focus on our real investigation. So anything that seemed suspicious? Any reason for them to not want the book to come out?"

"That's an understatement."

Meredith stopped her attack on the beignets. "Really?"

"Oh yes. Seems these ladies are convinced the evidence that Ambrose Sedgwick had anything to do with the layout of Savannah is fake."

Meredith frowned. "Wasn't it confirmed by historians? The age of paper can be determined. And the ink used to create documents."

Julia nodded. "I know, and so do they. They think the person the family used to test the materials is in on it."

"But what does that get the family? Fifteen minutes of fame? It doesn't make sense."

Julia shrugged. "They become important. It elevates them in society, I guess. Not that I understand that." She paused for a moment. "But I think the real reason is that there is a family feud between the descendants of Oglethorpe and Sedgwick."

"Because of the diary and the letters?" Meredith asked.

"Yep."

"Are we talking Hatfields and McCoys?"

"Maybe not quite that dramatic," Julia said. "But it seems the Sedgwick family feels justice is finally being done. They're angry that Oglethorpe took credit for something Ambrose Sedgwick actually did."

"Are the Oglethorpes angry enough about Sedgwick's claim that they'd try to stop the book from coming out?"

"That's the thing. It doesn't seem like it. They've released a statement that throws some doubt on the Sedgwick's claim, but that's it. The Sisters of the South appear to be the fury behind this storm."

"Why?"

Julia shook her head. "I think these are rich ladies that need a cause, you know? Everyone needs to feel they have a reason for living. The Sisters of the South are determined to keep Southern history correct. And they vehemently stand against the claims of the Sedgwick family."

"Enough to write a threatening letter and try to call Davis's publisher?"

"Yes, but…"

Meredith waited but Julia was silent. Finally, she said, "But what?"

Julia wiped her mouth and took a long sip of coffee. "Look, Meredith. No one knows better than you about the kind of women that are part of SOS. Most of them are rich, part of Savannah high society. One of the ladies is the mayor's sister, for crying out loud. I think they could put a real kink in the publication of Davis's book. I would imagine they could go directly to the publishing company without writing letters or making phone calls that stop with an administrative assistant. It just doesn't match up."

"I can see your point, but this is a good lead, Julia. This group has a real reason to stop the book. If they're angry about the Sedgwick family's claim, they have motive to stop publication."

"I guess. One of Oglethorpe's descendants is part of the group."

"You mean someone besides Dixie?"

"Dixie's claim is many times removed from James Oglethorpe. This woman is more directly connected."

"But I thought you just said the family isn't that interested."

Julia sighed. "And I meant that. Except for this woman who claims to be directly related to Oglethorpe."

"So tell me about her."

Julia flipped through her notes. "Her name is Fancy Devereaux. And yes, I'm being serious." She shook her head. "One of the women at the meeting told me she fits her name pretty well. Blond, perfectly coiffed, designer clothes, perfect nails, and a Southern accent that fits her station in life. Cultured. You know the type. Was probably a debutante when she was a teenager."

"I get it." Meredith turned to a new page in her notebook. "You said someone told you about her. She wasn't at the meeting?"

"No. Wish I could have met this gal. She sounds like the kind of person who could get really upset about someone dissing her famous relative."

Meredith raised an eyebrow. "Dissing?"

Julia shrugged. "It's a word."

Meredith smiled. "Okay, let's go over our suspects. So the threats could be coming from someone in the Sisters of the South. Maybe *Fancy* is trying to protect her family history. Regardless of her feelings, the Sisters of the South as a whole is opposed to the statue of

Ambrose Sedgwick because they believe the evidence presented in his favor is fake. Then there's Patricia Ivers. She was hurt by Alex Hemmings when she was fired. She is trying to stop the changes at the Book Worm for personal reasons. Is she trying to ruin their chance at some great support through Davis's book? We also have attorney Scott Dallas."

"And what is his motive?"

"I don't know," Meredith said. "But something about him is… wrong. I want him on our list. I'll take him off if my instincts prove incorrect."

"I can live with that. Your instincts are usually pretty good."

Meredith smiled. "Thanks. Now, finish your breakfast. We're going to the Georgia Historical Society. I want to see the display honoring Ambrose Sedgwick myself."

Julia began working on the cream puff she'd been trying to eat, while Meredith stared at her notes. Something kept tugging at Meredith, trying to get her attention. But what was it?

Chapter Fifteen

As they got ready to leave for the historical society, the phone in Meredith's office rang. She picked it up and found Maggie Lu on the line.

"I've been doing some digging on this Ambrose Sedgwick," she said when Meredith answered. "I'm not sure it will help, but I wanted to do what I could to assist y'all."

"Julia and I are getting ready to head to the Georgia Historical Society," Meredith said. "Do you want to come with us?"

"Yes, I do. I'm in the area. I'll meet you there."

"Great. Thanks, Maggie Lu."

"Not a problem, honey. I'm glad someone is questioning this instead of just accepting it as gospel truth." With that, she disconnected the call.

Meredith was left staring at her phone, wondering just what she meant.

She and Julia drove to the Hodgson Hall, the society's research center. Walking in the rain might be good for Gene Kelly and Debbie Reynolds, but Meredith preferred to stay dry.

They parked, got out, and jogged to the entrance with their umbrellas over their heads. The rain had started in the early morning and was still going strong. Although it wasn't really a downpour, it was steady.

Meredith was always impressed by the stately building that housed an unparalleled collection of Georgia history. They ran up the steps to the entrance. Inside Hodgson Hall were more than four million manuscripts, one hundred thousand photographs, thirty thousand architectural drawings, fifteen thousand rare and non-rare books, and thousands of maps, portraits, and artifacts. They preserved family papers and military records of every Georgia war, the papers of Georgia's major political leaders, colonial account books, diaries, plantation records, papers of social and cultural organizations, and business records ranging from the 18th through the 20th century. It was an awesome collection that would now add Ambrose Sedgwick's diary and letters to its assets.

When they got inside, they closed their umbrellas and took off their coats before hanging them up on hooks mounted on the wall next to them. These items weren't allowed inside the building. Both women had left their purses in their car as well. The inside of the society looked more like a library than a museum. They began to look for the Ambrose Sedgwick display. They found it quickly because Maggie Lu was standing in front of it. She waved them over.

"So what do you think?" Meredith asked quietly when they reached her.

Ambrose's letters and diary were in a long glass case. Maggie Lu was looking at the display with a frown on her face. "It certainly looks genuine," she said in a whisper, "but I think it's as phony as a three-dollar bill."

"Why?" Julia asked.

Maggie Lu shook her head. "Not here. Look it over, then we'll talk."

Meredith stared at the display, trying to get a feel for it. It certainly seemed real to her. The paper was aged and the ink looked right. The letters and the entries in the diary were written in the kind of script used many years ago. Meredith always marveled at how beautifully people wrote in the 1700s. That art seemed to be lost today.

Meredith was aware that, through the years, several forged documents had been accepted as authentic by people considered experts in their fields. It was certainly possible to fool people, but the more counterfeits were passed off as real, the easier it became for experts to spot them. The documents stored here were all professionally authenticated before being placed in the archives. If something was wrong with the Ambrose Sedgwick collection, the society's skilled historians would find it before it was accepted. Whatever Maggie Lu saw, it didn't ring a warning bell in Meredith's head, and she'd seen many historical documents during her time as president of the Savannah Historical Society. Why did Maggie Lu think the collection was fake?

A sign on the display case stated that the display would only run through Sunday. After that, images would be added to the society's online records, which were extensive. The thought crossed Meredith's mind that the society would be devastated if they added forgeries to their archives. She had just finished perusing the display when she heard a familiar voice.

"Why, Meredith Bellefontaine," a voice dripping with Southern sweetness said from behind her. "What are you doin' here, sugah?"

Meredith turned to face Beatrice Enterline, her replacement at the Savannah Historical Society. Her carefully penciled eyebrows were raised as if surprised to see Meredith. Beatrice's short black hair was worn in a pixie style. Her overblown attempt to appear *Southern* had a tendency to get on Meredith's last nerve, but she steeled herself and smiled widely.

"Why hello, Beatrice," she said. "We heard about the display and wanted to see it."

"Well, bless your little heart. I wouldn't think something like this would interest you."

"And why wouldn't it interest her, Beatrice?" Julia asked in a low voice. "This is a rather historic find. Of course she would want to see it."

Beatrice's phony smile disappeared. "Well, I declare. Y'all don't need to have a hissy fit. I wasn't trying to cast aspersions." She moved up next to Meredith. "Isn't this excitin'? To find out that our very own James Oglethorpe wasn't actually responsible for the layout of Savannah?"

Meredith shook her head. "I don't know, Beatrice," she said. "There's a ways to go to prove that yet, I think."

Beatrice stared at Meredith with her mouth open and then turned on her heel and hurried away.

Meredith forced her attention back to the diary. "I still don't know why you think this is…" And then she saw it. She looked at Maggie Lu with wide eyes. "It really is a forgery. We need to tell someone." She gulped as she realized that the correct person to report it to would be Beatrice since the Savannah Historical Society was in charge of the exhibit.

"First let's go get coffee and talk this out," she said to Maggie Lu and Julia. "I don't want to make a mistake here. Calling this a fake is a big deal."

"Good. I hope someone explains this to me," Julia said.

Meredith looked around them to see if anyone was looking. She took her phone out of her jacket pocket and quickly took a picture of the open diary. "Let's go," she said.

The three women headed out of the building to Meredith's car. Because of the weather, they decided to go back to the office and talk there. The promise of beignets may have influenced Maggie Lu to agree.

Meredith parked in the back of the building and the three women went inside. Julia took Maggie Lu into the conference room while Meredith went to the reception area.

"We're meeting in the conference room," she told Carmen. "Any calls?"

"Not a peep," Carmen said. "Pretty quiet."

Meredith dropped off her coat and umbrella in her office before heading to the conference room. When she walked into the room, Maggie Lu and Julia were helping themselves to pastries and coffee from a carafe that Carmen brought in. Meredith was still full from that morning, so a cup of coffee to warm her up was all she was interested in. With the rain, the temperatures had dropped. Meredith put a couple of logs in the fireplace and lit it. A fire would warm the room, but it also added a nice ambiance that made her feel relaxed. This case was a little confusing. There were lots of motives, but none of them strong enough to make her feel confident. Hopefully, things would become clearer.

She walked over to the table and sat down. After a couple of sips of her coffee, she said, "Okay, now let's talk about how we're going to inform the Sedgwick family that we can prove their claims about the artifacts are false."

"I don't think we should call them 'false,'" Maggie Lu said. "Better to say that the family is *mistaken*. We don't know who is behind this forgery...yet."

"So what did you two notice that I missed?" Julia asked.

"It's this page," Meredith said, taking her phone from her purse.

She passed the phone to Maggie Lu, who looked carefully at the screen. "Yes. Good picture." She gave it back to Meredith.

Meredith looked at Julia. "Do you want to look at this?"

Julia scooted her chair closer to Meredith's. "Show me."

"Forgers can buy old paper, they can even buy old ink," Meredith said. "Whatever they need to make documents appear real. But what they forget sometimes is to make the vocabulary appropriate. Different words or phrases we use come from certain times in our history."

"And that's how they messed up here?" Julia asked.

"Yes," Meredith said. "Right here. The line reads 'Our unfortunate neighbor was caught stealing and was sadly sent up the river.'

This phrase originally referred to prisoners sent to Sing Sing prison in New York. The river is the Hudson."

"So?"

Maggie Lou wiped the powdered sugar from her mouth. "So… Ambrose Sedgwick lived in the 1700s, and Sing Sing prison was built in 1826. This diary is definitely a forgery."

Chapter Sixteen

MEREDITH LEANED BACK IN HER chair and sighed. "So now what? This is going to cause a big stink. That statue is already in the park even though it's covered up by a tarp. The unveiling is tomorrow."

"We need to tell Beatrice," Julia said. "Then leave it to her to sort out. We also need to make Davis aware. He'll want to tell his publisher. The chapter about Ambrose Sedgwick should be removed."

"Y'all have no choice, Meredith," Maggie Lu said. "It's sad, but if the family is purposely trying to defraud the public, you have to make things right if you can."

"But how does it tie into Davis's book?" Meredith asked. She tapped her fingers on the table. The Sedgwick family *wanted* their ancestor showcased in Davis's book, so it made no sense to think they were the ones behind the threats. As Meredith took a sip of her coffee, something occurred to her. "What if the Sedgwicks thought the diary and the papers were real, but then they found out the truth? That they were fakes? Wouldn't they want to stop Davis's book so the forgery wouldn't be discovered?"

"That makes some sense," Julia said. "I realize I sound like a broken record, but shouldn't we turn this over to Davis and Beatrice? Keeping this information to ourselves makes me nervous."

"I understand," Meredith said. "I just want to think about it before we do anything. We need to handle this correctly. If the family doesn't know, telling someone else first could cause some real damage to their reputation. I don't want to do that."

"But Meredith, we can't let them dedicate that statue tomorrow if the whole story is false."

"Well," Maggie Lu said slowly, "seeing one page of a diary isn't a great reason to throw the baby out with the bathwater. I think you need to find out more about the family and this Ambrose Sedgwick before you make it look as if the family was trying to get away with something. Find out who discovered the diary and the letters. Be certain before you do something that makes this family look dishonest."

"I guess so," Julia said. "It just doesn't seem right to let them dedicate a statue to Sedgwick if the reason behind it isn't true." She took a deep breath, and her eyes widened. "When the Oglethorpe family finds out…"

"Yeah, I thought about that," Meredith said. She snapped her fingers. "Maybe we *should* tell Beatrice. Maybe she can just postpone the dedication and give us a little time. In the meantime we can interview the families."

"I found out there's someone else besides Miss Dicey who is directly related to Oglethorpe," Julia said. "From what I heard, she's the self-elected representative for the family." Laodicea Oglethorpe, referred to as Miss Dicey, was over one hundred years old. She and her nephew, Jubal, had been helpful to them in the past because of their knowledge about Savannah history.

"Funny Miss Dicey never mentioned her," Maggie Lu said, a frown creasing her forehead. "What's her name?"

"Fancy Devereaux," Julia said.

Maggie Lu sighed. "I know her. Her father owns a large advertising firm in Atlanta, very successful. She does have a few issues. I think she's desperate to gain his approval. It's sad. They are related to Oglethorpe, but they don't have much to do with any other branch of the family."

"I've never met her," Julia said, "but I think I'm relieved."

"I honestly can't see her involved in a plot to stop the release of Davis Hedgerow's book," Maggie Lu said. "Fancy likes suing people to get her way. I know of at least three times she's sued someone who didn't bow down to her wishes."

"Maybe we need to put Fancy on the back burner," Meredith said. "Frankly, if I have to confront one more Southern belle, I may lose my lunch." She paused for a moment. "I think I'll call Jubal and see if he's heard anything about Ambrose Sedgwick."

"Good idea." Maggie Lu sighed. "I've been invited to a *soiree* this weekend to benefit at-risk children in the Savannah schools. I'm certain Fancy and her husband will be front and center there. They planned the whole thing, you know. Maybe I could talk to her. See if she knows anything about Davis's book."

"That would be great," Meredith said. "If you don't mind."

"Of course I don't. If it will help, I'm willing to do whatever I can."

"When is it?" Julia asked.

"Tomorrow night. I'll call and let them know I can come."

"Isn't it kind of late to RSVP?"

Maggie Lu shrugged. "They won't mind. They always leave some open places at the tables in case someone with money decides to come at the last minute. I think I can slip in. I'll do my best to ask Fancy about the statue, but I doubt she's going to break down and confess to anything. All I can really do is watch her reaction. If it's...unusual, at least it will mean you can add her to your list of suspects." She frowned at Meredith. "But as I said before, writing a letter doesn't sound like Fancy. She's much bolder in her attacks."

"Thanks, Maggie Lu," Meredith said. "It might be a dead end, but at least I'll feel as if we followed every lead." She hesitated a moment as she looked back and forth between Maggie Lu and Julia. "We need to keep the rumor about Dixie dipping her fingers into the till to ourselves. We have no proof and even if we did, Dixie's relationship with the SOS isn't our case."

"I agree," Maggie Lu said. "I have no intention of bringing it up. And if my friend says anything else, I'll tell her to confront Dixie one on one. Give her a chance to explain."

"That sounds right," Julia said. She sighed. "As annoying as Dixie is, I hope it's just a misunderstanding."

"Me too," Meredith agreed. She sucked in a deep breath and let it out slowly as she tried to figure out what to do next. "Let's get back to the Ambrose Sedgwick diary. We have proof that at least *some* of the evidence pointing to him as the person who helped to create Savannah's layout is forged. But we need more information before we start accusing people."

"Turning this over to the proper person isn't *accusing people*," Julia said, sounding a little frustrated.

"I know, and you're right. I guess I want to completely trust whoever we share our suspicions with. I like Davis Hedgerow, but he was Ron's friend. Not mine."

"I don't understand," Julia said, her forehead furrowed. "You're surely not throwing suspicion on Davis."

Meredith sighed. "Of course not. But do I need to remind you that he works for a newspaper? This would be a story, wouldn't it? I'd hate to see it end up on the front page before we know if the family is involved. It could cause a lot of damage."

Meredith knew she sounded a little confused, but she really was. Just when she thought she had a handle on this case, it went another way. Who had forged the diary and why? And what about the letters? Could they be real? The answers to these questions were important, but none of this had a clear connection to the person threatening Davis Hedgerow. *He* was their client. It was important to remember why they were hired. Amid all these other things, that purpose seemed to be getting lost in the shuffle.

"I've got some work to do," she said getting to her feet. "You two stay and finish off the pastries." She pointed at Julia. "I'll see you and Beau at four o'clock."

"I can't eat another bite," Maggie Lu said. "I'm as full as a tick."

"Okay," Julia said. Meredith saw her eyeing the last cream puff. She left Julia behind to snag the last treat. She needed to make a couple of phone calls. She prayed Beatrice would postpone the dedication and give her the contact information for the Sedgwick family. Beatrice had a tendency to overreact. Right now, Meredith needed her to be levelheaded.

When she got to her office, she called Beatrice's cell phone. Thankfully, she answered right away.

"Beatrice, I need to talk to you," Meredith said. "It's important. Could we get together for lunch today?"

"I couldn't possibly," Beatrice said in hushed tones. She sounded like Meredith had just requested her firstborn child. "I'm at the Georgia Historical Society right now."

"Okay. I'll come to you. Surely you can give me a few minutes. What I have to tell you is very important."

A long sigh came over the phone. "Oh, all right. As long as it's quick. You'll have to get here soon. I'm getting together with the Sedgwick family for lunch. We'll be going over the memorial tomorrow."

Just in the nick of time. "I'll be there in a few minutes." Before Beatrice could argue with her, she hung up. She looked at the clock in her office. Ten o'clock. She had a lot to do before going to the B and B.

She picked up the phone and dialed Jubal Early Jones. She'd thought about calling Miss Dicey, but sometimes it was difficult for her to hear conversation on the phone. Meredith was glad to hear Jubal's voice after a couple of rings. She told him about the letters, the diary, and the dedication, leaving out the part about the diary being forged.

"I can't give you much information about this," he said. "I haven't heard about it, and I'm sure Miss Dicey hasn't either. Is it important? Should I tell her about it?"

"No, I wouldn't mention it. I just wondered if you knew something that might help us with a case."

"Well, I'd sure like to hear what you find out. Sounds real interesting."

Meredith assured him she'd keep him updated and promised to visit Miss Dicey as soon as she could. When she hung up, she sighed. It seemed Fancy Devereaux was going to have to stand in for the Oglethorpe family.

She stepped out into the hall just in time to see Julia going to her office and Maggie Lu headed toward the back door. She hurried over and gave Maggie Lu a big hug. "Thanks so much for all your help. It's much appreciated. Can I give you a ride?"

Maggie Lu hugged her back. "No, thank you. Charlene is picking me up. And you're very welcome. I have confidence you'll figure this out. And you let me know when you do, you hear? I'd like to find out what's going on myself. I'll call you after the party tomorrow night and let you know if I uncover anything helpful."

"Thank you. Pray for us, will you?"

Maggie Lu smiled. "Absolutely. I do anyway, you know. Just remember that you can do all things through Christ. He will give you the strength you need."

"Thank you, dear friend." Meredith sighed. "I needed that reminder." Maggie Lu was right. She needed to cast the care of this case on the Lord. His shoulders were bigger than hers.

Charlene's car pulled up in front of the building, and Maggie Lu opened her umbrella and stepped out into the rain. As she hurried toward Charlene's car, Meredith thanked God for Maggie Lu's friendship. She was definitely a treasure.

Meredith hurried to Julia's office and told her she was heading back to the Georgia Historical Society to talk to Beatrice.

"Do you want me to go with you?" Julia asked.

"No, I'm hoping if it's just me it will be less confrontational. You know how Beatrice can get."

"Yeah, I certainly do. You have fun."

"Not sure it will be fun, but you're right. It has to be done." Meredith started to walk away but turned around before she reached the door. "Do you want me to bring lunch back?"

Julia shook her head. "I'm full of beignets and cream puffs. I may never eat again."

Meredith laughed. "I doubt that. If you change your mind, call me, okay?"

"Okay."

Meredith grabbed her umbrella and her coat and left the office. She hoped this was the right move. Dealing with Beatrice was tricky, but Meredith was fairly certain she wouldn't want to do anything that would shed a bad light on the Savannah Historical Society. Since they were sponsoring this event, most people would assume they should have done a better job of confirming the diary and the letters were real.

Meredith could only pray this wouldn't blow up in her face.

Chapter Seventeen

WHEN SHE REACHED THE GEORGIA Historical Society, Meredith was still able to park fairly close to the building. It seemed the exhibition wasn't drawing a lot of visitors. She hadn't seen anything in the paper about it. If Meredith was still in charge, she would have contacted the *Tribune*. They had always been interested in historical exhibits and discoveries about Savannah. Meredith couldn't help but wonder why Beatrice hadn't done that. Especially with the donation from the Sedgwicks. Strange, indeed.

When she got inside, she headed straight for the display. At first, she didn't see Beatrice, but then she spotted her sitting at one of the long tables set up for those reading and doing research. She didn't look happy.

"Here you are," Meredith said with a smile. "How are things going?"

"We should have had more visitors," Beatrice said. She must have been really upset. She'd forgotten her thick Southern accent. "I sent an article to the paper. You know, to the editor who handles local events. Can't think of his name right now…"

"Jerry Steadman?" Meredith said. "He was always so easy to work with." As she sat down, something Beatrice said jumped out at her. "Wait a minute. Did you say you sent him an article?"

Beatrice nodded. "Yes. It was perfect. All he had to do was publish it. We would have had people packed toe to toe in here."

"But Beatrice, you don't write the article for them. Not without permission. You invite them over, let them interview you, and let them write it."

"I realize that's how you should do it, but sometimes the information is wrong. This way there are no mistakes." She frowned at Meredith. "I have a degree in creative writing, you know. That should qualify me to write my own articles. The paper should respect my work enough to simply print them as is."

Meredith just stared at her. What was there to say? Although sometimes an editor would accept an article submitted by an outside source, it was usually only after they had developed a relationship. It was a safe bet that the editors at the paper hadn't appreciated Beatrice's assumption that they would print her article. Meredith decided to ignore this and focus on the other problem Beatrice faced.

"Beatrice, I realize you plan to dedicate the statue to Ambrose Sedgwick tomorrow, but I…I think you need to wait."

Beatrice arched one perfectly formed eyebrow. "Excuse me?"

Meredith took a deep breath and said a silent prayer. "I have reason to believe the diary…and maybe the letters…are forgeries."

Beatrice's expression turned to stone. "I know you're jealous of me, Meredith, but to stoop this low…"

"Oh, don't be ridiculous, Beatrice. You didn't take my job. I retired, remember? Why in the world would I be jealous of you?"

Now both of her eyebrows shot up. "I'm doing a much better job than you did. I've been able to bring in exhibits that are far better than anything you ever could. Like this one. That's obviously why you want to ruin it. Well, I just won't let you."

Meredith had a notion to just let her stew in her own juices. Let the truth come out and allow her to look inept. But in her heart Meredith knew she couldn't do it.

"None of that is true. I honestly don't know if the entire exhibit is faked, but you need to call in an expert. If I can tell the diary is forged, I know others will as well. If you allow the dedication of the statue to go forward and then the truth is discovered, you will look incompetent, Beatrice."

"The diary and the letters were already authenticated by an expert," Beatrice insisted.

"Who hired the expert?" Meredith asked. "The family?"

"Yes."

Although Beatrice attempted to sound confident, Meredith could hear the hesitation in her voice.

"You have the diary opened to a page where this sentence is used." Meredith reached into her jacket pocket and took out a small notebook. She found the page she wanted and read, "'Our unfortunate neighbor was caught stealing and was sadly sent up the river.'"

"So?" Beatrice shook her head. "That verbiage sounds appropriate to the time."

"But it's not. That phrase, *sent up the river,* refers to prisoners sent to Sing Sing prison in New York, the river being the Hudson."

Beatrice glared at her. "What is your point?"

"Ambrose Sedgwick lived in the 1700s, right?"

Beatrice sighed as if she were growing bored. "I'm meeting the Sedgwick family for an early lunch. I need time to prepare. You need to leave."

"Beatrice, the building of Sing Sing prison was completed in 1826. There's no way someone in the 1700s would have used those words."

Meredith almost felt sorry for Beatrice. Almost. The color faded from her face, and her eyes looked as if they might pop out of her head.

"Do you…do you need something?" Meredith asked.

"But…but…"

"You accepted this display as authentic because an expert said it was. He lied. That's not your fault, Beatrice." Although she didn't like the woman, at the moment, Meredith felt the need to comfort her. "We just need to figure out what to do now."

"You wouldn't have used an expert hired by the family," Beatrice said, her eyes shiny with tears.

Well, phooey. Now Meredith really did feel sorry for the woman. "There isn't anyone out there who hasn't been fooled by so-called *experts*. Don't beat yourself up."

"So what do I do?"

"First of all, you put off the statue dedication tomorrow."

"How can I do that?"

Meredith thought for a moment. Then she snapped her fingers. "I should have thought of this before. Blame it on the weather. It's supposed to rain all day tomorrow. Tell people you'll let them know when the dedication is rescheduled."

"Okay. Maybe it's a good thing the paper didn't carry the story."

Meredith nodded. "Yes, it is. Everything will work out." Meredith had an idea, but she wasn't sure Beatrice would agree with it. "Can I go to lunch with you? Talk to the Sedgwick family?"

"That's not necessary. I can tell them."

"Okay, I understand. But there's something else going on. Something Julia and I are investigating. I'd really like to meet them. Maybe you can help me...."

Before Meredith could finish her sentence, Beatrice interrupted her. "Please, come to lunch. I'd like to help. You may have kept me from being publicly humiliated. Maybe even saved my job." She sighed. "Thank you, Meredith. I realize that sometimes I'm...a little difficult to get along with."

Now it was Meredith's turn to be shocked. She wondered if Beatrice would mind repeating that so she could record it on her phone. Julia would never believe it. "Thank you for saying that, Beatrice," she said with a smile. "Now let's fix this, okay?"

"Okay." Beatrice stood to her feet. "We're having lunch at Justine's. I'll drive."

"Sounds good."

Meredith followed Beatrice out of the building and to her car. A few minutes later they were walking into Justine's. The French restaurant was beautifully decorated. In the dining room, one wall was designed like a waterfall with water flowing down from the top into a tray at the bottom that sent the water back up to the top again. Seating consisted of dark wood tables and booths with padded blue velvet chairs and white tablecloths. The room was kept rather dark and every table had a lighted candle covered by a small hurricane glass shade. Meredith couldn't help but think how much

Ron would have enjoyed the restaurant. He'd loved places with ambiance.

"There they are," Beatrice said, pointing toward a table near the back of the dining room. As they approached, Meredith was relieved to see there were only two people. An older couple. It was obvious by the way they dressed that they were well-to-do. The man was distinguished looking, with thick silver hair. His dark navy blazer highlighted his brilliant blue eyes.

"I brought someone with me," Beatrice said to him. Her voice shook slightly. It was obvious that she was nervous. "This is Meredith Bellefontaine. She was the president of the Savannah Historical Society before me." She turned to Meredith. "This is Sylvester Sedgwick and his wife, Paula."

Sylvester reached out to shake her hand. He had a sincere smile, but Meredith was fairly confident that it would vanish before lunch was over.

Chapter Eighteen

MEREDITH AND BEATRICE HAD BARELY taken their seats when a waiter came up to them to get their drink orders. Meredith asked for iced tea. When he offered her a menu, she said no. Frankly, she wasn't sure the Sedgwicks would want her to stay after she told them about the diary.

"We're excited about the dedication tomorrow," Paula said. She matched her husband perfectly. Meredith guessed the Sedgwicks were in their seventies, but they looked younger. Paula wore her silver hair in a bun with tendrils framing her lovely face. Her makeup was flawless, and her slim and obviously fit body was clothed with the latest fashion. It was clear she'd been a great beauty in her youth. Age certainly hadn't dulled her looks.

Beatrice cleared her throat. "I'm…I'm so sorry, but we've moved the dedication back a bit. The forecast is for rain all day tomorrow. We want to make sure we get media attention and that people turn out for the event. I hope you understand."

"Well, I'm disappointed, but it makes sense," Paula said. "What's the new date?"

Beatrice swallowed hard. Meredith could tell she was faltering. Time to jump into the fray.

"We need to discuss something with you," Meredith said. "I'm afraid it will upset you, but I'm sure you'll understand why we need to bring it up."

Sylvester frowned at her. "Please, tell us."

"First, will you tell me how Ambrose Sedgwick's diary and letters were found?"

"Certainly," Sylvester said, "although Beatrice already knows the story."

"I realize that," Meredith said, "but I'd like to hear it, if you don't mind."

Before he could respond, their waiter returned. Not knowing how long she would be staying, Meredith just ordered a Caesar salad.

When the waiter walked away, she turned her attention back to Sylvester. She noticed that Paula seemed nervous. She kept fidgeting with her bracelet and refused to meet Meredith's eyes. What was that about?

Sylvester took a drink and put his glass down. "The diary and the letters were found under the floorboards of an old house in St. Mary's. We're not sure how they got there, and the diary doesn't explain it. We assume either they were given to someone after Ambrose died or else he moved there before his death. We're not sure. The original title for the house was lost in a fire."

"So the people living in the house found the documents and contacted you?"

Sylvester nodded. "I'd written an article about Ambrose. He was an aide to Oglethorpe and was acknowledged for helping him with his plan to found Savannah. That's how the Wilmores found us."

"The Wilmores?"

Sylvester nodded. "Marcie and Todd Wilmore. They were restoring an old house. As they were working in the attic they pulled up rotten floorboards and found a small chest with the diary and the letters."

"What do the Wilmores do?"

"They own an antiques store. That's how they knew they'd found something important."

Meredith sighed deeply. Things were becoming clearer.

"Mr. Sedgwick…"

"Sylvester," he said, interrupting her.

"Thank you. Sylvester, how did you obtain the papers?"

He shifted uncomfortably in his chair, and Paula wrapped her arms around herself, refusing to look at anyone. It was clear she suspected something.

"Well, they were going to take the items to auction. We…we asked if we could buy them directly. Getting historical documents to auction takes quite a while, and we didn't want to wait that long." He stared at Meredith through narrowed eyes. "We did have everything authenticated, you know."

Meredith nodded. "May I ask who authenticated the documents?"

"His name is Barton Whatley. He works all over Georgia."

"And how did you find him?"

Sylvester cleared his throat again. "He…he was recommended by the Wilmores."

"Do you mind if I ask how much you paid the Wilmores?"

"We gave them one hundred and twenty thousand dollars. We were assured by Mr. Whatley that this was much less than the items were really worth. That we were getting a really good deal."

He leaned forward, his eyes trained on Meredith. Out of the corner of her eye she thought she saw Beatrice push her seat back several inches.

"Why are you asking all these questions?"

There was nothing else she could do but pull the bandage off quickly. "I have reason to believe the diary, and perhaps the papers, are forgeries."

Sylvester's mouth dropped open. "That's impossible. How would they know so many details about Ambrose? The diary was full of factual information about his whereabouts, what he was doing, things I never mentioned in my article."

"Could they have gotten that information from their own research?"

Sylvester's jaw went slack, and he leaned back in his chair. "What...what are you saying?"

Even though she felt she'd already said it, Meredith felt the need to put the pieces together for Sylvester and his wife.

"First of all, you should never use an appraiser who is known to the people you're buying something from. Even if they seem legitimate. The Wilmores probably paid him a portion of the money they received from you."

"How can you be sure the diary and the papers aren't real?" Paula asked.

"I can't say anything about the letters, but there's something wrong with the diary." Meredith explained the use of a phrase that wasn't around in the 1700s.

"But it's not impossible that Ambrose used it before... I mean, maybe there was another prison and river..." Sylvester groaned.

"Okay, even I can see how ridiculous that sounds." He looked at his wife. "You tried to tell me, but I wouldn't listen." He reached over and took Paula's hand. "I'm sorry, honey. Seems I goofed up." He swung his gaze back to Meredith. "What do we do now?"

"Put off the dedication until you can have an unbiased expert look over the documents. We have several highly qualified people in Savannah who would be happy to help you. *If* they prove that the documents are forgeries, contact the police. They'll guide you from there."

"I'm not sure I want the authorities involved," Sylvester said. "This makes me look like a fool."

"That's what they're counting on," Meredith said. "If you don't go after them, they'll bilk someone else."

"They said they needed money to finish restoring their house," Paula said. "Perhaps it was a onetime thing."

"Maybe, but I doubt it. The work done to make those documents look real was crafted by experts. The only place they failed was in checking out that phrase. It was a fluke that the diary was open to that particular page. There may be other mistakes as well, but we have no idea since we haven't gone through the rest of the diary."

"Why didn't you notice that when we gave the papers to you?" Sylvester asked Beatrice.

"I'm sorry. I truly am. I didn't read every page. I opened it to that page because it seemed interesting. Unfortunately, that particular phrase wasn't familiar to me." Beatrice looked crestfallen, her heavy accent forgotten.

"Like I said, these documents were created by experts," Meredith said. "It was just a lucky break that we noticed that one phrase out of all the papers on display. This was not my colleague's fault."

"Yes," Paula said, crisply. "This is *your* fault, Sylvester. Not Beatrice's. You were so frantic to feel connected to Savannah's history that you didn't pay attention to all the warnings along the way."

Sylvester stared at his wife for a moment before turning to Beatrice. "As always, my beautiful wife is right. I apologize to you, Beatrice. We appreciate everything you've done for us."

"You're welcome," Beatrice said. "I'm just sorry it didn't turn out the way we'd all hoped."

"No use crying over spilled milk," Paula said, straightening her shoulders. "But now we need to clean it up."

Their waiter came to the table with their orders. When he left, Sylvester said, "Not feeling very hungry right now. Frankly, I feel a little sick."

Meredith certainly understood. She had one more important question to ask. "Sylvester and Paula, I understand you and the Oglethorpe family have had some…tension…in the past. Can you tell me about that?"

Paula put her cloth napkin in her lap. "Not until we came out with this supposed evidence. Then things did get a little uncomfortable."

"Did they dispute the claims about Ambrose coming up with the idea of the grid layout?"

"Yes. Strongly. Turns out they were right."

"That's the problem," Meredith said. "There might be a grain of truth here somewhere, but it will probably be lost because of misinformation. I'm sorry about that."

Paula shrugged. "To be honest, I just want to get out of this with as much grace as possible. We will have to apologize to the Oglethorpe family."

Meredith took a bite of her salad. "Have either of you heard of a group called the Sisters of the South?" she asked after she swallowed.

Paula looked at Sylvester. They both shook their heads. "I've never heard of it," Sylvester said. "Should I have?"

"Do you know a woman named Fancy Devereaux?"

"Yes," Paula said. "When the news about Ambrose came out, she sent us several letters. They weren't…nice. She was certain the diary and the letters were forgeries. Accused us of having something to do with it." She sighed. "I don't look forward to letting her know she was right."

"Somehow she found out we donated a large sum of money to the Georgia Historical Society," Sylvester said. "It had nothing to do with Ambrose, you know. We committed to that donation several months before the diary and letters were discovered. In Fancy's mind, however, we were trying to buy our way into her family history. She is a very angry woman."

Paula frowned. "We haven't heard from her in a couple of months, but I'm sure she hasn't given up."

"Her husband is a very successful surgeon," Sylvester said. "I met him once and found him to be a kind and gracious man. I'm surprised by his wife's actions. Of course, we have no idea if he is aware of the situation."

Meredith just nodded. Fancy Devereaux was now a solid suspect. Not only had she already written letters, her husband was a physician. Did he write BID on a pad of paper used next by his wife? Had they found their letter writer?

Chapter Nineteen

MEREDITH MET JULIA AND BEAU in the small parking lot of the Magnolia Blossom Inn. If it had been a busy tourist season, they would have had to park on the street. Many B and Bs only had street parking.

The outside of the home, restored and turned into a lovely bed-and-breakfast, was done beautifully with obvious attention to detail. It was the house that Meredith had passed by many times. She'd noticed it because her home was also Italianate-styled. At one time painted an awful orange color, now it was a lovely buttercream with black shutters and white and light blue accents. Meredith approved of the changes. They'd kept the spirit of the original house. The large wraparound porch with white rocking chairs would have been inviting if not for the chilly rain still falling. They grabbed their bags and ran up the stairs to the porch.

"Well, we won't have to make up excuses to stay in," Julia said as they stood by the front door. "We really will be hunkered in tonight."

"What's our reason for being here if they should ask?" Beau asked.

"We're celebrating Julia's birthday," Meredith said.

"But we already did that," Julia reminded her.

Meredith laughed. "I know that, but this is just an extension. I have some surprises for you."

"More than one? Oh, Mere. Really. I'm trying to ignore my birthday, and you're doing everything you can to make it go on and on."

Meredith laughed. "Tough. I for one am very glad you were born."

"And that goes double for me," Beau said, kissing Julia on the cheek.

"Just remember that somehow we've got to talk to the owner, Elise Sedgwick," Meredith said.

"Sedgwick?" Beau asked. "Related to *the* Sedgwicks?"

"The estranged daughter," Meredith said.

"Interesting," Beau responded, drawing out his response.

Meredith nodded. She thought it was interesting too, but how did it apply to their case? Hopefully, they'd find out something that would either rule Elise out or make her a possible suspect.

Beau opened the front door with his free hand. He stood back, allowing the women to enter first, then he wheeled in the small suitcase they'd brought with them.

They walked into gleaming marble floors, long windows, cream-colored walls, and staircases with black iron railings. The furniture was correct for the architecture and time period. Victorian with an Italian flavor, overstuffed red velvet furniture and various leather pieces. They could see into the dining room where breakfast would be held. A huge crystal chandelier hung over a shiny rosewood table, the padded chairs done in cream-colored brocade. A large mirror with an intricate gold-painted frame was the stunning centerpiece of the room.

The living room where they stood had a massive fireplace on one side. A fire crackled behind an ornate grate that sat on the large hearth. Meredith could see herself sitting in the brown leather chair near the fire, reading until she fell asleep.

"Sorry, I was in the kitchen," a voice called out.

They turned to find a small dark-haired woman who looked to be in her thirties coming toward them. She was wearing an apron. She held her hand out. "I'm Elise Sedgwick. I own and manage the Magnolia Blossom."

"We've passed by this house many times," Meredith said, shaking her hand. "I'm so impressed by the work you've done here. It's absolutely gorgeous."

"Thank you," Elise said with a smile. "It was a daunting task, but I just couldn't let this beautiful old lady die. I'm very proud of her now."

"You should be," Julia said.

"I take it you're the Foleys and you're Mrs. Bellefontaine."

"Yes," Meredith said.

"You're our only guests tonight," Elise said. "I'm sorry about the rain. I expected a call canceling your reservation."

"I hope it's okay that we came anyway," Meredith said. "We have a birthday to celebrate and didn't plan to spend much time outdoors anyway."

"I have an assistant manager, but I gave her the night off. I'm afraid you're stuck with me. I'm a pretty good cook, so I don't think you'll be disappointed by breakfast."

"We look forward to it," Julia said.

Elise smiled at them. "Let's get you settled in your rooms."

They grabbed their bags and followed Elise up the winding stairs to the second floor.

"I'm putting you in our Hibiscus room, Mrs. Bellefontaine." She opened the door to a lovely room, decorated in cream and maroon. A large four-poster bed sat near the tall windows that looked out on the streets of Savannah. Two of the windows were actually doors that opened onto a small balcony. If it wasn't raining, guests could sit outside with a mint julep and enjoy the carriages that passed by. There were two high-backed chairs near the gas fireplace that had been turned on. There was a mahogany half desk against the wall, near the bed. And a flat-screen TV over the fireplace. The bathroom was large and fully stocked, with a jetted tub. Meredith found herself wanting to return someday when she wasn't on a case.

"Will this suit you?" Elise asked.

"It's just beautiful. I could stay here forever."

Elise laughed. "I'll take that as a yes."

She motioned to Beau and Julia. "You're right next door." She indicated a door next to a large armoire. "This is a connecting door. Not sure if you want to use it, but if you're planning to celebrate together, this would keep you from having come in through the hallway." She grinned at them. "And of course, you wouldn't want to run into Colonel Lincoln Morgan and his wife, Clementine. They're known to wander the halls." She frowned at them. "Did you want the tour? My assistant manager usually does those. Of course I can fill in...."

Meredith smiled. "I think we can do without that, but thanks."

Elise looked relieved. "Great. And if you don't mind, I won't walk down the hall while you're trying to sleep and knock on your door. I'll just leave the ghosts to fend for themselves."

"We would appreciate that," Beau said, laughing.

"Let's get you into your room," Elise said, gesturing to Beau and Julia.

"Sounds great," Beau said. "Can we just go in through here?" He pointed toward the door Elise had indicated earlier.

"Sure."

Elise took a set of keys from her pocket and unlocked the door. She swung it open. Meredith followed Beau and Julia into their room. It was similar to hers, but it was done in blues and cream. It also had a balcony.

"Did you decorate the inn yourself?" Meredith asked Elise.

"Yes. I knew from the beginning how I wanted each room to look. As strange as it sounds, I felt called to save this old house. I love it. I even live here. My quarters are off the kitchen. You won't run into me if you want to go downstairs and sit in the living room. I lock myself in after six o'clock so you won't feel as if I'm keeping an eye on you."

Meredith turned around and smiled at her. "Actually, I'd love to talk to you about the house. What it took to turn it into…this." She waved her arm, indicating the room around them. "But if you're busy…"

"No. Not at all," Elise said. "Did you bring anything for supper or were you planning to go out?"

Meredith laughed. "No supper. But…there might be a birthday cake in the car."

"Oh my," Julia said. "Lemon Charlotte cake?"

Meredith shrugged. "Who knows? It just might be…."

"Let me suggest something," Elise said. "I have some homemade chili and corn bread in the kitchen. If you're interested, we can eat that and then you can serve your cake. You can use my plates."

"Are you sure?" Julia asked. "We don't want to cause you any trouble."

Elise shook her head and pointed to a nearby window streaked with rain. "In my opinion, you're not getting your money's worth. You can't sit out in the garden or even on the front porch. And if you don't want the ghost tour… Well, I owe you something. I'm getting off cheap with chili and corn bread."

"That's so generous of you," Meredith said. She looked at Beau and Julia. "That sounds great."

Julia and Beau nodded their agreement.

"Good," Elise said with a smile. "You unpack and relax. I'll have dinner ready at six thirty. Will that work for you?"

"Thank you," Beau said. "You're very gracious."

"Actually, I get lonely here by myself, especially when we don't have guests. Having someone to talk to is a blessing." She walked to the door but turned around before leaving. "Six thirty in the dining room. See you then." She walked out and closed the door behind her.

"She's so nice," Julia said quietly. "I don't think she'd threaten anyone. Besides, I think we have our suspect. Fancy Devereaux."

"She may be the strongest possibility we have," Meredith agreed. "I'm still not sure why she'd try to stop Davis's book from being published, though. Hopefully, Maggie Lu will be able to ferret out something at the party tomorrow night."

"Maybe she's very protective of her family?" Beau asked.

Julia nodded. "She seems to be, but why not just dispute the book after it's published? She has money and is well known in the community. People would listen to her. And since she likes to sue people…"

"You're right." Meredith sighed. "It sounds like that would be more her style. I don't know, I think my brain needs a break."

"Well, I certainly don't think Elise Sedgwick is involved," Julia said. "She's lovely."

"We've learned the hard way that not everyone is who they seem to be," Meredith reminded her. "We need to keep our radar up tonight. We have to check out every new site being highlighted in Davis's book. That's what we were hired to do."

Julia nodded. "You're right. So what's the plan?"

"Are you going to bring up her family?" Beau asked.

"Hopefully she'll mention them herself. If we start talking about our families, maybe she'll just chime in."

Beau grinned. "Sounds like a plan."

"I almost forgot to tell you," Meredith said to Julia. "This afternoon I ran a background check on Carl Finney. You know, the cook at Peachie's?"

"And?"

"He got out of prison a few months ago."

"Oh my goodness," Julia said, her eyes wide. "Does Kathy know?"

Meredith nodded. "I called her and brought up Jeffrey saying Carl was 'mean.' That it concerned me. She told me in confidence that Carl had done time in prison and that she was giving him a second chance. I guess he's doing well."

"What did she say about Jeffrey's comment?" Julia asked.

"I guess Jeffrey reminds Carl of his own son who died while he was in prison. Kathy thinks it's because seeing Jeffrey hurts him. She plans to talk to Carl about it."

"That's an interesting story," Beau interjected. "But couldn't he still be the person you're looking for? Maybe he doesn't want people to know where he is. Or that he was in prison."

"Except he isn't in any of the pictures."

"And the reason he doesn't want anyone to know his last name," Julia said slowly, "is because he'd like to keep his past...in the past?"

"Exactly."

"So you're taking him off your list?" Beau asked.

Meredith nodded. "There's another compelling reason to look elsewhere. Kathy happened to mention that Carl can't write. She's teaching him, but from what she told me there's no way he could have written the letter to Davis. They're still working on the alphabet."

"He's fortunate to have found a boss like Kathy," Julia said.

"Yes, he is," Meredith said with a smile. "Hey, give me a little time." She walked over to the connecting door. "I'll knock when I'm ready."

"Okay," Julia said. "I really hope we can rule Elise out. I'd like to come back here sometime. It's so charming."

"I agree." Meredith walked through the door and closed it behind her. She had so many ideas swirling in her head. Right now Fancy Devereaux was still on their list, but there were other possibilities. The Sedgwicks seemed so sincere, but what if their reaction to the news about the forgery was an act? They'd promised to contact Davis and share this new information with him so he could ask his publisher to remove the entry about Ambrose Sedgwick. She wondered if they'd followed through. She dialed Davis's number but only got his voice mail. She left a quick message, asking Davis to call her. That it was important.

When she hung up, she couldn't squelch a feeling of concern that kept trying to work its way into her thoughts. Would they ever uncover the person behind the threats? She was beginning to wonder.

Chapter Twenty

AS THE RAIN CONTINUED TO fall, Meredith, Julia, and Beau enjoyed Elise's delicious chili and perfect corn bread. Elise shared with them how she'd fallen in love with the house long ago and had dreamed of owning it someday. Finally she made an offer that was accepted, and now the house was hers.

"I was so excited when I found out that the woman who'd owned the house wanted me to have it. As I'm sure you know, real estate in this area is hard to come by. I'm sure there were bids higher than mine, but I submitted the plans I had for the house. How it would be fully restored and that it would be a place where people could come and enjoy this beautiful old lady." Elise shrugged. "Seems that was just what the owner wanted to hear. I feel it was meant to be." She looked around her. "I can't imagine living anywhere else."

"Was your family involved with the restoration?" Meredith asked.

Elise's open expression tightened. "What do you mean?" she asked.

Meredith feigned surprise. "I would think this was such a big undertaking that perhaps you had help from family...or friends."

Elise shook her head. "No. I hired people to help with the restoration. I don't see my family much. I have a few friends, but to be honest, I've spent so much time working on this house, I'm afraid I haven't invested much in my friendships. Right now it's just the house, me, and…" A faint meow came from somewhere under the table. Elise laughed. "Perfect timing!" She reached down and pulled up a large black cat that purred loudly. "This is Simon. My friend and constant companion. He's supposed to stay in our part of the house. I must have left the door unlatched." She pushed back her chair. "Give me a minute to feed him. I think his escape was caused by hunger. It's his dinnertime too."

She carried Simon to the door at the back of the kitchen. When she closed it behind her, Julia leaned toward Meredith. "Did you hear the way she reacted to your question about her family? Touchy subject."

"Yes, I noticed. You know, it's sad. The Sedgwicks seemed like great people, and I really like Elise. I can't imagine what could have happened to separate them like this."

Julia nodded. "It really is. I wish we could help them somehow."

"If she gets that upset when we just mention her family, I don't believe she's going to react well if we tell her that we've talked to them. I think we need to back off of this. Give her a chance to bring them up on her own."

"I agree," Julia said.

Meredith took out her phone. "I've been trying to reach Davis. I want to find out if the Sedgwicks contacted him." She pressed redial and waited for the phone to ring. Once again it went to voice mail. "Davis, this is Meredith. I'm sorry to keep calling, but it's really important that I talk to you." She hung the phone up and put it back in her pocket. "I wish he'd call me back."

"People get busy," Julia said. "I'm sure he'll contact you when he can."

"I guess so," she said slowly. "I keep feeling that we're missing something important. I can't seem to get it off my mind."

"Well, I don't know what it would be." Julia lowered her voice. "Let's sit down and write everything out. If we could narrow down our list, it would help."

"I'm sure you're right, but—"

The door opened, and Elise came back into the room. "Sorry," she said with a smile. "Anyone want more chili? More corn bread?"

"Oh, Elise," Meredith said, "I couldn't eat another bite. You're an incredible cook." She turned to look at Beau. "Would you please get that large box I left in the back of my car? And be careful. You've got to hold it by the bottom."

Beau grinned. "You mean as if I were carrying a cake?"

Meredith smiled. "Exactly."

"I'll take our dinner plates to the kitchen and get us some dessert plates," Elise said. "Anyone for coffee or is it too late for you?"

"I'd love a cup of coffee," Beau said, as he headed toward the front door.

"Me too," Meredith said.

Julia sighed. "I guess I'll have to join in. Just hope I won't be up half the night."

"I've got decaf if you want it," Elise said. "Besides my regular coffee-maker I have a single-serve machine. I found a wonderful decaf that is so good you can't tell the difference between it and regular coffee."

"That sounds perfect," Julia said with a smile. "Thank you so much."

Elise stood up. "Not a problem." She began to gather their plates and bowls.

"Please let me help," Meredith said. "You get the dishes on that side of the table, and I'll get the rest."

"Thank you," Elise said. "I appreciate it."

Once she'd gathered the dirty dishes, Meredith followed Elise through the door she'd gone through earlier with Simon. There was a short hall that led them into a bright and spacious kitchen that opened up to the living room. It was more modern than the rest of the house. The kitchen had gleaming white cabinets and granite counters. The small island echoed the style of the cabinets. The dark wood floors made the lighter colors pop. It was very appealing.

As she carried the dishes to the sink, Meredith glanced into the living room. A large beige sectional couch was situated near a large fireplace with two overstuffed wing chairs placed close by. Although Elise's portion of the house wasn't large, her use of the space showed off her decorating talent.

"Those stairs lead to my bedroom," Elise said, noticing Meredith's interest. "There's a full basement below that hasn't been finished. For now it's the perfect place for storage. Simon and I have plenty of room."

Simon, who was eating his supper, looked over at them and meowed, causing both women to laugh.

"I guess he agrees," Elise said.

"I have a Russian Blue named GK," Meredith said. "I was so glad he was with me after my husband died. He was so comforting, even though he's not really affectionate. Our relationship is built on *his* terms."

Elise placed the dishes in the sink. "That's the way it is with most cats. Simon has been such a blessing to me." She hesitated a moment before saying, "I used to be very close to my parents, but we had an argument. A big one. Since then I've rarely seen them. I was going through a very rough time, and one day Simon appeared on my front porch. He wasn't in good shape. Skinny. His fur was matted and dirty. I started feeding him. Then one afternoon, he ran past me when I opened the door. He sped straight over to a spot in front of the fireplace, turned around a few times, and lay down. Went to sleep. I got the feeling that for the first time in a long time he felt safe." She turned to look at Meredith with tears in her eyes. "I couldn't take that away from him. It didn't take long for me to realize that having him here made me feel better. I guess we help each other."

"He's so beautiful it's hard to believe he's ever gone through difficult times. You've turned his life around."

"He's done the same for me." Elise took a deep breath in an obvious attempt to calm her emotions.

"I'm sorry about your falling-out with your parents. I hope the rift can be mended."

Elise reached up into a cabinet and brought down four dessert plates. She handed them to Meredith and then slid a drawer open where she took out a cake cutter.

"I don't know. I want to reach out to them, but...I guess I'm afraid. I'm stronger now, and I don't want to put myself in a position where I might get hurt again."

"I can understand that," Meredith said, leaning against the island. "Do you mind if I ask what the argument was about?"

Elise let out a slow sigh. "I wanted to marry someone. They didn't approve. My father told me that if I married him he'd cut me out of his will."

Meredith frowned. "But you're not married."

"No. About a week before the wedding, I found out that everything my parents said was true. He was only interested in our money. I broke off the engagement and bought this house. Except for a couple of short, necessary phone calls, that was the last time I spoke to them. It's been almost three years now."

Meredith was silent. She couldn't imagine not speaking to her sons or her grandchildren. Just thinking about it brought tears to her eyes. "I'm truly sorry," she said sincerely. "I really hope you'll contact them. Family is so important."

"I agree. Well, enough of this. Let's get these plates in the dining room before we have a riot on our hands."

Meredith laughed. "We certainly don't want that."

The women took the plates back into the dining room and handed them out. Meredith's beautiful Lemon Charlotte cake sat in the middle of the table. "I'd wanted to bake this earlier for your birthday," she told Julia, "but I was so busy I just couldn't get it done. So here it is. Happy belated birthday."

Julia smiled. "Thank you, Mere. I love it."

"There's one more thing, but I have to go back to the room to get it. Why don't you cut the cake, Julia, while I get your other present?"

"Okay. How much do you want?"

"Just a tiny slice. Like I said, I'm stuffed."

Meredith left the room and went upstairs where she got one of her bags, opened it, and took out the additional gift she'd gotten for

Julia's birthday. As she headed downstairs, she heard her phone ring. She'd left it on the table. What if it was Davis? She hurried down the stairs but by the time she got there, the ringing had stopped.

When she got to the table, the cake and coffee had been served. "Before I give you this," Meredith said, "I want you to know that I purchased it before your birthday, but it arrived the day after your celebration. I didn't want to give it to you at work. I wanted it to be a little more special." She handed the package to Julia and then sat down.

"Before we have cake and Julia opens her gift, shouldn't we sing 'Happy Birthday'?" Elise asked.

Meredith nodded. "She wouldn't let us sing it at the Mansion on her birthday. I think this is the perfect time."

The three of them began to sing while Julia laughed at them. "Thank you. That was really lovely." She looked at Meredith. "Can I open this now?"

Meredith nodded. Julia removed the birthday paper wrapped around the gift and gasped at what she found. "It's *Jo's Boys*," she said.

"An illustrated first edition. Now you can add it to your first editions of *Little Women* and *Little Men*."

"Oh, Meredith. I can't believe you found one. It's in beautiful shape." She held it to her chest, a tear falling down her cheek. "This is the third book in the *Little Women* saga," she explained to Beau. "I have a copy of it, but it's not a first edition. They're hard to find in this condition." She smiled at Meredith. "I love it. I'll always treasure it."

In that moment, with Julia and Beau and the rain falling down outside, Meredith was able to put the case on the back burner. She felt great peace and contentment in this lovely house with her dear friends beside her.

As everyone began to enjoy the cake, Meredith picked up her phone so she could see who'd called. Sure enough, it was Davis. She excused herself from the table and carried the phone into the other room. She didn't want Elise to overhear her since they hadn't talked about Davis and the book yet. She pressed the CALL BACK button and listened as the phone rang. She expected to hear Davis's voice, but instead a woman answered.

"I'm sorry," Meredith said. "I was trying to reach Davis Hedgerow."

"Is this Meredith?" the woman asked.

"Yes, it is."

"This is Sylvia," the woman said. "Davis asked me to phone you. He's in the hospital. He was jumped on the way to his car this evening. He was beaten badly. For a while we weren't sure he was going to make it."

"Oh no," Meredith said. "I'm so sorry to hear this. Did the police arrest the person who attacked him?"

"No. And Davis couldn't identify him. He wants to talk to you," Sylvia said. "Can you come by the hospital in the morning?"

"Yes. Of course. I'll be there. I'm sorry I didn't recognize your voice, Sylvia."

"That's okay. It's been a while." Sylvia gave her Davis's room number before saying, "Whatever you've been doing, Meredith, please stop it now. You've put him in danger, and I won't stand for any more of this. I hope you hear me clearly." With that, she hung up.

Chapter Twenty-One

MEREDITH WENT BACK TO THE dining room. She tried hard to hide how upset she was. Was Sylvia right? Had they rattled the wrong cage somewhere? Had it triggered the person they were looking for to commit an act of desperation? Meredith felt sick to her stomach. Her wonderful cake felt like cardboard in her mouth. She was trying hard to pay attention to what everyone was saying, but Sylvia's voice kept echoing in her mind. *You've put him in danger, and I won't stand for any more of this.*

"Meredith, did you hear me?" Julia asked.

Meredith forced a smile. "I'm sorry. I was distracted. What did you say?"

"I was telling Elise how we found out about this wonderful place. That Davis Hedgerow graciously gave us an ARC of his upcoming book. About how Davis and Ron were friends."

Meredith nodded. "Yes, that's right." She smiled at Elise. "The description sounded so appealing." She took a deep breath and tried to refocus on what she needed to do now. Julia had obviously opened the door. She needed to go through it. "I noticed another chapter of his book, Elise. About a statue of an Ambrose Sedgwick being dedicated in Forsyth Park? Any relation?"

Elise sighed. "Unfortunately, yes. This is another thing my parents and I disagreed about. The people who said they discovered a diary and some letters from my much-removed ancestor? I didn't trust them. I felt they were taking my parents for a ride. They gave these people a lot of money, and it made me angry to think they were being taken advantage of." She shrugged. "They had an expert look at everything, and he claimed it was legitimate. I still have my doubts, but after that, there was nothing I could do. They wouldn't listen. Then we had the other argument I told you about. It was just too much for our relationship." She took a bite of her cake and swallowed it. "I'm glad it turned out the way they wanted. My parents care a lot about our heritage."

"And you don't?" Beau asked.

Elise smiled. "I'm interested, of course. I love history. I think that's evident in this house. But this thing…about Ambrose Sedgwick. I don't know. Maybe I have a bad attitude because I'm upset with my parents." She straightened up in her chair. "Let's find another topic of conversation, okay? I really don't want to talk about this."

"Of course," Meredith said. "I understand. But you must be thrilled about the mention of the Magnolia Blossom in Davis's book."

Elise smiled widely. "I'm beyond thrilled. I'm doing pretty well through word of mouth, but this should be a game changer. I'm very hopeful this book will be the thing that brings the kind of attention this old lady deserves."

"You keep referring to her as an old lady," Beau said. "Is that how you see her?"

Elise chuckled. "Well, she's old and she's just had a makeover. Sounds like a woman to me."

They all laughed.

"Meredith, this cake is scrumptious," Elise said. "Before you leave, will you give me the recipe? I would love to serve it here."

"Of course. I'll write it down tonight and get it to you in the morning." She pushed her chair back. "I'm beat. Time for bed. Let me help you with these dishes," she said to Elise.

"No. There's not that much. Besides, I have my way of doing things. Having someone in my kitchen just makes it harder."

Meredith nodded. She certainly understood that. She felt the same way about her kitchen. She had a system that worked for her. She didn't enjoy having someone get in her way and disrupt her process.

"If you're sure." Meredith stood up and waited while Beau and Julia thanked Elise for supper and for her kindness.

"Don't worry about the eleven o'clock checkout time in the morning," Elise said. "We don't have anyone else booked tomorrow. Leave when you want to."

"Thank you, Elise," Meredith said. She got the box the cake had come in and put what was left inside. "Can we keep this in your refrigerator overnight?" she asked.

"Of course. Not a problem."

"And please take another serving for yourself," Meredith said.

Elise chuckled. "I'm not about to argue with you."

Meredith thanked her again and left. When the three of them reached their rooms, Meredith said, "We need to talk. Why don't we do it in my room?"

Beau and Julia agreed and soon they were sitting at the small table not far from the mini kitchen. Meredith told them about the phone call.

"I certainly didn't expect this," Meredith told them. "Usually when a person sends threatening letters, it's because they don't want to confront someone face-to-face. I feel terrible. Why didn't I see this coming?"

"It's not your fault," Beau said. "I agree with you. Someone who uses letters and anonymous phone calls is a coward. Not inclined to physically attack anyone."

"Is he going to be okay?" Julia asked.

"Seems so. I need to go to the hospital in the morning."

"Oh, Meredith," Julia said. "Will Sylvia allow you to talk to him?"

"She asked me to come. Davis wants to talk to me. I'm not sure why." She sighed. "I also have to find out if the Sedgwicks contacted him. I wanted to ask Sylvia, but she didn't give me a chance."

"I'll go with you," Julia said.

"No. You and Beau stay here and enjoy this beautiful place. I think we can cross Elise off our list. She has no reason to stop the book from being published."

"I don't know," Beau said. "She certainly has a strong opinion about her parents getting involved with the Wilmores."

"Maybe so, but that doesn't give her a strong reason to stop Davis's book from being published, especially since she's set to ben-efit from it. Besides, I don't think Elise Sedgwick is capable of sub-duing and beating Davis up. She's barely five feet tall and probably doesn't weigh one hundred pounds soaking wet."

Beau shrugged. "Good point. Maybe she had someone do the job for her?"

"Perhaps, but her beef isn't with Davis," Julia said. "It's with her parents."

"She did mention the word *bids*," Meredith said. "Maybe it wasn't a prescription. Maybe it actually meant bids for renovations."

Julia cocked her head to the side as she considered Meredith's point. "No," she said finally. "It just doesn't work. Besides, what if that word isn't actually *bids*. What if it's *birds* but we can't make out part of the indentation?"

Meredith wasn't sure the scribble was *birds*, but Julia's point was a good one. She went over to the small desk in the room and got out her notebook. She turned the chair around so she could face Julia and Beau.

"Okay, let's go through it. Who among these suspects could have attacked Davis?"

"Or hired someone to do it," Beau reminded her.

"Right." She held her pen over the notebook she had on her lap. "First of all, *why* would someone physically attack Davis Hedgerow?"

"Obviously because they want him to stop the publication of his book," Julia said. "But so far we haven't found anything that would cause someone to become violent. Have we?"

Meredith shook her head. "No. Not that I can think of." She thought for a moment. "So who can we write off? Elise Sedgwick and anyone at Peachie's. The only person we suspected there couldn't be our suspect. So let's cross those names off. Do you both agree?"

Beau and Julia nodded their agreement.

"There's the Book Worm," Meredith said slowly. "But Patricia Ivers is angry with Alex, the bookstore owner, not Davis. Besides, hating someone so much you'd hire a thug to beat them up just so the store wouldn't get publicity?" She shook her head. "I don't see it. Patricia may not want the Book Worm to change, but that's not incentive enough for her to have Davis brutalized. To tell the truth, that group doesn't seem the least bit dangerous, although I didn't like Patricia's attorney."

"What attorney?" Beau asked.

"I guess she's suing the Book Worm owner for unlawful termination."

"Sounds to me as if that's her way of getting back at him. I don't think she'd have Davis beaten up because of her beef with Hemmings."

"I agree," Meredith said with a sigh. "So far, we just don't have a clear suspect. We have several possibilities, but none of them has a *direct* beef with Davis Hedgerow. They're angry at someone else, and beating Davis up because of a mention in his book? It just doesn't compute."

"Okay," Julia said. "So we're marking off Peachie's, the Magnolia Blossom, and the Book Worm Warriors. But what about Dixie and her friend Fancy? They may not want their relative, James Oglethorpe, to lose any of his prestige. And they both have enough money to hire someone to assault Davis."

There was a small silence as Meredith turned Dixie's and Fancy's names over in her mind. "But why would Dixie not want the book to come out?" she asked, slowly. "How does it affect her directly?"

Julia took a deep breath and said, "Well, if the statue was being dedicated tomorrow, wouldn't someone mention SOS? You know, that there was a group opposed to this new information about Ambrose Sedgwick?"

"But that would be in the media. It has nothing to do with Davis's book."

"You're right," Julia said.

"And as far as Fancy Devereaux? It's a really weak link. I just don't see a clear reason for her to fight the book's publication except some kind of family pride thing. But beating up the author? It seems illogical. And as far as Dixie, as I said before, the Oglethorpes still have influence in Savannah. Franklin could have shut down Davis's book if he wanted to."

"You're right about that," Beau said. "Franklin is very influential with the upper crust in this city."

"But that's if he knows about what Dixie's doing," Meredith said slowly. "Maybe that's it. Dixie's trying to keep her theft away from him."

"That's possible," Julia said. "Look, if Dixie started this thing because of the statue, she can stop now. The statue won't be dedicated, and the mention in the book will be deleted. Then we may never know for certain who was behind the attempt to stop the book." She sighed. "I don't like that possibility."

"I don't either," Meredith agreed. "I need to make sure she knows about the forgery. Maybe it will bring an end to all of this. You know, the thing that bothers me most about Dixie is that she has the money to hire a thug to beat up Davis."

"But how would she know a *thug*?" Julia asked.

Something obvious occurred to Meredith. "And if she has to steal money from SOS, doesn't that mean she doesn't have much money?"

"Maybe Franklin controls their wealth," Beau said.

"So she took the money so she could hire someone to attack Davis?" Julia asked.

Meredith felt sick to her stomach. Was that what happened? But why?

"I know Franklin Vanderkellen pretty well," Beau said. "If Dixie has really taken money, he would be furious. Even with all the airs he puts on, he's a moral person. A good man. And one other thing. He's very controlling, not in an abusive way. He was brought up to believe the man rules the roost. You're right about the money. Franklin pays all the bills. He mentioned once that he gives Dixie an allowance. There's no way she could come up with money for a hit man."

"Unless she took the money from SOS," Meredith said softly.

"But we have to go back to motive," Julia reminded her. "Protecting your family against a very small thing, like who developed the layout for the city of Savannah? Really? Who cares? Oglethorpe will always be credited with the founding of Savannah."

"Doesn't the same thing apply to Fancy Devereaux?" Beau asked.

Meredith sighed. "You're right. Let's leave Dixie and Fancy on the list for now but with a very big question mark. My gut tells me it isn't one of them." She pointed at Beau and Julia with her pen. "It's important to remember that right now all we have are suspicions. When we bring something to Davis we'll have to have clear-cut evidence. We're not anywhere close to having anything like that."

"So we've talked about the Book Worm Warriors, Dixie and the SOS, Peachie's, this place…none of them clear suspects." Julia paused for a moment. "What about the Sedgwicks? They have money, and they've lost one hundred and twenty thousand dollars. I'm sure they don't want the publicity that could come from an exposé piece about how they were bamboozled by the Wilmores."

"Good point," Meredith said, trying to suppress a yawn. "That might be the first time we have a direct reason to stop Davis. If he finds out the diary and the letters are forgeries, and he will know it soon, will he write an article about it, exposing their mistake? Would they go that far to protect their reputations?"

Julia shrugged. "I think it's the best motive we've found, but…"

"I know. The Sedgwicks weren't aware of the forgery until we told them. So why send Davis a letter and call his publisher about something they didn't know about? Doesn't make sense. Besides, I'm not usually wrong about people and I liked them."

"*I like them* might not be a good reason to rule them out," Beau said with a grin.

Meredith laughed. "You're right. Let's table this for now. Tomorrow night I'll visit the last place on our list. After that we'll go over everything we have. After hearing about Davis, I'm really motivated to find out who did this. I'm angry that someone would hurt him."

"I agree," Julia said, getting to her feet. "What time are you going to the hospital in the morning?"

"I'll head out of here around eight thirty. I want to get there about nine. After I'm done I'll call you."

"Sounds good." Julia went over to Meredith and gave her a hug. "See you in the morning, and thanks for the cake and the awesome book. Oh, and for a night at this wonderful place."

"You're welcome," Meredith said with a smile.

After her friends went into their room, Meredith took a quick shower, put on her pajamas, and climbed into bed. The mattress was soft and comfortable. She tried to drift off to sleep, but something kept bothering her. It was as if she knew there were two pieces of a puzzle that fit together, but she hadn't managed to connect them.

She had just started to drift off to sleep when she suddenly sat upright in her bed. She was pretty sure she knew who had assaulted Davis. She swung her feet off the side of the bed, found her laptop, and sat down at the desk. A few minutes later she was able to confirm her hunch. Meredith picked up the phone and called the police.

Chapter Twenty-Two

WHEN SHE ARRIVED AT THE hospital the next morning, Meredith had prepared herself to run into Sylvia. She prayed she could find a way to convince her she'd had no idea that Davis was in physical danger. As it turned out, his attacker wasn't connected to their investigation.

When she got to Davis's room, she found him alone. She tried not to gasp when she saw him. His face was bruised, and one eye was swollen shut.

"Oh, Davis," was all she could get out.

He offered her a feeble smile. "It looks worse than it is. I'm doing pretty well. Besides, the pain meds are pretty good."

Meredith sat down in a chair near his bed. "Anything broken?"

"No, just bruised and battered. The doctors were afraid I had internal bleeding, but thankfully I don't. I won't be running any marathons for a while, but I think I'll get to go home tomorrow."

"That's wonderful. Is Sylvia here?"

"No, she went home to get some sleep. She'll be back around noon. I'm sorry for the way she talked to you. She's sorry about it too. She was just worried about me."

"I understand. I really do."

"We're both very grateful to you, Meredith. The police were here last night and again this morning. They've made an arrest and have a confession." He frowned. "I still can't understand how you figured it out."

"Two pieces of a puzzle..."

"Huh?"

Meredith laughed. "Sorry. I heard something that stuck in my mind. Then when I was wondering who would do something like this to you...who could be this angry...the pieces came together. I remembered what you said about the brother of the girl you hit all those years ago. And then I recalled reading something about the person who attacked you. That he had a sister that died around the same time. A little research proved my suspicions."

"We could have stopped him earlier if I'd just told you the girl's last name. I guess I thought I'd mentioned it. A name I'll never forget. Amanda Dallas."

"Scott Dallas's sister."

Davis nodded then groaned. "Ouch," he said.

"So he confessed?"

"Yeah. The police picked him up last night, and he told them everything."

"But why wait until now?" Meredith asked. Although she'd put two and two together and realized that Scott was Amanda's brother, she still couldn't understand why he attacked Davis over twenty years after the accident.

"Seems he's been in Atlanta since shortly after the accident. He cared for his sick mother until she died just recently. With her gone, he decided to move back to Savannah and set up his practice. He's always loved this city, but because of the accident, it was hard for him to think about coming back. Then as luck would have it, he was hired by the local chamber of commerce. That's where he saw an ARC of my book. I guess all that stored up anger boiled over. He was already devastated by the loss of his mother and still carried all that anger from losing his sister. He never could accept that it was her fault. I guess he needed a scapegoat. Me. When he realized I was doing well, it was too much for him. He started watching me. Figured out what time I normally got home. He waited for me last night, and when I got out of my car, he assaulted me. Thank God Sylvia heard me yelling and came outside. When Dallas saw her, he ran away." He sighed. "If she hadn't scared him off, I...I think he would have killed me."

"Oh, Davis. I'm so glad you're going to be okay."

"Yeah, me too."

"Davis, do you know if Scott sent the letter and called your publisher?"

Davis shook his head. "I asked the police to bring that up. He said he had nothing to do with that. I believe him. He's not the kind of person to approach a problem like that. I guess he talks with his fists."

"I guess his connection to Patricia Ivers had nothing to do with his anger toward you."

"It may have exacerbated his resentment because her group was also connected to the book, but no. Not directly connected." He shook his head. "That's why I find your realization that it was Scott who attacked me so...incredible."

Meredith smiled at him. "I'm glad you feel that way, but as far as the other threats against you, we still have no clear suspect. We're still working on it."

Davis chuckled. "Do you think any of them plan to beat me up? I'm not sure I can take much more."

"I don't think so. People who use letters and phone calls as a way to fight back against things they don't want usually don't resort to violence. But keep your eyes open. Lock your doors at night. Just general common sense. I think you'll be fine."

"I'll never be able to thank you enough, Meredith."

"Don't worry about it, please. I'm just so glad I could help. Davis, did you talk to the Sedgwicks yesterday?"

"The Sedgwicks? Not sure which Sedgwicks you mean, but no. They may have tried to call. I don't think I checked my phone since early afternoon yesterday."

"Then I'm afraid I'm about to give you some bad news."

Davis frowned. "There's bad news? Is it worse than being beaten to a pulp?"

"Well, no."

"Good, bring it on."

Meredith took a deep breath and told him about the Sedgwicks and the forgeries.

"Wow. I need to contact my publisher and have them remove that chapter from the book."

"I'm sorry. I hope it won't hurt the publication in any way."

Meredith was surprised when Davis laughed. She didn't expect that kind of reaction.

"Once again, you've saved me a great deal of embarrassment," he said, still smiling. "If the forgery had been discovered after the book was published, it would have been much worse. Removing it now is no big deal. Trust me, my publisher will be grateful to find this out now instead of later. I'll call them this morning and let them know."

"I think the Sedgwicks are truly sorry about this. The Wilmores, the people who supposedly created the forgeries, used a rather respected appraiser to look over the documents. I suspect either he was negligent or part of the scheme."

"I hope the Sedgwicks can get their money back."

"They probably won't, but I got the feeling it wasn't anything that would break them."

"Boy, I wish I had so much money that one hundred and twenty thousand dollars would just be a small blip in my bank account."

"I agree. When you're better, you might give the Sedgwicks a call. I think they're a really nice couple who feel awful about what's happened."

"I'll do that, thanks."

Meredith stood up. "Is there anything I can do for you, Davis?"

"Just find our letter writer if you can. After what's happened, I'd just like to be certain there's no one else out there who feels the need to interfere in my life."

"I understand. I'll be in touch in the next few days." She sighed. "I hope I can locate this person, Davis, but so far…"

He reached out a hand and she took it gently, not wanting to hurt him. "Meredith, I'm so thankful for everything you've done for me. If you don't find this other person, it's okay. I've decided to sit down with my publisher and tell them about the accident. I don't think they'll stop publication of my book because of something that happened so long ago and wasn't my fault. Even if they did, I'd just look for another publisher. I'm pretty sure I can find one if I need to."

"That's your choice, Davis. But to be honest, I'm not convinced that the person who called your publisher knew anything about this. Didn't you say this *secret* they wanted to tell your publisher was vague?"

"Yes, very."

Meredith nodded. "Almost everyone has something in their past they'd rather keep to themselves. I have my doubts that your letter writer has any idea about the accident. If they did, they probably would have named names."

Davis squeezed her hand and let it go. "Good point."

The door opened behind them, and a nurse came in. "How's your pain level, Mr. Hedgerow?" she asked.

"I'm ready for a little more happy juice," he said, winking at Meredith.

"I'll talk to you soon," Meredith said with a smile. She picked up her purse and walked out of the hospital room. She was relieved that Davis's attacker had been arrested and that he was grateful to find out about the Sedgwick forgeries. But even though he'd said he'd be all right if she didn't find the letter writer, Meredith was more determined than ever to uncover the truth.

Chapter Twenty-Three

"It looks like I missed out," Meredith said teasingly when she returned from the hospital and walked into the dining room at the Magnolia Blossom. The table where Julia and Beau sat was covered with food. Meredith spotted a big bowl of grits with melted butter on top. There was corn bread, Southern spoon bread, and a bowl of scrambled eggs. Bacon and sausage filled up a large platter. A carafe of orange juice and the aroma of freshly brewed coffee made Meredith's mouth water.

Meredith pointed to an empty chair. A place had been set for another person. "For me?" she asked.

"Of course," Julia said with a smile. "We hoped you'd make it back."

At that moment Elise walked in from the kitchen with a large platter of pancakes. "Well, there you are," she said when she saw Meredith. "We were hoping you'd get back in time for breakfast."

Meredith slid into the empty seat and sighed. "How can four people eat all of this food?"

"Hush," Beau said. "I'm giving it the old college try. I've even loosened my belt."

"Oh, Beau, you hush," Julia said.

Meredith and Elise laughed.

"I'll get you some coffee," Elise said to Meredith. "Help yourself. Everything should still be hot."

Meredith sighed happily. "Thank you so much. This is perfect."

She helped herself to scrambled eggs and sausage. Then she filled the bowl near her plate with grits. After a few bites she was ready to talk. Elise was still in the kitchen.

"Davis will be fine," she said quietly to Julia and Beau. "Scott Dallas was arrested earlier this morning. He admitted to the beating."

"According to the police, Dallas said he didn't have anything to do with the letter and the call to Davis's publisher, so we're still looking for that person."

"Why would this Dallas person wait all these years to go after Davis?" Beau whispered.

"I'll tell you more later, but when he moved back to Savannah he saw the ARC of Davis's book. Just went nuts thinking that Davis was doing so well."

Meredith heard Elise's heels tapping on the hard flooring. She shook her head quickly and popped a big scoop of buttery grits into her mouth. They were so good. She thanked Elise as she put a coffee cup next to her. "Oh, Elise. These might be some of the best grits I've ever eaten."

"Some people put sugar on them," she replied. "But I like them with just butter." She looked at Beau and Julia. "I put sugar on the table just in case someone wants to add it."

"Well, not me. They're absolutely perfect."

Elise smiled. "Thank you. I'm so glad you all came to stay with me."

"We are too," Julia said. "Except I think I'm going to have to go on a diet when I get home. Where did you learn to cook like this?"

Elise sat down on the other side of the table, and a shadow crossed her face. "My mother taught me. She's an incredible cook."

"That reminds me." Meredith reached into her pocket and took out a piece of paper. "Here's the recipe for my cake." She handed it to Elise.

"Thank you," Elise said softly. "You remind me a little of my mom. Being around you has made me really miss her."

"You know," Meredith said gently, "sometimes healing an estrangement can happen as quickly as one person picking up the phone."

Elise met Meredith's eyes. "I know you're right. I guess I feel...I don't know. Vulnerable. What if they don't accept my apology?"

Meredith had to bite her lip. She came very close to saying *they don't seem like the kind of people to do that.* Instead she said, "From what you've said, they sound like loving parents. Maybe your father could have handled it better, not threatened you financially if you married that man you were engaged to, but was he saying it because he wanted to control you? Or was it because he was worried about you?"

Elise's eyes filled with tears. "The latter. I've been so foolish. If they told me they didn't want anything to do with me, I wouldn't blame them."

It was Meredith's turn to get weepy. "Oh, Elise. The love of a parent for a child is one of the strongest bonds in this world. I would walk through fire for my sons and my grandchildren. I'm certain they'll welcome you with open arms. And they will be so proud of what you've accomplished here with this beautiful house and the business you've created." She took a deep breath. "I lost my husband a few years ago. There are still so many things I wish I would have told him. Things I wanted to say that I never got the chance to say. You can't always count on tomorrow. People can be gone in an instant, and then it's too late. I hope you'll call them soon. I really do."

Elise wiped away a tear that fell down her cheek. "Reaching out to them has been in my heart for a while now. I guess I needed to talk about it to someone. Unfortunately, Simon hasn't been a big help in this area. He tends to keep most of his opinions to himself." She offered Meredith a tremulous smile. "Thank you, Meredith. Thanks to all of you. I'll call my parents later today."

Meredith picked up her napkin and dabbed at her eyes. Helping to heal a family rift wasn't something she'd anticipated when they'd begun this investigation. She said a silent prayer of thanks to God.

After finishing Elise's incredible breakfast, Meredith went upstairs to pack. She was almost done when someone knocked on the connecting door. She opened it to find Beau standing there.

"I'm here to get your bags," he said with a grin.

"That's nice, but not with your ankle. I'll get them."

"Well, at least give me the small one."

"Are you sure?" Meredith asked.

"Positive. My ankle's feeling much better."

He reached out his arms so Meredith passed the lightest bag to him. "Thanks, Beau. Let me check my room one more time. Then I'll meet you downstairs."

Beau saluted her, almost conking himself on the forehead with Meredith's overnight bag. She laughed at him as he marched away. After a quick look around, she walked out of the room, keeping the key with her. She wasn't sure if she was supposed to leave it in the room, but just in case, she decided to turn it over to Elise.

She met Julia downstairs and paid for their stay, telling Elise they would definitely be back and would also recommend the Magnolia Blossom Inn to their friends.

Once they were loaded into Meredith's SUV, it didn't take long to get home. First she dropped Julia and Beau off at their house.

"Are you sure you don't want me to come along with you tonight?" Julia asked before getting out of the car. "I really don't like the idea of you going there alone."

Meredith chuckled. "Oh, Julia, I'm not going to the *Psycho* house. It's a nice bed-and-breakfast."

"Yeah, with a ghost who is looking for his body."

"Don't be silly. You and Beau have a good evening. I'll call you tomorrow afternoon and let you know how it went."

"Are you Skyping with the grandkids today?"

"No. Carter and Sherri Lynn are taking them to the Children's Museum. I'll miss talking to them, but I'm so distracted right now I'm not sure I'd be much fun anyway."

"Okay. But you call me if you get cold feet and want me along tonight, promise?"

Meredith smiled at her. "I promise. Now go spend some time with that handsome husband of yours. I'll talk to you tomorrow."

Julia and Beau got out and walked up the steps to their large wraparound porch with its ceiling fans and rocking chairs. The gorgeous two-story house was painted moss green with black shutters. Although it was much different than Meredith's stucco Italianate-style home, the house fit Julia's personality.

As Meredith drove away, she still had a nagging feeling there was something she'd seen or heard that she needed to pay attention to. She'd been certain the feeling came from not connecting Scott Dallas to Davis's past. So why was it still there?

Chapter Twenty-Four

MEREDITH SPENT THE DAY WASHING clothes and cleaning house. The weather forecast was for continued rain, and the dark clouds above them looked ominous. Although GK seemed unconcerned about her absence, she noticed he stayed close to her throughout the day.

She was packed and ready to go by three o'clock. She made sure GK had food and water. He allowed her to pet him even though he tried to look somewhat annoyed by the attention. He'd likely noticed the bags and knew what they meant. Meredith felt a little guilty about leaving him again, but she knew he'd be okay. When she got back she planned to spend extra time with him.

This was the last of the sites in Davis's book. She still wasn't convinced they'd found their primary suspect, but at least they'd been able to bring some justice to Scott Dallas. Even though what he did was despicable, Meredith couldn't help feeling a little sorry for him. He was obviously in great pain over the loss of his sister and his mother. She'd prayed for him, asking God to help him recover not only from his grief but also from his actions against Davis.

A few minutes later she drove up to the John Douglas Farmer House. There were parking spaces in the front of the inn so Meredith pulled into one. She sat for a moment and looked at her lodging for the night. The inn was boxy, which was expected with the federal style, but the two-story townhouse had been beautifully restored. The outside was painted a shade of taupe. The entrance was a small covered porch, charmingly done. White wooden stairs led to the main entrance on the floor above the basement area. The windows all around the building had black shutters. The arched roof had two dormers. Someone had put a lot of effort into the restoration. Meredith could certainly see why Davis had included it in his book. She was grateful to have discovered the Magnolia Blossom Inn, and now this one. If the inside lived up to the outside, she was in for a treat.

She got out of the car and grabbed her two small bags and her purse. As she started up the stairs, she realized it was starting to rain again. She was fortunate that it had waited until now.

Meredith pushed open the large door and walked into a short hallway. A sign above the door to her right said OFFICE. She turned in to the room, which was deliciously decorated. Hardwood floors, a large maroon and gold Persian rug, a beautifully carved fireplace on the far wall, upholstered chairs near the fire. She loved that they didn't match, but they fit the style of 1834 furniture. She found matching furniture a little boring.

To her left was a large bookcase that took up the entire wall. In front of the bookcase was a rosewood counter. An oversized book lay open near a shiny silver bell, probably the B and B's guest register. Except no one was there. Meredith walked over and clicked the bell. Someone had taped a handwritten card to the counter that read PLEASE RING FOR SERVICE.

After her second attempt to rouse someone, a large woman came around the corner. She wore a brightly flowered dress. Her flaming red hair clearly originated from a bottle. Her bright red lipstick matched the floral display on her dress.

"Why, honey!" she exclaimed. "I'm sorry I wasn't here to greet you." She held out her hand. There was a diamond so large in her ring, Meredith wondered if she had trouble lifting her hand. "I'm Lulu Belle Dawson." As Meredith shook her hand, she gave her a large smile.

"Thank you."

The woman finally let go of her hand. "I take it you're Mrs. Bellefontaine?"

Meredith acknowledged her identity. Lulu was not what she'd expected. With a house so expertly restored, she assumed the owner would mirror the same elegance.

"Let's get you situated, honey," Lulu said. She pushed the large book toward Meredith. "Would you sign in?"

Meredith picked up the pen next to the book and wrote her name, address, and her car information. After doing that, she handed Lulu her credit card so she could place a hold against it. This was standard operating procedure.

"That's it, honey," Lulu said when they were finished. She pulled a small cell phone out of her dress pocket. She punched in something and then waited a moment. Someone obviously answered and she hollered, "Freddy, come get the bags!" She hung up the phone and shook her head. "My husband, Freddy, will get your luggage." She laughed. "Good thing we weren't full. We weren't expecting anyone else this weekend."

"I hope it wasn't a problem."

"Why, no, honey. We have two other couples that booked a long time ago, but except for their rooms and yours, we're empty."

Meredith started to tell her that she could carry her own bags, when around the corner an odd little man popped into the room. He was barely over five feet tall and his black handlebar mustache matched his coal-black hair that was plastered down with some kind of grease. Unfortunately, his bushy gray eyebrows had escaped the same touch of hair dye. Freddy wore a dark suit with a black tie and shiny black shoes. He reminded Meredith of an undertaker in the 1800s. She bit her lip to keep from laughing.

"How do you do?" he said in a rather high voice. "We're so glad to have you."

"Thank you. I was going to tell your wife that these bags are light. I can carry them myself. Please don't bother."

"Now, Freddy," Lulu said, "you get those for her. This pretty lady shouldn't be luggin' those things upstairs."

Freddy sighed. "Better let me carry them. It will be easier for all of us."

This time Meredith was unable to hold back a nervous giggle. She immediately coughed into the crook of her arm, trying to cover up her uncontrolled amusement. When she met Freddy's gaze, she was surprised to see him give her a small smile. He picked up her two bags and said, "Follow me, please."

Meredith turned around. "Thank you for your help, Lulu. I appreciate it."

"You're very welcome, honey. We hope you enjoy your stay."

Although she didn't say it, Meredith was fairly sure it was going to be interesting if nothing else.

Freddy led her down the hall to the stairs. They passed a beautiful sitting room with a fireplace. The Victorian-styled furniture was lovely and perfect. Then they passed the kitchen on one side and a dining room on the other side. Although she couldn't see much of the kitchen because of the door only being halfway open, she gasped when she saw the dining room. The polished table was surrounded by carved chairs with rich brocade seat covers. The walls were painted a light celery, and the fireplace mantel was marble. A beautiful painting hung over a serving table that hugged one wall. The image was of a young girl sitting in a field of flowers. It was enchanting. Another painting hung over the fireplace.

"Did you want to look around?" Freddy asked.

"Yes, please. It's…it's gorgeous."

Freddy put the bags down and followed Meredith into the room. A green and dark red patterned rug lay on the wood floor. The colors were perfect and accented not only the wall color but also the chair covers. Above the table was a large crystal chandelier that sparkled as it reflected the flames from the fire. The painting above the fireplace was of a stately older gentleman with kind eyes and a half smile. The female version of the Mona Lisa?

"That's John Douglas Farmer," Freddy said.

"Very distinguished." Meredith grinned at him. "Did he really disappear?"

"Believe it or not, it's true. He left his home, this house, to go to his office. Never showed up. No one ever found him…or his body."

"My goodness. That's quite a story." Meredith decided it might be now or never to bring up Davis's book. "I saw an advanced copy of a book by Davis Hedgerow. Your lovely inn was featured in it."

Freddy nodded. "Yes. Lulu's excited about that. She thinks it will bring us lots of customers."

"How long have you been open?"

"The final renovations were six months ago. Then we spent a couple of months learning the ins and outs of inn keeping."

"So this is your first B and B?"

"This has been Lulu's dream for years. You see, we won the lottery a couple of years ago. We lived in Minnesota, but Lulu always wanted to live in Savannah. Her mother was born and raised here. Hence my wife's name. They were very close. She passed away a few months before we won all that money. I think Lulu regrets not being able to do something special for her mom. Don't get me wrong, it's a wonderful city. After we moved, we looked around for just the right house. Then we found this. Outbid some other people who wanted it. Now, Lulu is finally living her dream."

"How exciting for you. You must enjoy what you do."

Freddy was quiet for a moment. "Sometimes…" He turned to look at her, his eyes wide. "I…I'm sorry. I didn't mean to make it seem as if I'm unhappy. You see, like I said, this is Lulu's dream…"

"But not yours?"

"No. To be honest, I wanted to stay in St. Cloud, near our kids and grandkids. I thought we could take them all to Disney World. Or some other place they'd like to go. A big family trip. But we never got the chance. Now we can't leave the inn. Owning a business means you have to be around to run it." He frowned. "Do I sound selfish?"

"No, of course not. It's not the least bit selfish."

"I…I've said too much." Freddy went back out into the hall and picked up Meredith's bags. "There's something about you that makes me want to share my problems. I suspect I'm not the only one. Must be a bother."

"No, not at all."

"Please don't say anything to Lulu. She would be so unhappy if this failed. I love her, and I want her to have the desires of her heart."

"I understand," Meredith said. "This will stay between us."

"Thank you. Please join us in the sitting room at four thirty. We'll have cold beverages and appetizers. We're running a little late, but we waited to see if the rain would stay away so we could set up in the garden. Unfortunately, it's moved back in and is supposed to hang around all evening."

"I'll be happy to do that. Lulu mentioned that there are other guests?"

Freddy nodded. "Two other couples. They're celebrating a birthday. They won't be here later this evening since they're going out to eat, but I think you'll be able to meet them downstairs before they leave."

Freddy trudged toward the stairs, and Meredith followed behind him. For the first time since getting involved in this investigation, she realized she may have found the perfect suspect. Was Freddy the one trying to quench the book so he and Lulu could go back to St. Cloud and spend time with their family?

Had she finally found their letter writer?

Chapter Twenty-Five

MEREDITH WAS PLEASED WITH HER room. She could look out her window and see the garden area below. It was beautiful. There was a lovely water fountain in the middle. The flower and plant beds were edged with red bricks. The same bricks had been laid over the ground. Cast-iron chairs and two benches were placed around the garden, giving it an inviting look.

Her room consisted of a large four-poster bed with a cream-colored satin bedspread. A large cherrywood armoire hid the television set. There was a lovely rolltop desk and a small fireplace with a settee and two high-backed chairs nearby. A beautifully carved coffee table sat in front of the settee.

The bathroom was spotless and offered a large shower as well as a claw-foot tub perfect for soaking. Candles had been lit on the counter. It was charming. Had Lulu planned and decorated the inn? Or had they brought someone else in? They seemed so odd. Rather out of place, yet the inn was perfect.

As she unpacked, Meredith pondered the idea that Freddy might be the letter writer. He obviously wasn't happy here and wanted to go back to St. Cloud. He also seemed like the kind of person to approach the problem in a nonviolent way.

Meredith checked her watch. Four fifteen. She sat down in one of the chairs near the fire and called Julia. When she answered, Meredith told her all about the John Douglas Farmer House and its unique innkeepers.

"They sound interesting," Julia said.

"At the very least. But here's the thing, Julia. Freddy, the husband, is very unhappy here. He wants to go back to Minnesota, where their kids and grandkids live. Yet he doesn't want to dash his wife's dreams."

"You think he doesn't want Davis's book to come out because he believes it will make the inn successful?"

"Well, maybe. He's a nice man. Definitely not violent."

Julia was silent for so long that Meredith wondered if they'd been disconnected. "Are you there, Julia?"

"Yeah, I'm here. You say he's a nice man, but the letter and the call to Davis's publisher... I mean, are they the acts of a *nice* man? It seems desperate to me. Would he risk getting caught and being charged with harassment just because he misses his grandchildren?"

Meredith realized Julia was just thinking out loud, analyzing the situation. But she had a point. Actually, Meredith couldn't see Freddy going to those extremes to get his way. Especially if it would hurt his precious Lulu Belle. "Just when I think there's a flicker of light, you have to extinguish it, don't you?"

Julia laughed. "Just asking the same questions you'd ask me if the situation was reversed."

"I know." Meredith sighed. "I have this bad feeling that we're not going to find the person threatening Davis. It would be much easier if the perpetrator would just jump out in front of us and yell, 'It's me! I did it!'"

Julia snorted. "I'm not sure you should put much hope into that scenario. Besides, don't forget Fancy Devereaux. Maggie Lu may find out something tonight that will point us in the right direction."

"I hope so," Meredith said, "but I still struggle with the idea that someone with that much money and prestige would try to stop Davis's book with an anonymous letter and phone call. I think they'd be much more up-front about it."

"You could be right. We'll have to wait and see."

"I should be going, Julia. I'm going downstairs to the drinks and appetizers spread in the sitting room. You really should see this place. It's amazing."

"Seems Davis knows what he's doing."

"Yes, he certainly does," Meredith said. "I'll be paying closer attention to his column in the future."

"Me too. So what are your plans for later this evening?"

"I don't know. Depending on what there is to eat, I might go out and grab something. I did stuff a few granola bars in my bag. If it's raining, I might munch on those and try to make some sense out of our suspect list."

"Good luck with that."

"I don't want to tell Davis we failed."

"Except we didn't fail," Julia said. "You figured out who Scott Dallas was. What if he'd attacked Davis again, Meredith? Davis might not have survived."

"Maybe. I don't know. Davis said the same thing. I just have this weird feeling, Julia, like I've seen something...something important, but I can't pull it up."

"You've had those feelings before," Julia said. "And in the end you've been able to figure out what it was that bothered you. I have confidence the same thing will happen this time."

"I hope you're right. Well, have a good night, Julia."

"You too."

After she hung up the phone, Meredith changed into some comfortable dark blue slacks and a white blouse with scallops on the bodice. A red sweater matched her pumps. She brushed her hair with a sigh. The humidity in the air had turned her curls to frizz. She did her best to tame it and then applied a light mist of hairspray, hoping it would stay in place for a couple of hours.

As she walked down the stairs, she could hear voices coming from somewhere below her. When she walked into the sitting room she found Lulu standing behind a table with a white tablecloth. It was loaded down with trays of food. A smaller nearby table held a variety of drinks and glasses.

Four other people were in the room, two seated on the settee and two in the chairs. Meredith noticed they looked surprised when she walked in.

"I thought we were your only guests," a man with blond hair said.

"Oh, you were," Lulu answered. "This lovely lady made a reservation at the last minute. And we're happy to have her."

Lulu had changed clothes and wore black velvet slacks with a shiny gold blouse. She'd piled her crimson hair on top of her head and secured it with a rhinestone comb. Her lipstick was toned down to peach, but she'd added fake eyelashes that looked...fake. She wore a pearl necklace and matching earrings. Although her outfit was rather flamboyant, it was much more appropriate for a proprietress than the dress she'd worn earlier. Actually, Lulu was an attractive woman. Once again, Meredith felt a flash of guilt. She wasn't trying to judge Lulu. Meredith really liked her. She decided to make a point of encouraging her during her stay.

Meredith smiled at her.

"How's your room, honey?" Lulu asked.

"Perfect. What wonderful taste you have."

"Actually, we hired someone to decorate the inn. I knew what I wanted, but I'm afraid my first ideas weren't…appropriate."

From behind her she heard someone snicker. It took effort for Meredith not to turn around and glare at the person who'd been so rude.

"Well, you were very clever to get a second opinion. And you were savvy enough to know whether or not the person you hired was doing a good job. Not everyone can do that."

Lulu, who had obviously heard the offending sound from one of her guests, gave Meredith a tremulous smile, her cheeks red with embarrassment. "Thank you so much, Meredith. You're a very kind person." She waved her arm toward the assortment of food on the table. "What can I get you? We have deviled eggs Southern style, spiced pecans, cheese straws, sliced honey ham, and different kinds of cheeses." She pointed to three metal pans on warming trays. "These are cheesy grit fritters with hot pepper jelly." She smiled. "They're very good. And of course fried green tomatoes. The crab hush puppies are served with an avocado aioli. The hush puppies and fritters are my mother's recipes. I hope you enjoy them."

Meredith looked at Lulu in astonishment. "This looks incredible. *You* are amazing."

Once again, Lulu's cheeks flushed but hopefully this time it was for a different reason.

"Actually, these are probably the best appetizers I've ever had."

A deep male voice came from behind her. Meredith turned around and saw a man in his thirties getting to his feet. "I'm Anson Foster and this is my wife, Vicki." He extended his hand, and Meredith shook it.

"Meredith Bellefontaine. Nice to meet you."

Vicki, a lovely woman with dark hair and sparkling brown eyes smiled at her. "You're here by yourself?" she asked.

"Yes. I needed some time away to work on a few things," Meredith said. "I thought this would be the perfect place." She swung her gaze to the other couple. He was about Anson's age, but where Anson's hair was dark brown, this man's hair was a very light blond. Probably bleached. Definitely streaked.

He raised one eyebrow and nodded at her. "Eric Foster," he said curtly. Then he cocked his head toward the woman sitting next to him. "This is Dolly, my wife."

Meredith smiled at the woman, whose blond hair matched her husband's. She was dressed in a white pantsuit, a tasteful diamond pendant dangling from her neck. Her earrings matched, of course. This was the snickerer. Was that a word? Probably not.

"Nice to meet you," she said. Dolly didn't even bother to look at her. Just shoved a hush puppy into her mouth.

"You're both named Foster?" Meredith asked, directing her question to Anson.

He nodded. "Cousins. Believe it or not, we were born on the same day so every year we get together to celebrate our birthdays."

Dolly sighed. Meredith got the feeling she was letting everyone know that this get-together wasn't her idea. What a rude woman.

Meredith turned back toward Lulu and allowed her to pile her plate with goodies. She wouldn't have to worry about supper. Lulu carried her plate over to a small table next to the high-backed chair in the corner.

"We have several beverage choices," she said.

"Water will be fine," Meredith replied.

Lulu looked a little disappointed but quickly filled a goblet with ice and water and handed it to her. Meredith picked up a fork and a napkin and headed for the chair. Once settled, she picked up her plate and began eating. Anson was right. Everything was perfect. Delicious. The crab fritters were out of this world. Lulu was a talented cook. Meredith couldn't help but think of Elise. Two women from completely different backgrounds, but both had dreamed of running a B and B, and both were fantastic cooks.

"I hear you're all going out for dinner to celebrate your birth-days," Meredith said, trying to start a conversation.

"We only have reservations for four," Dolly said, rolling her eyes.

"I...I wasn't trying to invite myself."

"Of course you weren't," Anson said. "Sorry. And yes. We have reservations at 45 Bistro. Our first time there. Have you been?"

"Oh yes. It's wonderful. Whatever you do, don't miss the Georgia Pecan Dacquoise for dessert. It's incredible."

"Thank you," Vicki said. "We'll be sure to try it."

Meredith ignored the dirty looks coming from Dolly and her husband. She'd had enough of the childish Dolly. Meredith really didn't care what she thought about anything.

"So what do you do, Meredith?" Vicki asked.

"I run Magnolia Investigations," Meredith said with a smile.

"What?"

Meredith was surprised to see the blood drain from Dolly's face.

"Wh-what does that mean?" she asked. "I mean, what do you actually do?"

"We're investigators," Meredith replied. "We take cases from all kinds of clients. Missing people, misplaced valuables, lost heirs, almost anything that either doesn't fall under the jurisdiction of law enforcement or has gone cold. Of course, sometimes we work with the police as well."

Dolly fell silent, but Meredith caught her throwing glances at her husband, who also seemed nervous.

For some reason, Meredith had just thrown a bomb at one-half of the uptight Fosters. They were spooked. What was that about? Suddenly, this visit had gotten much more interesting.

Chapter Twenty-Six

"Would anyone like coffee?" Lulu asked. It was clear she hadn't noticed Dolly's and Eric's odd reactions. Meredith wasn't sure about Anson and Vicki. Had they seen it?

"I would," Anson said. "Can I help you get it?"

"Oh, thank you, but I'll find Freddy. He can help me." She flashed a smile at her guests. "I'll be right back."

"I can hardly wait," Dolly said under her breath. She refused to look at Meredith.

"Dolly, knock it off," Anson said sharply.

"Don't tell my wife what to do," Eric said. He glared at Meredith. She'd certainly rocked their boats. But why?

"When she shows some good manners, I won't have to say anything," Anson responded, scowling at his cousin.

Lulu scurried from the room, obviously embarrassed.

"Well, why in the world does she dress like that?" Dolly said under her breath. "No one with any sense would make herself look so…weird."

"That's not a nice thing to say," Vicki scolded. "When you have thoughts like that, just keep them to yourself. Otherwise you hurt people's feelings."

Meredith noticed that Eric was getting ready to react, so she quickly said, "So how did you all hear about this place?"

"I have a friend who works for the *Tribune*," Anson said. "He knew we always try to make today a celebration so he lent me an advanced copy of a book coming out soon. Have you ever heard of Davis Hedgerow?"

"Yes, I have. He writes a column about special places in Savannah, right?"

"Exactly. He seemed to really like this place. And the story of John Douglas Farmer's ghost... Well, that sealed it. Sounded like fun."

Dolly took a deep breath and blew it out, obviously not agreeing with Anson's idea of *fun*.

Meredith ignored her. "I agree. I saw the same book. Once it's published it should bring a lot of people here, don't you think?"

Anson smiled and nodded. "I do. And I think they'll all be glad they came."

At that moment, Lulu and Freddy came into the room. Freddy had a large carafe of coffee, and Lulu carried several cups.

Anson stood to his feet and took them from her. "Thank you, Lulu," he said. "The perfect thing on a rainy afternoon."

Meredith found herself agreeing. She needed to stay up tonight and work. Coffee would certainly help. When Lulu handed her a cup of coffee, Meredith thanked her. "The food is wonderful, Lulu. I hope you won't think I'm a pig if I go back for seconds."

Lulu's expression brightened. "Oh no, honey. I'd be happy to see you fill that plate up again. Can I get it for you?"

"Thanks, Lulu. I can do it. Why don't you sit down? I'll get *you* a cup of coffee."

"Well, I don't know…" She looked flustered.

"Here," Anson said. "Take my seat. I'll sit on the hearth."

"Oh no, I couldn't."

Meredith took Lulu's arm and led her to the chair Anson had vacated. She gave him a smile of thanks, and he winked at her.

"Now, I'll get you some coffee," she said. "Do you take anything in it?"

Lulu had carried in cream and sugar with her when she'd carried the tray with the coffee cups on it.

"No, just black," Lulu said. "Thank you, Meredith."

"Happy to do it."

As she poured the cup for Lulu, she heard Dolly's whiny voice. "I'd like some more too."

Meredith smiled at her as she handed Lulu her cup. "There's plenty," she said. "Help yourself."

Meredith ignored Dolly's exaggerated sigh.

"Actually, we need to be going," Anson said. "Please let me at least carry these dishes to the kitchen for you, Lulu."

"No, please. Just leave them. Freddy and I will get them. You all go on and have fun."

Anson frowned at her. "If you're sure."

"I am."

"All right." He stood up. "Everyone ready?" he asked. "We don't want to be late for our reservations."

Vicki stood up and took a jacket from the back of the couch. Anson helped her into it. Eric ignored Dolly, who slipped on her own coat. It was made to look like real fur, but Meredith could tell that it wasn't. It didn't mean anything. Many women didn't believe in wearing real fur. Somehow, the seemingly self-centered Dolly hadn't struck her as one of them.

Lulu got up and hurried to the front door so she could hold it open for them. Once they were all gone, she came back into the sitting room and collapsed on the sofa. Meredith had returned to her comfortable chair.

"Oh my goodness," Lulu said. "I had to bite my lip so hard I think I bit all the way through."

Meredith laughed. "I admire you more than I can say. I was about ready to read Miss Dolly the riot act. What an obnoxious woman."

Lulu shrugged. "I'm used to it, I guess. After we won the lottery, I bought stuff. Stuff I'd always wanted, but I guess my tastes aren't… refined enough for some people." She looked down at her clothes. "Some people think I dress funny. I guess I do, but I like it."

"If you like it, that's all that matters, Lulu," Meredith said. "People like Dolly may think the way they look is perfect, but they're really ugly on the inside. Treating people with kindness is more important than anything we'll ever wear. I think you're a lovely person. Don't let someone like Dolly make you feel like anything else."

"Thank you, honey. You know, once we got that money, I bought this ring." She held her hand out so Meredith could see it. "Then we bought the necklace and earrings that match. I realize now it might seem silly, but I grew up so poor. I'd never had any real jewelry." She shook her head. "Someday I'll sell it. But for now…well, it just reminds me that I'm not poor anymore. That I don't have to feel less than anyone else."

"You're certainly not less than anyone else," Freddy said, stepping into the room. "And if you want to keep that jewelry forever, it's fine with me." He smiled at Meredith. "They wrote an article in the paper about us after we bought this place. It wasn't real nice. Laughed at us for buying the jewelry. I guess most people think lottery winners go crazy and lose all their money because of silly purchases." He shrugged. "They might be right sometimes, but we invested in this B and B. It has value. Almost all of our money is in savings accounts and stocks and bonds. We have an investment guy who helps us. The papers don't print that. Focused on that jewelry. The diamond in the necklace is famous, I guess." He frowned at his wife. "What is the name of that thing? I never can remember."

Lulu smiled. "The Blue Lake Diamond." She held up her hand again. "If you look closely at the ring you can see a blue tint too. The necklace is an even deeper color."

"That's wonderful," Meredith said. "I'm happy for you. It's your money. You should spend it however you want."

"Lulu's a little afraid of putting anyone in charge of the whole amount. We keep some cash around. You know, for emergencies."

Lulu nodded. "I want to *see* the money, you know? Make sure it's still there."

"Our investment guy doesn't agree," Freddy said. "Tried to get us to put everything in the bank, but Lulu wouldn't have it. He finally had to give up. When Lulu makes up her mind…"

Meredith chuckled. "You might as well give in?"

Freddy nodded and laughed. "And you know, it's one of the reasons I love this woman so much. When she made up her mind she was going to open a B and B here… Well, look at what she's accomplished."

"It really is marvelous, Lulu," Meredith said.

"Oh, thank you, honey. One of these days we'll go back to St. Cloud," Lulu said. "I know Freddy misses our family. I do too. But first, I want to make this place a success. When I was a kid, my mom cleaned for a woman who owned a B and B. That's when I decided that one day I'd own one."

Meredith smiled. "I'm so glad I came." She gestured toward the table with the hors d'oeuvres. "I was thinking I'd have to go out tonight and pick up supper. But your delicious spread took care of that."

"Let me fix you a sandwich and some other goodies," Lulu said. "You can take it to your room if you'd like."

Although she wasn't hungry now, Meredith knew she would be later. "That would be perfect. Thank you, Lulu."

"You're very welcome." She stood up and squared her shoulders. Then she pointed at Freddy. "Help me get this food back to the kitchen, dear." She smiled at Meredith. "If you want to go up to your room, honey, we'll bring up a tray."

"I hate to have you do that."

Lulu chuckled. "Not a problem. We both need the exercise. You go on. And what would you like to drink, honey? We have iced tea, coffee, sparkling flavored water, hot tea...."

Meredith held up a hand. "Whoa. If you offer me too many things it will just confuse me." She sighed. "I shouldn't drink coffee this late, but yours is delicious. Maybe some coffee...and some ice water?"

"You've got it. Come on, Freddy. Let's get in gear."

Freddy winked at Meredith. "I better obey. I'll bring your tray up in a bit."

Meredith laughed as Freddy scurried after his wife. What a great couple. She felt bad for being too judgmental when she first met them.

By the time she climbed the stairs and entered her room, Meredith realized she really was tired. Now she was glad she'd asked for coffee. If she was going to work tonight, she'd need it.

She planned to look over everything their investigation had uncovered. Meredith hoped that tonight she could figure out just who had been threatening Davis. But as much as she hoped she could come up with something solid, she still had doubts that the person they were looking for was among the new attractions in Davis's book. Could the perpetrator be someone they'd never considered?

She sighed as she put her laptop on the desk. Tonight promised to be a long one, and there was no promise her efforts would reveal the truth.

This case frustrated her. Would it end in victory or defeat? At this point she wasn't sure.

Chapter Twenty-Seven

After changing clothes, Meredith got the file she'd put together for this investigation as well as her notebook with all her notes and questions. She'd just sat down when her phone rang. She picked it up. "Hello?" she said.

"So where are you?" Maggie Lu asked.

Meredith could hear some noise in the background. Voices and light orchestral music. "I'm at the John Douglas Farmer House," she replied. "One of the nicest B and Bs I've ever seen. Where are you?"

"Still at the party, although I'm trying desperately to make my escape. I've had enough. I'm worn slap out."

"Boy, you really don't enjoy those things, do you?" Meredith asked.

A sigh of exasperation came through the phone. "No, I sure don't, honey. I have some information for you though."

"Is Fancy there?"

"Yes, in all her glory."

"Did you get a chance to talk to her?" Meredith asked, hoping Maggie Lu had some news that would help them.

"Yes, I held court with the divine Ms. Devereaux."

"Oh, Maggie Lu, stop," Meredith said, trying not to laugh.

"All right. Well, y'all can cross her off your list. She and her husband just got back from their villa in Tuscany. They've been there for the last two months. That's the story anyway."

"You have a reason to doubt that?"

"Let me answer that by telling you that if Ms. Fancy's skin stretches any tighter she'll be able to lick her own ear."

Meredith giggled so hard she had tears in her eyes. "Maggie Lu King! That's terrible."

"You might be right, honey. But it's the plain truth. Wherever they really were, I can assure you she wasn't writing letters or making phone calls to any publisher. When I brought up Davis Hedgerow's book, she had no idea what I was talking about."

"Thanks for doing this. At least that's one name I can take off my list."

"I hope my pain was worth it," Maggie Lu said, chuckling. "Now, I'm gonna get myself out of here, go home, take off this fancy dress, and get comfortable in my sweats."

"You do that. Thanks again. I'll talk to you soon."

Meredith hung up and went back to her notebook, drawing a line through Fancy Devereaux's name. Although she was certain the Dawsons weren't involved, she was curious about the lottery they'd won and the Blue Lake Diamond. She'd never heard of it, which meant nothing. She didn't have much interest in expensive jewelry. She owned some nice pieces, but they weren't worth a great deal of money.

First she found articles about the Dawsons' lottery win. There was a picture of Freddy and Lulu holding a large duplicate of a check.

Meredith gasped at the amount. One hundred and sixty-three million dollars? Wow. They really were rich.

It didn't take long to find articles about the Blue Lake Diamond. When she saw a picture of the necklace, she couldn't help but be impressed. It was huge. Definitely had a blue tint. Meredith wondered what caused that. The article didn't say. But there was a picture of Lulu wearing it. She wore a shiny red blouse that was too tight for her and black pedal pushers with red high heels. Her makeup was overdone, and her lipstick didn't match her clothes. One of her fake eyelashes was partway off.

Freddy wore black slacks and a gray sweater. He looked nice. His hair was salt and pepper and not slicked down to his scalp. He still had his handlebar mustache, but it fit his face just fine.

Meredith had just started to read the article when someone knocked on the door. She closed the computer and went to open it. Freddy stood there with a large tray. Meredith held the door open, and he came in.

"Please don't think you have to finish all of this," he said. "Just eat what you can and set the tray out in the hallway when you're done." He grinned. "Lulu went overboard because she likes you so much."

He set the tray on the coffee table. Then he removed the cloth napkin covering everything. There was a ham and cheese sandwich, a small bowl of spiced pecans, some cheese straws on a small plate, four deviled eggs, and a plate of crab hush puppies with a small bowl of avocado aioli.

"Oh, Freddy. There's no way I could eat all of this."

"I know. This is just Lulu's way of saying thank you for your kindness and encouraging words."

"I hate wasting this wonderful food."

"Just put what you can't eat in the fridge. Then you can take it home with you tomorrow."

Meredith frowned. "Fridge? I have a refrigerator?"

"Sorry. I should have mentioned it when you checked in. Just forgot."

He went over to the armoire and opened a door next to the drawers on the lower part of the piece revealing a small refrigerator. There were two bottles of water inside.

"Oh my. That's great."

"Remind me in the morning and I'll give you a to-go box for whatever's left over."

Meredith smiled at him. "Thank you. And I have an important question to ask you."

"Yes?"

"Will John Douglas Farmer walk the halls tonight?"

Freddy laughed and arched an eyebrow. "I can't guarantee it, but I wouldn't be surprised."

"Good. Thanks again, Freddy."

"My pleasure and if you need anything, just call us." He pointed at a phone on the small nightstand next to the bed. "Just dial one."

"I will. Good night."

"Good night, Meredith. I hope you sleep well."

After Freddy left, Meredith went over to the tray. She put the sandwich and the deviled eggs in the fridge to eat later. Then she carried the pecans, cheese straws, and crab hush puppies over to the desk where she had her laptop. After setting the food down next to her, she went back to the article she'd been reading. She sipped the coffee and then popped some pecans in her mouth as she continued to read. Although the person who wrote the article didn't say anything actually snarky about the Dawsons, what he wrote dripped with sarcasm.

Lulu talked about buying the Blue Lake Diamond. When the reporter asked what else they were going to do with the money, Lulu told him about buying a B and B in Savannah and taking their grandkids to Disney World.

After that article Meredith found another one. The writer focused on what was called the Lottery Curse. Supposedly almost everyone who'd won big ended up losing it all. There were stories of divorces, suicides, and illnesses. The Dawsons were mentioned, and his comments were far from flattering. He talked about the Blue Lake Diamond, making it sound as if the Dawsons were foolish for buying it. Meredith didn't agree. No matter what happened, they had the diamond. It seemed like a great investment. Like they said, they could always sell it. Supposedly the diamond was worth three million dollars.

Lulu talked about the B and B. At least the writer was complimentary about the John Douglas Farmer House. He mentioned that it was beautifully restored and that the renovations were spot-on. But as she munched on a cheese straw, Meredith almost choked when she read one of Lulu's comments. When asked what they intended to do with the rest of the money, Lulu actually said she planned to invest most of it, but that "It would probably be a good idea to keep a few million in cash. What if the stock market crashes?" she asked. "It's too big a risk."

Had she really told the world that she and Freddy had a large amount of cash in their home? Meredith shook her head. That was just asking for trouble. Thieves would see this as a challenge. Meredith decided to try to talk to Lulu and Freddy tomorrow. Maybe she could find a way to mention the article and suggest that a bank would be a much safer way to protect their cash...and themselves.

Meredith checked the date of the article. Only two months ago. The inn must have just opened.

Curious about the house itself, Meredith found an article that reported on the restorations. The woman who oversaw the work mentioned several interesting things about the house. She confirmed that the 1834 federal-style townhouse really had belonged to John Douglas Farmer. She displayed pictures of different parts of the house during and after renovations.

When they got to the sitting room, Meredith was surprised to see that the large painting of John Farmer had been swung open. Behind it was an old wall safe. "The owners decided to keep the safe since it was an original feature of the house. Once opened, the safe was restored and reset. The painting was cleaned by a professional, and Mr. Farmer still protects the safe and its contents."

Meredith sat back in her chair. The Dawsons shouldn't have alerted thieves that there was a safe in their B and B. Surely they had some kind of protection. She hadn't seen any signs. No notices of a security company. Although she didn't want to treat the Dawsons like children, she felt the need to discuss this with them in the morning. Their actions were incredibly reckless.

After finishing her research on the Dawsons, Meredith pulled her notebook over and opened it. She'd put each of the new attractions in Davis's book on its own page. Then she'd written down reasons they might have written the letter and phoned the publisher.

Then reasons they wouldn't. She had just reached the page for the Magnolia Blossom Inn when there was a knock on the door. Must be Freddy looking for the tray. She'd meant to put it outside but had forgotten. She grabbed the tray and headed for the door. But when she opened it, Anson Foster stood there, holding a paper cup.

He looked at the tray in Meredith's hand and grinned. "I guess you were looking for someone else?"

Meredith laughed. "I'm sorry. I thought you were Freddy."

He reached out and took the tray from her. Then he set it down on the floor outside her room. "That should do it. Sorry to bother you, but we had the most delicious hot chocolate at a little shop near the restaurant. It was the best I've ever had. We got some for the Dawsons and for you. Kind of an apology for Dolly's rudeness earlier. She can be difficult. I'm truly sorry." He held out the cup. "Peace offering."

"Totally unnecessary but appreciated. To be honest, I'd just told myself I needed to quit drinking coffee or I'd be up all night." Meredith took the cup from Anson. "Thank you."

"You're very welcome. I hope we'll see you at breakfast in the morning."

"Oh, I plan to be there. After tasting Lulu's appetizers, I can't imagine how delicious breakfast will be."

"I agree. I'm already anticipating it." He smiled at her. "Well, good night, Meredith. I'm so glad we've met."

"Me too. Thanks."

He turned and headed down the hall to his room. Meredith closed her door and then pulled the lid off the cocoa. The aroma of dark chocolate wafted from the cup. Meredith smiled. Perfect. She took the cup back over to the desk and sat down again. Frankly, looking through everything hadn't helped at all. It had just given her a headache. There wasn't one person who stood out as a solid possibility. She still wondered about Freddy, but her gut told her he wouldn't mess up the chance to be in Davis's book. It would disappoint Lulu, and that was something he would never do. He loved her too much.

As she sipped the delicious hot chocolate, she had to face the truth. She had nothing solid to tell Davis. Dixie looked the most guilty, but in her gut Meredith didn't buy it. She wasn't that connected to Oglethorpe even though she liked to pretend she was. There just wasn't a good enough reason for her to do it. And the idea that Dixie might have taken money from SOS bothered her. The Vanderkellens were rich. Why did Dixie need to steal? It didn't make sense.

Frustrated, Meredith picked up the ARC of Davis's book and looked through it slowly. She'd stared at the pages so many times. Still, she couldn't shake the feeling that there was something she'd missed. Something important.

Suddenly, she heard a low voice out in the hallway. "Where is my body? Where is my body?"

Although she'd expected it, nevertheless she was startled and knocked over her cup of hot chocolate. She ran toward the bathroom to get a towel to soak it up. As she returned to the mess on the floor, a knock came on her door. Wanting to play along, she called out, "I don't know where your body is, John Farmer!"

Seemingly satisfied, the voice moved down the hall and called out again. Meredith found it amusing. Charming really. She cleaned up the floor and was relieved to see that the rug was just fine.

Meredith carried the wet, chocolate-laden towel into the bathroom and rinsed it out. Then she hung it on a rack to dry. She was grateful that except for a wet spot on the carpet, there was no indication that an accident had happened. She was sorry that she hadn't been able to finish the hot chocolate, but at least she'd gotten about half of it down. That was better than nothing. In the morning she'd ask Anson for the name of the coffee shop. She couldn't remember one near 45 Bistro. Maybe it was new.

Meredith suddenly realized she was hungry. She went to the small refrigerator and took out the sandwich. She also grabbed a bottle of water and carried everything over to the small table. After she ate she put the dirty dishes on the tray outside. She began to wonder how much more she could do tonight. She wasn't getting anywhere, and she was so tired she couldn't think. She yawned and rubbed her eyes. The room around her spun a bit. Boy, she was more exhausted than she'd realized.

When she sat down again her gaze moved to Davis's book, which was open to one of the pages highlighting the John Douglas Farmer House. She picked it up and realized she'd missed something important. A sudden realization struck her, and she gasped. Her fingers reached out for her phone, but for some reason she was having a hard time making her hand move. As she stood up again, a wave of dizziness overtook her. The room spun wildly. Meredith barely made it to her bed before she felt herself losing consciousness.

Chapter Twenty-Eight

WHEN MEREDITH AWOKE, SHE FORCED herself off the bed and over to the desk where she opened Davis's book to confirm what she'd noticed earlier. When she got to the section about the John Douglas Farmer House, she looked through the pictures again. She saw exactly what she'd expected.

She stumbled over to the door and made certain it was locked. Then she put her ear to the surface. Sure enough, she could hear someone moving around downstairs. Holding on to the furniture, she made her way back to the desk and found her phone. This time she was able to grasp it. She glanced at the clock. A little past three o'clock in the morning.

She started to call the police, but her thoughts were so cloudy, she found herself calling Julia instead. It was okay, she reasoned. Julia could call them. Meredith realized she was having trouble forming coherent sentences. She tried several times to rehearse what to say to Julia, but her mouth was so dry her tongue stuck to the roof of her mouth. She knew she wasn't making sense. She heard Julia's phone ring. A few seconds later a sleepy voice said, "Hello?"

"Julia, issss…need hel…help. Please…mub mumb…some…"

"Meredith Bellefontaine. Are you drunk?" Julia asked loudly.

Meredith could hear Beau's voice in the background. "Meredith's drunk?"

"Noooo. Noooo. Not...drun...drunk. Drugs."

"You're high?" Julia's voice had risen at least two octaves.

Meredith's mind was fuzzy, but she still knew what she needed. What was going on? Why couldn't she say it?

"Call...call 911111..."

There was a brief silence. "Are you in trouble, Mere?"

"Yeahhh. Thieves. John Farmer House. Send po...po...police."

"Okay. You stay on the line."

She could hear Julia tell Beau to call the police and send them to the B and B. "Tell them there's a robbery going on. And for goodness' sake, ask them to find Meredith right away. I think she's been drugged."

Meredith could feel her body relax with relief. She kept her phone on as she once again checked that the door to her room was locked. Then she made her way to the coffeemaker in the room and brewed a cup. She sat down at the desk and sipped the coffee, grateful she hadn't finished the entire cup of hot chocolate given to her by Anson Foster. Although several times she felt as if she wanted to lie down, she fought the urge and waited for the police to come.

***

Not long after the police left, Julia and Beau showed up.

"Are you okay, Mere?" Julia asked. Her face was pale, and her eyes were wide with concern.

"I'm fine," Meredith said. She sat in one of the wing-backed chairs. Lulu and Freddy were on the couch.

"Shouldn't you be in the hospital?" Julia asked. "If you were drugged…"

"Sleeping pills," Meredith said. "Luckily I didn't drink the entire cup of cocoa the drugs were in."

"We don't have chocolate in the evening," Lulu said. "Sugar and caffeine keep us up." She sighed. "It looked so good we only tasted it then put the rest in the refrigerator so we could have it today. We gave the cups to the police."

Meredith realized that Julia and Beau hadn't met the Dawsons, so she introduced them.

"Meredith told us you called the police," Freddy said. "Thank you."

Lulu wore a long satin robe with images of brightly colored peacocks, and Freddy was decked out in red pajamas. Even in their pj's their eccentricity came through.

"You're welcome." Julia sat down in the chair near Meredith, and Beau took the corner chair where Meredith sat the night before. So much had happened last night it seemed like ages ago instead of only a matter of hours.

"So what did they give you?" Julia asked.

"A pretty strong dose of sleeping pills. EMTs came by, but since we hadn't taken the whole dose they didn't take us to the hospital. We were told to go to the emergency room if we felt any lingering weakness or disorientation. The police located the pill bottle in Anson Foster's room." Meredith shrugged. "But he admitted to everything anyway."

Julia shook her head. "I was so worried about you," she said, her voice choking. "You could have been killed."

Meredith shook her head. "They didn't want to kill us. They just wanted us asleep so they could steal the jewels and the cash."

"So the police got here in time?" Beau asked.

"Caught them in the act. They'd just opened the safe when the police came in." Meredith frowned. "The front door is a little worse for wear. Boy, the Fosters weren't too happy when they discovered the safe was empty."

"Empty? Really?" Julia looked surprised.

"I figured out that the Fosters had heard about the Blue Lake Diamond and then read up on the Dawson's B and B. They realized there was still a safe behind John Farmer's portrait. They were convinced it held the diamond."

"Yeah, that's what they thought," Freddy said, grinning, "but they were wrong. We're not idiots. We know the safe is public knowledge. We have a much better hiding place for the jewels."

"Where?"

Meredith giggled. "Under their mattress."

"What?" Julia's mouth dropped open. "Seriously?"

"Yep. Seems Lulu sliced open the material on the mattress and added a zipper. That's where the Blue Lake Diamond is kept."

Julia didn't say anything, but Meredith could see she was shocked.

"The police talked to her about it," Freddy said, shaking his head. "They suggested a safe-deposit box, but Lulu is happy keeping it in the mattress. She figures no one would actually think a three-million dollar diamond would be hidden there."

Meredith laughed. "The police weren't too happy with that response."

Lulu grinned. "I was pullin' their chain a little. I heard what they said. I may rethink my hiding place."

"Good for you," Julia said.

"I need to go home," Meredith said. "I'm very tired."

"You're welcome to stay here," Lulu said. "Sleep. You've had a busy night."

"Thanks, but I just want my own bed. Besides, I miss my cat."

Lulu smiled. "Now I can certainly understand that. I've been asking Freddy for a cat. I think it's time."

Freddy sighed. "I have a feeling we'll have a cat soon. Thanks, Meredith."

Meredith said, "So glad I could help," causing Freddy to laugh.

Julia stood up. "I'll help you pack, Mere."

"I'm so grateful no one was hurt," Beau said. "This could have been much worse."

"Who knows what they might have done next?" Julia asked. "What if they'd forced the Dawsons to show them where the diamond was hidden?"

"I don't think that would have happened," Meredith said. "I don't believe they're violent. Just greedy."

"Maybe."

"Why didn't they bring guns and force the Dawsons to open the safe?" Meredith asked. "They put us to sleep because they didn't really want to harm us."

Julia sighed. "You could be right. I don't know. I just want to get you home where you can recover. If you're well enough, we'll take you to breakfast first."

"We owe you breakfast," Lulu said. "We can put something together...."

"No," Meredith said with a smile. "You've been through a lot. I won't have you putting yourself out for my account. You two need to rest and regroup. Don't forget that after Davis's book comes out, you're going to be very busy."

"We're not so sure that's what we want," Lulu said, frowning. "I think maybe it's time to head back to St. Cloud."

"I hope it's not because of this," Meredith said.

"It has something to do with it," Freddy said. "There are bad people in the world. People who want to take what others have. We don't want anything to happen to us. We'd miss so much. We want to watch our grandchildren grow up. We've decided to sell the inn *and* the diamond and go home. After we've settled down we'll pack up the family and take them all to Disney World." He smiled at Lulu. "We want to spend our money on our family. Make sure all the grandkids go to college. Pay off our kids' houses."

Lulu nodded. "That means more to me than this inn. I guess this incident helped us to figure out what is really valuable and precious in life. And it isn't a big diamond."

"That sounds right to me," Meredith said. "Good for you." She suddenly remembered something. "It's Sunday." She looked over at Julia. "I just don't think I'm up to going this morning."

Julia laughed. "I'm not sure, but I think being drugged by a group of thieves is a pretty good reason to miss a service."

Meredith sighed. "I guess so."

She and Julia headed upstairs, where Meredith packed her bag. She didn't bring much, so it didn't take long. Julia took the remaining food out of the refrigerator and put it on the tray that was still outside the room. There wasn't much left, and if they were going to breakfast Meredith had no way to keep it cool. She didn't want to mess with it.

Next Meredith packed up her notes and Davis's book. She slid everything into a briefcase she'd brought with her. Then she unplugged her laptop and put it in its case.

"Went through all my notes and Davis's book last night," she called out to Julia, "but I didn't get anywhere." Meredith couldn't keep the disappointment out of her voice.

Julia came out of the bathroom, where she'd packed up Meredith's toiletries. "You figured out that the Dawsons were being robbed," she said. "I think that's enough for one night. We'll go over it all tomorrow. If we can't solve this one, it will be all right."

"I still keep feeling that I missed something," Meredith said slowly.

"You say that a lot, you know."

"I know. I'm sure you're tired of hearing it."

Julia smiled. "No, because it usually means you're on the verge of solving a case."

"I wouldn't count on it this time."

"We'll see." Julia pointed to Meredith's toiletry bag. "I think I got everything, but if you want to double-check…"

"No, I trust you. But I would like to brush my hair and check my makeup." She looked down at her clothes. "Am I too wrinkled?"

Julia bit her lip and tried to stifle a giggle. "Do you really want me to answer that?" she asked finally.

"Ha ha. Very funny. I mean my clothes."

"No, your clothes are fine." She handed Meredith her bag. "Brush your hair and your teeth, and fix your face. You'll feel better."

Meredith went into the bathroom and opened her bag. A few minutes later she felt presentable.

"Okay, let's go," she said when she came out. "I love this place, but I'm ready to leave."

"You know, it really is special. I'd like to stay here sometime. Hopefully Beau likes it too."

"Sounds like you better do it quickly. I'm not sure the Dawsons will be around long."

As they walked out the door to her room, Meredith took a look back. Although her visit hadn't revealed anything helpful about their case, at least something good had come out of it. She was beginning to accept the fact that she and Julia might fail to bring Davis Hedgerow the answers he needed. That didn't sit well with her. Meredith didn't like to lose.

Chapter Twenty-Nine

WHEN SHE CAME DOWNSTAIRS, THE Dawsons were talking to Beau. He looked up at them. "Freddy just told me that Eric Foster was trying to crack the safe when the police came in. He had special tools. But not only was the safe empty, it wasn't locked. Foster never checked."

Meredith's mouth dropped open. "So all he had to do was to pull the handle, and it would have opened?" She burst out laughing. "Not a very skilled safecracker, is he?"

"Actually, they weren't skilled at anything," Beau said. "It appears that this was their first attempt at a felony. They didn't even know enough to use fake names."

"Well, I'm just glad everything turned out okay," Meredith said to Lulu and Freddy. "Thanks for a very interesting experience."

The couple laughed. "At least you can say staying with us is something you won't soon forget," Lulu said. She got up from the couch and gave Meredith a hug. "Thanks again, honey. It was providence that you were here when we needed you."

"I'm just grateful I could help." Meredith hesitated a moment but decided to ask the question she'd wanted to ask ever since she met the Dawsons. She turned her attention to Freddy. "I need to know something," she said. "Please don't be offended."

Freddy frowned. "Of course. There's nothing you can't ask."

"Did you send a threatening letter to Davis Hedgerow, telling him not to publish his book?"

Freddy's eyes widened. "Of course not. Why would I do that?"

"To keep the inn from being successful so Lulu would want to go back to St. Cloud."

Freddy shook his head. "I would never do anything like that to Lulu, Meredith."

"We don't operate that way," Lulu said. "Besides, it doesn't make sense. Whether we stay...or go...the more the inn is worth, the better it is for us." She sought Meredith's eyes. "Do you believe us?"

Meredith smiled. "Yes, I do. I'm sorry to ask, but I wanted to leave with this off my mind."

"Is that why you came?" Lulu asked.

Meredith nodded. "But in the meantime I fell in love with this place and made two new friends. I think it was worth it."

"Oh honey," Lulu said, her eyes filling with tears. "We feel the same."

After another hug from Lulu, Meredith said goodbye again. Beau collected her bags, and Meredith followed Julia out of the house. Had God really sent her here to help the Dawsons? This case had led her to several people who needed help but had nothing to do with the original reason Davis hired them. She remembered a scripture that said one's steps are ordered by the Lord. Even though the situation with the Fosters hadn't been pleasant, it turned out okay in the end, even bringing Lulu and Freddy to a decision that would get them back to their family. Just thinking about that made Meredith feel pretty good.

"Let us drive you to breakfast," Beau said. "We'll bring you back to get your car afterward. If you're still a little drowsy, it's not a good idea for you to be driving."

Even though she felt okay, Meredith realized Beau was being sensible. A nice breakfast and a little more coffee couldn't hurt, so she agreed.

When Beau pulled into the parking lot at the Downhome Diner, Meredith smiled to herself. Perfect.

The diner, located in the historic district, was a favorite for Savannah residents. It had been around a long time. When they walked in, one of the waitresses, Justine, saw them and smiled. She hurried over to them.

"Glad to see you," she said. "Not sure I remember you coming in on a Sunday morning. Aren't you usually in church?"

"Yeah," Beau said with a smile. "But it's been a very unusual morning. We decided that God wouldn't mind if we enjoyed one of your great breakfasts even though we missed church."

Justine laughed. "I'm sure you're right. We just cleaned off a booth. Is that okay?"

"Sounds perfect," Julia said.

They followed Justine to a booth against the wall. Meredith loved the Downhome Diner. Maggie Lu's daughter, Charlene, had done a wonderful job with it. The walls were light yellow with framed pictures displayed prominently throughout the dining room. The tables and booths reminded Meredith of her teenage years. There was a long counter with red vinyl-covered stools in front of it. Actually, Peachie's and the Downhome Diner were similar in their decor.

Maybe the nod to her younger days was one of the reasons she loved both of these special places.

After Justine brought their menus and took their drink orders, Julia said, "That was brave of you. Just coming out and asking the Dawsons about the letter sent to Davis."

"I felt strongly that they would tell me the truth."

"And did they?" Beau asked.

"I believe they did," Meredith said. "They're good people. Not the kind to write letters like the one Davis got. Certainly not the type to make that phone call to his publisher."

"I agree," Beau said. "I talked to them for a while when you were upstairs. I like them very much. They seem sincere."

Meredith grunted. "So, that's it. We've met and talked to everyone that Davis suspected, yet we still don't have a clear motive or any evidence that will allow us to accuse any of them."

"I agree," Julia said with a sigh. "Maybe it's someone else. Someone not associated with these five places."

Justine came back to the table with their coffees. "Are you ready to order?" she asked after she put their cups and a carafe on the table.

Meredith and Julia ordered the shrimp and grits while Beau ordered a breakfast scramble. Meredith could hardly wait for her food to arrive. She was so hungry her stomach growled. She hoped Julia and Beau hadn't heard it.

"So what do we do now, Meredith?" Julia asked. "Do we give up?"

"No. Not yet." She frowned at Julia. "Have we heard anything more about Davis? I meant to check up on him."

"I called yesterday and he'd been released. He's home."

"Good. I wish I'd realized the connection between Dallas and Davis sooner. Maybe I could have prevented that awful attack."

"Meredith, don't think that way," Julia said. "There's nothing you could have done."

"I agree," Beau chimed in. "Let it go. Davis is recovering and Dallas is in jail. All you can do is go forward from here."

"That's just it. I'm not sure how to go forward."

"Let's just enjoy our breakfast," Julia said. "Put the case out of your mind. Tomorrow we'll go over it one more time. Pull it apart. Maybe we'll come up with something. If we don't, we don't. We've been going with Davis's hunches. Maybe he was wrong. If so, this is Davis's failure. Not ours."

"I know you're right," Meredith said. "But it still bothers me. And…"

"I know. You still feel as if you missed something." Julia sighed. "If you did, thinking about it too much won't bring you the answer. It will just make it harder. Rest your mind. Give it a chance to show you what the problem is."

"I guess." She took a sip of coffee and halfway listened as Julia and Beau talked about redecorating their guest room. Even though Julia's advice was good, the case wouldn't be banished so easily from her thoughts.

When Justine came to the table with their food, Meredith realized her previous hunger had disappeared. She stared at the delicious-looking shrimp and grits in front of her. Instead of enjoying one of her favorite meals, the realization that she might have to walk away, never finding out who had tried to stop publication of Davis's book, made her feel sick to her stomach.

Chapter Thirty

WHEN MEREDITH GOT TO THE office Monday morning, she hung up her coat and put her purse under her desk. She went straight to the coffeemaker and was surprised to find a pot had already been brewed. She got a cup and checked Julia's office. She found her partner hunched over her desk, which was covered with papers.

"Where's your car?" Meredith asked. "It wasn't parked outside."

"It needed an oil change, so Beau dropped me off and took it into the shop."

"Are you spring cleaning?" Meredith asked with a smile.

"Hardly," Julia answered. "Just going through the case again, trying to find something." She chuckled. "I guess I'm looking for that *thing you missed.*"

Meredith sat down in a nearby chair. "So did you have any luck?"

"No. Not really." She frowned at Meredith. "I have an idea, but I don't know what you'll think of it."

"At this point, I'm open to just about anything."

"Let's talk this over with Maggie Lu," Julia said. "I think we need fresh eyes. She already knows about the case."

Actually, it wasn't a bad idea. Maybe she and Julia had been working this case so hard they weren't seeing things clearly. Meredith considered Julia's suggestion. Maggie Lu's point of view had been useful in the past, and they needed help.

"Okay," Meredith said. "Can you call Maggie Lu and see if she's available for lunch today?"

"I'll do it now," Julia said, picking up the phone.

Meredith got up and headed toward her own office. She found Carmen getting herself a cup of coffee. They chatted for a few minutes before Meredith walked into her office. She sat down at her desk and ran her hand across the walnut finish. This was once Ron's desk. "Sure could use your help right now, honey," she said softly. She still missed him. Every day. Meredith took a deep breath and picked up her phone. She dialed Davis's number and waited. Sylvia picked up on the third ring.

"Sylvia, this is Meredith. How's the patient?"

"Stubborn and complaining. Which means he's healing."

Sylvia sounded so much better than the last time Meredith had talked to her. She breathed a sigh of relief.

"Meredith, I owe you an apology," Sylvia said. "Davis explained what happened and that you had nothing to do with it. Please forgive me for jumping on you. I was just so upset."

"Oh, Sylvia. I totally understand. I would have felt the same way. I'm not the least bit offended."

"I'm afraid you're more gracious than I would have been if our places were reversed," Sylvia said softly.

"I doubt that. I can pitch a pretty big fit if I'm pushed too hard."

Sylvia laughed. "Then remind me to never push you, okay?"

"No worries. It would never happen."

"Did you want to speak to him?"

"Yes, if it's okay."

"Sure," Sylvia said. "He's lounging on the couch waiting for me to refresh his coffee. He needs to get up and around, so I'm ignoring him. Don't expect him to be in the greatest mood."

"That's okay, I'll risk it," Meredith said, laughing.

"Okay, you've been warned. Hold on a minute."

A short time later she heard Davis's voice. "Meredith?" he said.

"Yes, it's me. How are you feeling?"

"Like someone beat me with a baseball bat."

"Is that what he used?" Meredith asked. She hadn't heard that detail.

"Yep. I guess I should be grateful he didn't have a gun or a knife."

"I'm so sorry this happened to you."

"I am too, but I'm grateful you figured out what was going on. Thanks for that. How is the other thing shaping up?"

"It's very slow, Davis. We're doing the best we can, but we don't have anyone we can definitely point a finger at yet."

"Well, you found someone who probably wanted me dead," he said. "I'm just lucky that didn't happen. If you don't find anything else, you've more than earned your fee."

"I appreciate that," Meredith said. She really did. It helped to relieve some of the tension she felt. But still, their assignment was to find the letter writer, and they hadn't done that yet. "I'll get back to you by the end of the week. We'll tell you everything we have. Hopefully, we'll have the one name you're looking for."

"I still believe it has something to do with the places I told you about," Davis said, "but I'm not infallible. If I missed it, it's on me.

Still, I don't like knowing someone is running around out there who means me harm."

"I totally understand," Meredith said. "I don't like it either. I'll talk to you later in the week."

"Thanks, Meredith. For everything. If not for you, I could be dead. Scott Dallas might have come back to finish the job. I'll be grateful to you and Julia forever. No matter what else you can find."

Meredith felt tears fill her eyes. Why was she getting emotional? She patted Ron's desk once more before she thanked Davis and hung up. She wiped away a tear that ran down her cheek. At that moment Julia came into the office. Meredith wasn't able to hide her emotion.

"What's wrong, Mere?" Julia asked, her face showing her concern.

"I don't know. I'm just being emotional today. Davis just thanked us for possibly saving his life."

"This case. It's…I don't know. Different. Even though we haven't found what we were looking for, some good things have happened. We figured out who beat up Davis. We discovered that the Ambrose Sedgwick diary was a forgery. The Book Worm Warriors have agreed to try to work things out with Alex. We stopped the Fosters from stealing anything from Lulu and Freddy, and I think Elise Sedgwick is thinking about reuniting with her parents. All great things."

"It's like that scripture," Julia said. "About God going before us. I think we were supposed to meet these people and do what we could to help. Meeting Scott Dallas—well, I truly believe that was divine intervention. Davis is right, you know. What if Scott had gone after Davis again?"

Meredith nodded, but she couldn't speak. The desire of her heart was to help people. And they had. She was certain she was exactly where she was supposed to be, and it brought her great comfort.

"I talked to Maggie Lu. She suggested we meet at Peachie's." Julia grinned. "She knows how much you love those lemon shakes and knows you've been through a lot this past week."

"That sounds great. Are you through with the file? I'd like to let Maggie Lu look through it at lunch."

Julia sighed. "I'll get it. I hope she has more luck than we have."

"Thanks, Julia."

As she waited for the file, Meredith prayed. She thanked God for using them. She also asked that He would give them wisdom to see whatever it was they'd missed. And that He'd reveal the person who'd threatened Davis. When she finished she took a deep breath and let it out. She was ready to bring this case to an end. At this point they could only trust God to bring it to a successful conclusion.

Chapter Thirty-One

JULIA AND MEREDITH WERE A little late getting to Peachie's. Julia had been on the phone with a possible client, and Meredith hadn't wanted to cut the conversation short. All she got from Julia was that it had to do with a missing person.

When they got there, the place was packed. Meredith hoped Maggie Lu had already secured a table. Sure enough, she waved from a booth. Meredith and Julia told the hostess they were joining her. As they made their way through the crowded restaurant, a voice called her name. Meredith turned around and was surprised to see Elise Sedgwick and her parents. She stopped in her tracks and Julia ran into her.

"Sorry, Meredith," Julia said. "But next time you might signal before putting your brakes on."

"Look," she said, pointing toward the table where Elise sat.

"Oh, wow," Julia said under her breath.

Meredith caught Maggie Lu's eye and held up one finger. The universal sign of *please wait a minute*. Then she walked over to the table where the Sedgwicks sat.

"I'm surprised and pleased to see you...together," she said.

Elise smiled. "I have you two to thank for it. I realized we don't have all the time in the world to spend with the people we love. I didn't want to lose any time with my parents."

"It was our fault," Paula said. "We should have trusted Elise more. She gave us a tour of the Magnolia Blossom. It's incredible. So beautiful."

"Thanks, Mom," Elise said.

Paula smiled. "We're very proud of you."

Sylvester said, "We're having the statue moved from the park. Not sure what will happen to it. It might just end up in our backyard. Maybe the birds can enjoy it."

"You know," Meredith said, "Ambrose Sedgwick did serve with James Oglethorpe. You might want to do a search through authenticated documents. Discover more about him. Oglethorpe must have valued him. When you find out more, you might want to donate the statue to the Historical Society. They can find a great place to put it."

Sylvester nodded. "That's a good idea." He laughed. "Maybe the birds will have to find another perch."

"I really want to thank you for what you've done for our family," Paula said. "You've both been a real blessing. By the way, we contacted the police, and the Wilmores are being questioned. We don't know what will come of it, but at least they're having to explain themselves to the authorities."

Meredith caught Julia's glance. Definitely another detour on the road God had led them to.

"We're so glad to hear that," Julia said. "Thank you for telling us."

"It's funny," said Elise. "I planned to call you later today and thank you, but I'm glad we got to talk in person. Such a strange coincidence to run into you today." She smiled. "Anytime you'd like to stay at the Magnolia Blossom, it's on me."

"Oh, Elise," Meredith said. "We can't accept that. It's so nice of you though."

"Well, you'll have to accept it because I won't change my mind. Please. I really want to do this."

Meredith smiled. "Okay, we'll remember that. We love the Magnolia Blossom. It's charming. Thank you so much."

"You're welcome."

"We need to join our friend," Julia said. "Talk to you soon."

Julia followed Meredith over to where Maggie Lu waited. As they slid into the other side of the booth, Julia said, "Wow. That was...awesome."

"What was awesome?" Maggie Lu asked. "Does it have something to do with the Sedgwicks?"

Meredith nodded. "They've had some family problems, but they seem to be doing better now."

"I'd heard there had been troubles between them," Maggie Lu said. "I'm so glad to see them together."

"We are too," Julia said.

Molly came over to the table. "Welcome back," she said.

"Thank you, child. How are you feeling?" Maggie Lu asked.

"Much better. Being more careful to track my blood sugar. Thanks for your concern the other day."

"You're very welcome. We can't have you passing out and hurting yourself." Maggie Lu was obviously concerned about the young woman.

Molly chuckled. "I won't, but thanks for caring. What can I get you to drink?"

Julia ordered a Diet Dr Pepper.

Meredith smiled at Molly.

"Let me guess. A lemon shake?" Molly asked.

"Please."

"Are you ready to order your food or do you want some time?"

"I'd like another cheeseburger," Meredith said.

"Same here," Julia said.

"Exactly what Maggie Lu asked for before you got here. You must like our burgers."

"After seeing them the other day, I knew I had to have one," Maggie Lu said. "I enjoyed my BLT, but I've been thinking about those big juicy cheeseburgers ever since we were here last time."

Julia wagged her finger at Maggie Lu. "That's the real reason you wanted to meet at Peachie's. It wasn't really Meredith's lemon shake was it?"

"Can't it be both?" Maggie Lu asked with a grin.

"So a Diet Dr Pepper, a lemon shake, and three cheeseburgers?" Molly read back.

The three women nodded.

"Coming up." Molly turned away and headed toward the kitchen.

Maggie Lu leaned back in her seat. "So tell me what's going on."

"We've ruled out the Dawsons, the people who own the John Douglas Farmer House, and Elise Sedgwick, the owner of the Magnolia Blossom Inn. We wondered about her parents, but they had no idea the items purported to have belonged to Ambrose Sedgwick were forged. Therefore there was no reason to try to stop Davis's book from being published. I don't believe it was an act. They've been nothing but up-front. They were only too happy to stop the statue dedication and have the story of Ambrose Sedgwick removed from Davis's book. We can't find a reason for anyone connected to the Book Worm to try to stop the publication of Davis's book. We looked at Fancy Devereaux, but thanks to you, we know she was out of the country when the threats began."

"So that leaves two potential suspects," Maggie Lu said slowly.

"Yes," Meredith said. "We haven't been able to cross Dixie Vanderkellen off our list. She was really upset about Ambrose Sedgwick's supposed letters and diary." She sighed. "Turns out she was right."

"But is she really so dedicated to some far-removed relative that she'd write a threatening letter and call Davis's publisher?" Maggie Lu asked with a frown.

"That's what bothered us," Julia said. "The Vanderkellens have enough pull in this city that they could probably quash that book deal if they wanted to."

"There's one other thing that might point to Dixie," Meredith said. She told Maggie Lu about the BID impression on the paper used to write the note. "We don't know if it's a doctor's notation or someone looking for a bid."

"Or even part of another word," Julia added.

Maggie Lu shrugged. "I really don't see Dixie as a very good suspect. She likes to throw James Oglethorpe's name around, but she doesn't care who designed the layout of Savannah. I mean, really? It's just not that important to her. James Oglethorpe founded Savannah. That's what she hangs her hat on."

"I keep wondering about the money she supposedly took," Julia said. "Could that have anything to do with the threats?"

"I really don't know, but I am sure it's not a problem anymore."

"What do you mean?" Meredith asked.

"Miss Dixie admitted to taking the money. Seems she'd planned to pay it back but couldn't get it done before someone found out. Her husband gave the SOS the full amount she'd *borrowed*. No formal charges will be filed. She was booted out of the SOS, but that's a small price to pay for what she did." Maggie Lu pointed her finger at them. "That doesn't mean she didn't write that letter, but I really don't think she had anything to do with it."

"Why did she take the money?" Julia asked.

"I heard it was because she felt Franklin gave her an allowance that didn't meet her needs. Hard to impress people when you're on too short a leash."

Julia sighed deeply. "This has been our problem all along, Maggie Lu. No one person stands out. I think we may have to admit defeat on this one. Unless you can come up with something."

"You two ladies are extremely talented investigators," Maggie Lu said. "Not sure I'll see something you didn't."

"Thanks, but neither one of us is feeling that confident right now," Meredith said. She reached down for her tote bag, then she pulled out the file on the Davis Hedgerow case. She handed it to Maggie Lu. "Just try not to get mustard or ketchup on it if you don't mind."

Maggie Lu laughed. "I'll do my best. You know, you've mentioned four possibilities. I thought you said there were five new mentions in this book."

"Oh, Peachie's is the fifth one," Meredith said, "but there's no reason anyone here would send the letter. We did wonder about the cook, Carl Finney, but we found out it wasn't him. I'm sorry I can't tell you more about that. I wouldn't feel right about it."

"You mean that he has a record?" Maggie Lu asked, smiling. "I swan. That wasn't hard to figure out. Why else would he want to keep his picture out of Davis's book?"

"He's not mentioned in the article," Julia said. "Nor is he in any of the pictures. There's no way he would have been compromised."

"Are you sure he saw the article?"

"Yeah. Kathy showed it to him. He didn't react negatively about it at all."

"Okay. Well, give me a few minutes to read through everything, okay?"

"Sure."

"Here we go," Molly said, coming up to the booth. She gave Julia her Diet Dr Pepper and handed Meredith her shake. "Your food should be out soon."

"Thanks, Molly," Julia said.

"Where's that ARC?" Maggie Lu asked when Molly walked away.

Meredith reached back into her tote bag and pulled it out. "Here," she said, handing it to Maggie Lu.

Meredith and Julia stayed quiet so as not to bother Maggie Lu as she looked through the file. Meredith was happy to simply enjoy her lemon shake. She'd have to limit her consumption. Too many could easily pack on the pounds.

Finally, Maggie Lu shut the file and opened the ARC. A few minutes later, she said, "Hmm."

"What?" Meredith and Julia asked at the same time.

Maggie Lu took the ARC and turned it toward them. "Here," she said. "I believe this is the thing you thought you missed, Meredith."

At that moment Molly brought their food. As she handed them their plates, her eyes fell on the opened ARC. This time when she went pale Meredith was sure it had nothing to do with diabetes.

Although she didn't know exactly why, Meredith had the strangest feeling that their case was about to be solved.

Chapter Thirty-Two

MEREDITH AND JULIA SAT IN Kathy's office with Morris and Molly staring back at them. They both looked worried. Kathy looked curious.

"We have some questions," Meredith said. "We're not accusing you of anything. Please don't assume we are."

No one said anything so Meredith continued. "Kathy told us that you two wanted the pictures reshot for Davis Hedgerow's book. She said you were upset about them but that she told you she thought they were okay. That they didn't need to be taken again."

"Yeah," Morris said. "There's nothing wrong with that." His tone was definitely defensive.

"No, there's not," Meredith said, "but something else bothered us." She opened the ARC to the article on Peachie's. She pointed to one of the pictures. "Morris, the tattoo on your neck is showing here, but it's not there now. And it wasn't there the last time we were here. When you leaned over our table when we came the first time, I noticed your earring, but there was no tattoo. I would have remembered. So I have to ask myself why you're covering it up. I know it's not because of your job. Molly told us Kathy has nothing against tattoos." She turned her attention to Molly. "I believe you really were experiencing low blood sugar the other day, but you reacted when you saw this ARC and you did the same thing today. I have to wonder why. There's something about this tattoo in the picture that upset you. Isn't that right?"

As Molly started to cry softly, Meredith stared at Morris. At first he wouldn't meet her gaze, but when he looked up, his defensive look crumbled.

"Okay, okay." He reached over and took Molly's hand. "It's all right. It's time to tell the truth."

"And what is the truth?" Kathy asked.

Meredith knew Kathy cared about Morris and Molly. She hoped the answer wouldn't do anything to destroy that relationship.

"Do you have a criminal background?" Meredith asked, trying to shake the truth out.

Morris's eyes widened. "No. That's not it." He took a deep, shaky breath. "Four years ago I worked at a casino in Kansas City. My boss was being pressured to cheat several of the big spenders at the casino. You know, VIP guests."

"Cheat them?" Julia asked. "What do you mean?"

"Cause them to lose big-time. Then this guy would come in and bail them out. Give them a loan. After that, he'd own them. He was targeting people with business connections he wanted to exploit."

"What did your boss say?"

"He said no. He didn't want to do it." Morris looked down. "So my boss had an *accident*. Someone ran him off the road, and his car rolled down an embankment and burst into flames. Thankfully, he was able to crawl out before the car exploded. He barely survived. Not long after that, the FBI showed up. They wanted him to testify against this guy. They said they could protect him and his family. He refused because the man behind the scam was notorious for going after the families of people who wouldn't do what they were asked. The Feds took his family into custody and hid them for their own protection. They learned that the only other person who knew about the situation—who had overheard many of their conversations—was me. I agreed to testify. The case went to court. I told them everything I knew. My testimony convinced my boss to speak out too. With both of us telling the court what this guy had done, he went to prison. For the rest of his life."

"But his associates were looking for revenge?" Meredith asked.

"Exactly. So my boss and I went into WITSEC, the Witness Security Program. The Marshalls moved us to different locations. Gave us new names. I think my boss was fine. I mean, he had his family. But I had no one. Stuck in a small town without friends or family... I just couldn't take it. So I ran away. Came here." He looked over at Molly. "Fell in love. Found friends. When I saw the book, I realized my tattoo was showing. It's very distinctive. I was afraid for my safety and for Molly's."

"And that's why you wrote the letter to Davis Hedgerow?"

Morris didn't say anything. Just hung his head. Then he nodded.

"And the telephone call?" Julia asked.

"Yes." He looked up at them with tears in his eyes. "I know it wasn't...right. But I didn't know what else to do. I knew if the wrong people saw it, they would recognize the tattoo. I'd be in danger again, and so would those around me."

"Did you know about this?" Kathy asked Molly.

"Not at first," she said. "When Morris kept pushing you to get new pictures, I knew something was wrong. I kept asking until he finally told me everything."

"Why didn't you two just leave town?" Meredith asked. "That would have solved everything, wouldn't it? Find a new place to live."

"We talked about it," Molly said. "But my mother's ill. I'm the only one left in the family to care for her. I just couldn't leave her."

"And I couldn't leave Molly," Morris said. "She's my life."

"Did you have anything else planned to stop the book?" Meredith asked.

Morris nodded, looking ashamed. "Another letter. But then we heard on the news that Mr. Hedgerow had been attacked. I just couldn't do it. He's been through enough. I was so sorry I'd ever started this. I should have just left. It was selfish of me."

"What will happen to Morris?" Kathy asked.

"I don't know," Meredith said. "It's against the law in Georgia to harass someone through a threatening communication. I would say your letter fits the bill. The phone call? It was never passed along so there may not be anything actionable there."

"What's the…I mean, how much trouble am I in?" Morris asked.

"It's a misdemeanor," Meredith said. "Let me talk to Davis and see what he wants to do."

"You…you don't have to contact the police?" Molly asked.

"In some cases, it would be the right thing to do," Meredith said. "If a serious crime isn't reported to the proper authorities, an investigator can be charged with aiding criminal activity. But with something like this? We'll turn it over to our client and let him make the decision. He's the one you hurt."

"I'm sure he's angry with me," Morris said. "And I wouldn't blame him."

"I'm certain he'll be relieved to know he and his family aren't really in any danger," Julia said.

"I...I didn't think it through," Morris said, shaking his head. "I just panicked. I was sorry after I called the publisher. If it makes any difference, I don't think I would have sent the last letter."

"Did you really think Davis would stop the publication of the book because of your actions?"

Morris rubbed his forehead. It was clear to Meredith that he was truly repentant for what he'd done. How would Davis view this? It was impossible to know.

"Look," Meredith said, "go ahead and get back to work. Let us talk to Davis. When he realizes the photo could put you at risk, I'm sure he'd be willing to have a new one taken. As far as pressing charges, it's up to him." She wagged her finger at him. "You stay put. It's time to set things right. Running away won't solve anything. And besides, you have a woman who loves you. You should treasure that."

"All right," Morris said. "You have my word. I'll stay here and take my medicine."

"And what about you?" Julia asked Kathy. "Does he still have a job?"

"Of course," she said with a smile. "As long as he wants it. What he did was stupid, but I've gotten to know Morris over the last few months. One stupid move doesn't change how much I like and respect him. We'll weather this together, Morris." She frowned at Meredith. "You said this was a misdemeanor? Does that mean he might not go to jail if Davis Hedgerow presses charges?"

"In Georgia he could face up to a year in jail, a fine of one thousand dollars, or both."

"Oh no," Morris said.

Molly grabbed his hand. "It will be all right," she said to him. "We'll do whatever we have to. We have the rest of our lives to look forward to."

"You're right," Morris said slowly. The blood had drained from his face, but he seemed buoyed by her words of assurance.

"I have two other questions," Meredith said. "We found an impression on the letter. It was caused by someone writing on a piece of paper on top of yours. BID in capital letters. What does it mean?"

Morris frowned at her for a moment, but then his expression cleared. "I used a piece of paper from a pad Kathy had under the counter." He looked at his boss. "I have no idea what was written on the paper before the one I took."

Kathy looked confused for a moment but then smiled and shook her head. "I was getting bids for work here. There was one that was so low I wrote down their name and then added *UNDERBID* in capital letters. I was very suspicious about the company because of that lowball bid. Turned out I was right. Lots of complaints about shoddy work."

Meredith wanted to laugh but felt it wasn't appropriate at the moment. Here they were convinced it was a note written by a doctor.

"You said there were two questions," Morris said.

"Yes, your tattoo. The name *Shirley* with vines and white flowers threading through it."

Once again, tears came to Morris's eyes. "My mom. She died when I was eighteen."

"I'm so sorry."

Morris shrugged, but it was obvious he'd loved her very much.

Meredith hoped Davis would show compassion, but she couldn't be sure. She got to her feet. "Thank you for telling us the truth. I hope things turn out okay for you."

Morris squared his shoulders and looked at Molly. Then he shifted his gaze to Meredith. "I'll face whatever I have to. I just...I just can't go back into Witness Protection. I just can't."

"Yes, you can if you have to," Molly said. "You won't be alone. Mom and I will go with you. She loves you, you know."

Morris nodded but didn't say anything. He was clearly overcome by emotion.

"Let's not get ahead of ourselves," Julia said. "Give us some time to get back to you. You'll hear from us soon."

Meredith and Julia left the office and went back to the table where Maggie Lu waited.

"So what happened?" she asked when they reclaimed their seats across from her.

"We finally know the truth," Meredith said. "We're hoping our client will be forgiving, but I can't guarantee it."

"Receiving a threat can be extremely disturbing," Maggie Lu said. "I wouldn't blame Davis if he wanted the person who did it punished."

"You're right," Julia said. "Balancing justice and compassion is tough." She shrugged. "But that's not our job. Our job is to deliver the results of our investigation to our client." She took a drink of her Diet Dr Pepper. "But I'll be praying that mercy wins out this time."

"You were right, Maggie Lu. That tattoo is what kept bothering me," Meredith said with a sigh. "I saw it…but I didn't see it." She smiled at Maggie Lu. "Sometimes a fresh set of eyes really can send us in the right direction. You're a blessing."

"My granny would have said, 'Child, if it was a snake it would have bit you.'" Maggie Lu laughed. "Let's finish our lunch. Then you two need a big break. You must be tuckered out."

"Not going to argue with that," Meredith said. As she ate her cheeseburger, Morris's stricken face filled her mind. What would Davis decide to do? She had no idea, but she intended to pray about it.

Chapter Thirty-Three

AFTER MEREDITH AND JULIA GOT back to the office, Meredith called Davis. She told him they needed to talk to him and offered to drive over to his house. Instead he told them he'd come to the office. About an hour later Carmen let them know he was there.

"Can you send him to the conference room?" Meredith asked.

"Sí." Carmen disconnected, and a couple of minutes later the door to the room swung open. Davis came in with Sylvia. His face was still bruised, and one arm was in a sling. After greeting Sylvia, Meredith gestured toward the chairs on the other side of the table. Davis sat down gingerly, and Sylvia slipped into the chair next to him. Meredith could tell Sylvia was worried about her husband. It was clear he was still in pain.

"We would have been happy to meet at your place," Julia said.

"He wouldn't listen," Sylvia said. She smiled at Meredith. "So nice to see you again. How are you doing?"

Meredith knew that she was referencing Ron. "Day by day. Step by step," she said.

"I understand," Sylvia replied softly. "My mom passed away recently. Some days all I can do is put one foot in front of the other." She blinked away tears. "You must come to dinner soon, Meredith.

I've been experimenting with Asian fusion recipes. You know, Asian and Indian cuisine. It's quite interesting."

"That sounds lovely," Meredith said. She didn't miss Davis's eye roll, done so Sylvia couldn't see.

"Thanks for offering to come over," Davis said, "but I've got to start getting around. I can't lie on the couch, waiting for the pain to stop." He frowned at Meredith and Julia. "What is it you want to tell me? Have you found the person who's been threatening me?"

Meredith nodded. "We have. You were right about this being connected to your book. I have to admit we weren't convinced you should have limited our investigation, but it turned out that your instincts were correct."

"So who is it?" Davis asked.

Meredith took the ARC that was on the table and opened it to Peachie's. She pushed it toward him. "See the waiter with the tattoo on his neck?"

Davis nodded. "He requested that we use a different picture. There was a waitress that asked the same thing. They were very insistent, but I told them the picture was great and that we'd go ahead and use it. I just thought they were being camera shy. I didn't think anything of it." He looked up at Meredith. "It's one of these people?"

"Yes." Meredith told him Morris's story. Why he wrote the letter and made the phone call. "He knows what he did was wrong. He finally has a life he loves and was so desperate to stay in Savannah with his fiancée that he acted out of fear. Didn't think it through. He's incredibly sorry for what he did and in his own words is *willing to take his medicine*."

"And what kind of medicine are we talking about?" Sylvia asked.

"If convicted he could get up to a year in prison. Or a thousand-dollar fine."

"He could get both if he gets certain judges," Julia added.

"You're trying to get me to drop this, aren't you?" Davis scowled at them. "No way. He frightened me and made me fear for Sylvia's life. It's inexcusable."

"Davis Hedgerow," Sylvia said. "These ladies figured out who beat you up. I think they deserve to be heard."

Davis's expression changed. "I'm sorry," he said, his tone softer. "I guess I've just had enough. A threat sent to my home, someone calling my publisher, and then getting beaten within an inch of my life..."

"And these ladies finding out who did it," Sylvia added.

"You just said that, dear," Davis said. "I get it."

Meredith found the couple funny. Davis came across as someone in charge of his life, confident and able to fend for himself. Yet Sylvia seemed to have him wrapped around her little finger. It was sweet, and it hurt. Ron had been the same way. Self-confident and strong but also tenderhearted when it came to her.

She took a deep breath and pushed thoughts about Ron away, into that inner vault that she tried more and more not to open. "You can do whatever you want, but we've spoken to this young man. He's extremely remorseful. When he couldn't get you to reshoot the photos, he became afraid. He didn't think clearly, and he regrets it. He was afraid of losing his girl, his job...and possibly his life. That's why he came up with this harebrained scheme."

Davis sighed deeply. "All right, all right. It's obviously three against one. I won't press charges, but it seems to me that he should suffer some consequences for his actions."

The thought flitted through Meredith's mind that they could ask him over for one of Sylvia's dinners, but she kept that to herself.

"Since you're a little incapacitated, why don't you ask this young man to help you clean out that garage you've been planning to take care of?" Sylvia suggested.

Davis's eyebrows shot up. "You want to stick me out in the garage with someone who threatened me?" he asked, his voice higher than normal. "Are you trying to get rid of me?"

"No, I'm trying to get the garage cleaned out." She gave Meredith a half smile. "Tell this young man that no charges will be filed. Also, Davis will make sure new pictures are taken. Without Morris in them. And please give him Davis's phone number. Ask him to call." Sylvia stood up. "Let's go. These women have other clients besides you."

Once again, Davis rolled his eyes, but the edges of his lips turned up. He was obviously smitten with his wife. Once again, a sharp stab of something close to pain pierced Meredith's heart.

"Thank you for your help," he said as Sylvia helped him out.

When the door closed behind them, Julia giggled. "What a couple." She sighed and shook her head. "And what a case. You know, somehow or the other, we've touched the lives of every single person we once suspected. Most of them in good ways. I suspect Scott Dallas isn't too pleased with our involvement, but he's where he needs to be and Davis is safe from him." She frowned. "Oh, except Patricia Ivers and her boss at the Book Worm. At least they're trying to work together, I guess. I hope there won't be any further protests."

"I haven't had time to tell you," Meredith said with a smile. "Patricia called and told me that she and Alex got together to talk. They came to an agreement about the coffee bar and the food he wants to serve. Alex finally realized that Pat didn't tell him about his wife and the other man because she didn't want to hurt him. He also admitted that he pushed her away because she reminded him of the pain his wife's betrayal caused him. Pat is starting back to work this week."

"Why, that's wonderful."

"By the way, I called an old friend," Julia said. "A US marshal. He's looking into Morris's situation. He thinks it's a good possibility that no one is looking for him anymore. He believes the members of the group working with the man Morris testified against are either in jail or out of the country. He's going to make certain but it's a possibility Morris won't have to hide anymore." Julia shook her head. "I truly believe God directed our steps all the way through this case."

"I do too," Meredith said with a sigh. "I'm exhausted. Let's take a few days off, okay?"

Julia leaned back in her chair. "We could do that, but I got an interesting call. A family looking for their father who died ten years ago."

Meredith frowned at her. "You just said they were looking for a dead man. That doesn't make sense."

Julia shrugged. "That's the interesting part. Seems a family member saw him working as a carny in a traveling carnival. They want us to investigate."

Meredith struggled mentally between a long nap and finding out why a dead man was working as a carny. How did he pull it off? And why?

She took a deep breath and blew it out slowly. "Okay," she said, picking up a pen and opening her notebook. "Tell me more."

Dear Reader,

Savannah, Georgia, is a gorgeous city that is full of history...and mystery. Although I've never visited Savannah myself, researching this amazing place made me want to visit. I would love to walk down the cobblestone streets and enjoy the unique architecture, sample Southern delicacies in Savannah's incredible restaurants, and view the fountain in Forsyth Park.

Our main characters, Meredith Bellefontaine and Julia Foley, not only adore their city, but they also love Magnolia Investigations. These wily women spend their time uncovering Savannah's secrets for their clients. You'll enjoy getting to know them and following their adventures in this fantastic series written by some of the best authors of inspirational fiction.

Have fun sampling Savannah's secrets.

And y'all come back now, ya hear?

Nancy Mehl

About the Author

NANCY MEHL IS A *USA Today* bestselling author. She's been a finalist for the Carol Award twice and won the award once. She was also a finalist for two Reviewers' Choice Awards from RT Book Reviews, and was a finalist for the coveted Christy Award. She lives in Missouri with her husband, Norman, and her Puggle, Watson. She's authored forty books and is currently working on a new series for Bethany House about an FBI profiler working with the BAU, and a cozy mystery series with Guideposts, set in Savannah, Georgia.

Readers can learn more about Nancy through her website: nancymehl.com. She is part of the Suspense Sisters: suspensesisters.blogspot.com, along with several other popular suspense authors. She is also very active on Facebook.

An Armchair Tour of Savannah

SAVANNAH, GEORGIA, IS HOME TO many wonderful attractions. Tourists come from all over the world to enjoy the old Southern ambiance of this beautiful city. In *Southern Fried Secrets*, I introduce a character who writes a column for the local paper called Searching Savannah. Mentioned along with places I made up for this story are some real spots that are particularly popular with residents and visitors alike. For example, Forsyth Park is the largest park in the historic district of Savannah, Georgia. The park features walking paths, open areas, beautiful trees, and a fragrance garden. Throughout Savannah are many other fascinating features like old cemeteries, beautiful homes, interesting museums, and incredible restaurants that serve delicious dishes like grits and shrimp, fried green tomatoes, and Southern-fried chicken. And if you're looking for ghosts? Savannah has them. They claim to have the most haunted location in the world, the Moon River Brewing Company. However, for me, one of the most captivating attractions in Savannah is Echo Square. It doesn't look unusual. Just a gray square in the concrete, but if you stand inside the square and speak, your voice will sound like an echo to you. But people on the outside of the square can't hear your voice at all. The site acts as an echo chamber. Not sure what causes it, but it sounds like a lot of fun. In fact, the city of Savannah is now on my list of places to visit. I hope you'll enjoy seeing Savannah through the eyes of our authors as we do our best to bring the flavor and character of this beautiful city to the books in the Savannah Secrets series.

FRIED GREEN TOMATOES

Ingredients

1 egg, lightly beaten

½ cup buttermilk

½ cup all-purpose flour, divided

½ cup cornmeal

1 teaspoon salt

½ teaspoon pepper

3 green tomatoes, cut into ⅓-inch slices

Vegetable oil

Directions

Mix together egg and buttermilk; set aside. Combine ¼ cup flour, cornmeal, 1 teaspoon salt, and pepper in a shallow bowl or pan. Dredge tomato slices in remaining ¼ cup flour; dip in egg mixture, and dredge in cornmeal mixture.

Pour oil to a depth of ¼ to ½ inch in a large cast-iron skillet; heat to medium high. Drop tomatoes, in batches, into hot oil, and cook 2 minutes on each side or until golden. Drain on paper towels or a rack. Sprinkle hot tomatoes with salt.

Read on for a sneak peek of another exciting book
in the Savannah Secrets series!

The Greatest of These
BY MARLENE CHASE

"Do you ever feel like the world is going faster and faster?" Julia Foley asked. She tucked her hand inside Meredith Bellefontaine's elbow as they walked through the park on the way to the City Market. "You try to keep up, but any minute you think you're going to fall off the edge."

"Happens every time I get on the treadmill," Meredith answered, her blue eyes merry. "But I know what you mean. Seems like just yesterday we were hanging our Christmas stockings from the mantel, and here it is nearly Valentine's Day!"

"I know. Go figure!" Carmen Lopez chimed in, catching up to Julia and Meredith. Their unlikely assistant pushed back her cloud of dark hair.

"Still chilly, though," Julia said, feeling the wind through her sherpa-lined jacket. But it was exhilarating too. It was good to be with friends—Meredith, who had reopened her husband's agency and brought her in as partner, and Carmen Lopez, their young assistant, whose life zest was nothing short of inspiring.

"Folks in the Midwest would call this weather downright balmy," Meredith said, turning to Julia, whose shiver must have been perceptible. "They would say you were lucky to enjoy temps like these in February. It's sixty-one degrees already!"

"What can I say?" Julia laughed. "I'm dyed in the warm wool of the South!"

Meredith laughed, lifting her head toward the sun. She pushed back a lock of blond hair that was already curling with the morning's humidity. "Well, it's a glorious morning anyway, and I love this trek through Forsyth Park at any season of the year."

"Me too," Carmen said, breathing the fresh air in deeply. "Even if it is Saturday, and I could be sleeping in." She rolled her dark eyes expressively.

Passing Mercer Museum, they turned onto Liberty Street, a straight shot for City Market, the attraction that drew hundreds of Savannahians year round and a host of visitors from everywhere. Today they would join the crowds delighting in the many colorful shops and galleries clustered in the four-block area.

The developer of the project, which began in 1985, had emulated the design of the successful Torpedo Factory in Alexandria, Virginia. Savannah's group of working artists occupied approximately nineteen thousand square feet of space in the Market. The environment was enhanced by food, entertainment, and retail businesses.

Carmen paused to cradle a pink camellia from a resplendent bush bordering the walk. Her dark brown hair lifted in the breeze and floated around her shoulders. She murmured her appreciation of the flower's beauty in her native Spanish, to which she resorted on occasion, though her English was more than adequate. "*Hermosa*, no?"

Julia smiled. She was glad Carmen had joined them for a Saturday brunch at the café/bakery that was a favorite of locals. As a juvenile court judge, Julia had seen in Carmen what was now evident to everyone. Despite a somewhat checkered past, the young woman in her midtwenties was intelligent and resourceful and had become a valuable assistant. Though separated in age from the two partners by four decades, she had quickly become a friend.

Carmen held out the flower for their inspection. "So gorgeous!" she raved. "If I were a flower, I would be a camellia." She pressed her face into the pink bloom which, against park rules, she had nipped from the bush. At Julia's disapproving glance, Carmen shrugged good-naturedly, brown eyes innocent. "It's just one, no? It was hanging loose; it would have dropped off any minute."

Meredith leaned in to study the flower in Carmen's hand and gave Julia an indulgent glance. "Where else than our beloved South can you find evergreen shrubs that flower during the dull days of winter?"

Julia nodded, grinning. Meredith knew a lot about flowers and tended them carefully around her Italianate-style home that overlooked Troup Square. Her camellias burst into flower weeks before Julia's garden came to life. "Long live our beloved South!" Julia quipped as they hurried on toward the Market.

The café/bakery proved to be every bit as enjoyable as everyone said. They breakfasted on frittatas and sweet crepes with caramelized pears. Meredith ordered a double chocolate muffin and cut it in threes to savor with their gourmet almond coffee. More than satisfied, they headed into the stream of eager shoppers.

"I'm dying to see the new designs at Pottery Paradise," Carmen said. "Their ads claim to have some of the best Talavera pottery pieces."

"I hope it's at least a block or two away," Julia said, patting her stomach. "Breakfast was fantastic, but I'll need to hit the treadmill from dawn to dusk to compensate." She grinned. Beau used their treadmill on occasion, but left to her ministrations, it was doomed to live out its days as a clothes rack.

"Treadmills should be good for something," Meredith put in knowingly.

"Just because you never need one," Julia said teasingly. Meredith wore her stylish clothes well, but she had even more to offer in spirit and character. Any man would be lucky to win her affection. Meredith had lost her husband far too soon. She had loved Ron and grieved deeply for him, but Julia couldn't help hoping her friend would find someone to share the rest of her life with. Someone as wonderful as her own Beauregard Eugene Foley.

Julia turned to Carmen, who had set a challenging pace. "I didn't know you were interested in pottery."

"Well, not just any pottery. It's the Talavera variety I like. I have a set of salad plates I bought at Crate and Barrell for forty-four dollars, but someday I may be rich enough to buy some authentic pieces."

Carmen could surprise you, Julia thought. After her Guatemalan parents were killed when she was only ten, she'd been shifted from one foster home to another. In a way, she'd practically raised herself, and she got into some early trouble with the law as a teenager. But she'd been amazingly resilient and had made giant steps to finish her education and advance herself. For Julia, Carmen's rise had been deeply satisfying to witness, and she'd been eager to help the young woman succeed.

"You know, the process for creating Talavera pottery hasn't changed much since the early colonial period," Carmen continued in her animated fashion. "They start by mixing black sand from Amozoc and white sand from Tecali. They wash it and filter out the best particles and shape it on a potter's wheel. Then it must dry for days before it's fired. Then comes glazing, more firing, and hand painting. It takes about three months for most pieces, but some can take up to six months. *Es muy bonito.*"

Julia raised her eyebrows, impressed.

"I googled it," Carmen admitted. "You can learn anything on the internet."

Carmen was a whiz on the computer, it was true. She could navigate sites with speed and determination. Her skills had come in quite handy in the investigation business.

"You know," Carmen continued, still rosy with praise for her favorite artistry, "the process of making Talavera pottery is so complicated and the pieces so easily damaged that during colonial times, artists prayed special prayers over them, especially during the firing process."

"Very wise artisans," Julia said. "It might be what's missing in a lot of arenas today. Not just art." She smiled apologetically. Did she sound like she'd donned her old judge's robe and was about to pontificate? Or like her pastor on a Sunday morning? "Prayer is certainly underrated by a lot of people," she finished, drawing in the strap of her purse as they bustled through the crowd.

Prayer unquestionably had made a difference in her life over the years, Julia realized, not for the first time, and especially in guiding her and Meredith in their work at Magnolia Investigations. Their first case had been a daunting one, by anyone's measure. They might have abandoned the venture if God hadn't shown up.

Sometimes she marveled over the way He sent just what and who they needed at the right time—like Maggie Lu, who had made it possible for them to solve the mystery of the young girl who disappeared from the Besset mansion sixty-five years ago. Since that first case, the intrepid woman had assisted them in solving others as well.

Julia had hoped she could ask Maggie Lu to join her and her mother for supper later that day, but Mom had said she wasn't up to it. She had pleaded for a quiet meal at her house with just her daughter for company.

Julia felt her chest tighten. Lately her eighty-four-year-old mother had been distant and sometimes even morose. Julia was aware that elderly people could fall prey to depression. Was that what was going on with Bonnie Jean Waverly—B.J., as her family and most of her friends called her? Julia shook away a vague sense of regret and guilt. She wouldn't think about her mother now. She would simply enjoy this part of the day with friends who knew how to find joy in life.

"Well, that style definitely wasn't designed for me," Meredith said wryly, interrupting Julia's reverie. They were passing a boutique featuring a model in a trendy high-waisted skirt. "I'd look like a reject from a Holland tulip field."

"But look at that ruffled blouse!" Carmen said, pointing to an adjacent window. "It's to die for. I'd love it in red." She mimicked a cha-cha-cha, swiveling her hips.

"Let's check out that pottery place you're so crazy about," Julia said, grabbing Carmen's arm and propelling her forward.

The streets were busy, even in February. Most were wide enough for a dozen people to walk abreast and still afford space for a horse-drawn carriage. Outdoor patios were set for alfresco diners with huge wooden planters blooming with flowers and greenery. Every window was designed to draw attention. The eye simply wasn't quick enough to take in the myriad sights.

Meredith stopped at a tall iconic clock, a gift to the citizens of Savannah that commemorated the hundredth anniversary of the founding of Rotary International. "They dedicated that clock in 2005 when I was director of the historical society," she said. "It's a real landmark and quite a draw for tourists."

"I'm sure Beatrice points it out to visitors of Savannah now. In her over-the-top Southern speak, no doubt," Julia said, not unkindly. Beatrice Enterline, the current historical society director, often set them musing over her flamboyant and sometimes unnerving demeanor. "I reckon she'd say it was enough to make a possum roll over dead."

"Or a frog spit in a rabbit's eye!" Meredith added.

Carmen laughed, rolling her eyes. "Come on, you two. Pottery Paradise is in the upper-level section. It's always fun to meet the artists and watch them create."

Julia had enjoyed doing just that on more than one occasion. There was always something new and exciting to see. Even Beau was willing to endure a shopping trip to observe the eclectic items on display at the Market. Paintings, pottery, wood turning, sculptures, glass works, jewelry—the variety was amazing.

"Let's check out the downstairs galleries first," she said before Carmen could begin climbing the black wrought-iron staircase to the upper floor.

"Looks like the Winston Gallery has reopened," Meredith said, pointing across the wide street to an attractive smoke-colored brick building with high-set windows in glossy black casements. "It's been closed for a while, but someone must have taken it over—unless Eduardo is back."

"Didn't I hear he was in a rehab facility after his stroke?" Julia asked, zigzagging through the crowd.

"Since last November," Meredith answered. "The Winston was one of the classiest in the Market. Apparently, there was no one to keep the place going in those intervening months."

Julia entered the high-ceilinged gallery and gazed around at the works of art placed on three long walls. Paintings were carefully arranged and illuminated to draw the eye around the room. "Lucky Eduardo didn't lose his lease," she said. "New businesses are always clamoring for a spot here. How did you find out? Was it in the paper?"

"Quin had something to do with helping to retain the lease for him." Meredith spoke somewhat absently as she peered at the dazzling display of color and form.

Arthur "Quin" Crowley was an attractive lawyer who had recently come from Columbus to Savannah. He and Meredith had met in the process of securing information about the owner of the Bessett mansion.

"I wonder what Eduardo would say about his gallery now," Julia said, drawing in her breath. "He definitely preferred beautiful landscapes and classic works from an earlier era."

"As I recall, he had some fine Winston Churchill paintings for sale," Meredith said, glancing around with a slight frown. "I always liked his *Lake near Breccles in Autumn*."

The gallery was quite changed, filled with modern works from the first half of the twentieth century and contemporary offerings produced after 1950 and even later into the twenty-first century. Such art, Julia knew, was globally influenced and culturally diverse. Of course, it would naturally reflect the advancing world of technology.

Julia released a surprised breath. "I guess it's a good thing Maggie Lu didn't come along today." She'd been invited since she loved art but had begged off to visit a good friend who was ill. The wildly chaotic forms in the Winston today might not be to her taste. *Or to mine either*, Julia thought. But it was a new age and keeping up with it could be a challenge.

Meredith surveyed each work with a critical eye. "Art really helps us look more closely at people and emotions, doesn't it?" she asked. "It helps us see what doesn't readily or easily appear to us."

Julia nodded, appreciating once again her partner's deep insights into things. Among her other fine qualities, she might make a first-rate philosopher.

Carmen had gone ahead and roved from one display to another without comment. Now as Julia caught up to her, they were a few feet from a large painting covering half the rear wall. It was a striking piece. Bold crimson and orange geometric shapes like stylized flames erupted from some black maw and penetrated an invisible sky. In the center of the squares and triangles a small white oval pierced the brilliant oranges and crimsons.

Julia felt a quick shudder—like fear. Yet something compelled her, drew her eyes back, held them. The forms were beautiful, entrancing, but at the same time dark with mystery and dread.

Something of hope shone through as well, and Julia was deeply touched. What was the artist saying? And why at this moment did she think of her sister, Cassie? Something of a runaway herself. Other visitors must have been affected too, for a small crowd lingered near the painting, whispering excitedly.

Carmen continued to peruse the art. Silence was uncharacteristic of the outspoken young woman peering now at the signature at the bottom, which read DESDEMONA.

Adjacent to the painting was a sign, which the three of them seemed to catch sight of at the same time. Meredith read in a hushed voice:

> Desdemona, known to some as the 'runaway artist,' has come to Savannah and is scheduled to appear on February 16 for a gala event to which everyone is invited. A collection of the artist's paintings titled *Spectrum of the Soul* will be available for purchase from 7 until 9:30 p.m. This is her signature piece, appearing at the Winston for the first time. Fans of her exciting work will want to be on hand to greet her.

"Runaway artist?" Julia repeated.

"Curious," Meredith agreed, narrowing her eyes. "I'm afraid where modern art—or should I say contemporary art—is concerned, I'm somewhat of a runaway fan. Realism and impressionism are more my line, but I'm no connoisseur, that's for sure."

"I read something about a 'runaway' artist," Julia said. "There was a showing in Chicago at a prestigious grassroots gallery. Since then it seems this Desdemona has developed a cadre of enthusiasts." Julia tried unsuccessfully to draw her eyes away from the painting.

Meredith studied it closely. "Everyone loves a good mystery, I suppose."

"A lot of theories have grown up about her too," Julia said. "Someone suggested that she's a descendant of the great Marc Chagall, an early modernist. Or a wealthy dowager who funds her own exhibitions and caters to the rich and famous."

"Or brings new clothes to the emperor," Meredith said wryly. She touched Carmen's shoulder. "What do you think?"

Carmen, who was still studying the painting, appeared not to hear.

"Carmen?" Julia urged.

She turned to look up at Julia, wonder in the olive oval of her face. "Desdemona," she said under her breath.

"What do you think?" Julia asked.

Carmen straightened. She stepped back with a troubled expression. "It reminds me of something—from a long time ago," she said quietly. She pursed her full lips, dark eyes nostalgic, as though peering into some long-forgotten memory.

"We should move along," Julia said, nudging Carmen. A group of admirers was pressing in for a closer look. The gallery was full. Besides, she was eager to get outside—away from whatever drew her to the strange painting. She felt edgy, uncomfortable. The gallery was so changed, so unexpected. She had been here before, often with Beau. Neither one was a collector of art, but it was fun to peruse and to "listen" to what the various paintings had to say. This display had unnerved her. "Come on. I'm ready for coffee."

They turned into the nearby Cinnamon Bear Country Store and settled at a table outside. It was a favorite place that also had locations in Hilton Head, Amelia Island, and Midtown Savannah. Beau was partial to this store in City Market and was content to enjoy a Cheerwine while Julia finished her shopping. Now she sipped her Coco Mocha Nut Delight and waited while Carmen slowly stirred a cup of Jamaican Dark.

"So, what do you think?" Meredith asked, as she wrapped her hands around her cup of Amaretto Light and watched Carmen. "You seemed interested in that exhibit. What did it say to you?"

Julia was glad Meredith hadn't asked her, for her thoughts were disparate, troubled, far too personal, even bringing Cassie to mind.

Meredith continued thoughtfully. "Art should speak truth, some reality to enhance the human condition. At best, art should bring beauty and light to a dark world. Maybe, too, art says something about the human condition of the artist."

"I don't know," Carmen began thoughtfully, still stirring coffee that didn't need stirring. "Like I said, that painting reminds me of something from a long time ago. When I was—you know—on the streets." She fluttered her eyelashes in Julia's direction. "Well, one of the girls I knew then was a talented graffiti artist. We used to hold cans of spray paint for her and hand them to her when she needed them."

"A graffiti artist?" Meredith repeated. "I suppose that large, sweeping style could have roots in graffiti."

"She didn't write bad words or stuff like that. She just made pictures—and they were so good that no one painted over them right away. Like maybe they realized they were special." Carmen's eyes glowed. "She never signed a name, but somewhere in every painting she would put this swirling white thing sort of like an alien bird." She cocked her head to one side. "That's how she got the name. We called her 'The Dove.'"

Julia had seen the swirl of white in the center of the bold red and black forms, though it didn't resemble any dove she'd ever seen. It did look alien, though. A fanciful, almost alien birdlike flourish.

"I—I don't suppose you ever ran into her on the bench?" Carmen aimed her question at Julia but kept her eyes down. "I mean, she did get into some trouble like I did."

Kids defacing property was a perennial problem, but Julia hadn't dealt with many such cases in Chatham County during her tenure in juvenile court. While practicing in Atlanta, she had tried a few instances—all involving boys.

A nostalgic mist hovered in Carmen's eyes. "She was a little older than the rest of us, but in a lot of ways she was a child. All she ever wanted to do was paint. Brick alley walls, abandoned billboards, anything she could spray. It was like an obsession with her. And she could climb like a mountain goat! She was fifteen; I wasn't quite thirteen. I thought she was beautiful. I looked up to her. But she was *ingenuo*, you know?"

"Naive," Julia translated.

Carmen nodded. "You could tell her anything and she'd believe it." She released a long breath. "She used to draw the white bird on everything she painted. We never knew why." She frowned. "It was a long time ago—twelve years or more since I saw something like that."

Carmen paused again to stir her drink, staring into it. "She said her name was Ophelia, but sometimes she called herself Virginia or some other name she thought was exotic. She was sort of mysterious." Carmen bit her lower lip. "There was a little boy too. He followed her around like a puppy. He was about seven or eight, and he could get in and out of any place quicker than you could blink." She clasped her arms around herself as though she were suddenly cold.

Her eyes flashed and filled. She was quiet for so long that Julia became alarmed. "What is it, Carmen?"

Carmen swallowed. Her whisper seemed to come from some deep, impenetrable distance. "He was climbing a scaffold of a building that was being renovated, and he—he fell." She gasped. "He was so small, so still."